The  across the helipad. The ̶_̶_̶_̶_̶_̶_̶_̶_̶_̶ ̶, ̶_̶_̶ ̶_̶_̶_̶_̶_̶_̶_̶_̶.̶ So Brannigan did the only thing he could, under the circumstances. Even as their presence registered to the lead Iranian rifleman, Brannigan snapped his AK-12 up and fired.

The two-round burst was a coughing *bark* amidst the thunder of the night, the rifle cycling faster than the recoil could push the muzzle off target. Flame spat from the rifle's muzzle brake, and the Iranian crumpled. Brannigan gave him a second pair, just to be on the safe side, then switched to the next man to the right.

By then, the other three had joined in, cutting the rest of the Iranians down in a rattling storm of rifle fire. Muzzle blasts flickered in the dark of the outer courtyard, and then the four Iranians were down on the ground and the mercenaries were sweeping toward the still-open door.

BRANNIGAN'S BLACKHEARTS

FURY IN THE GULF

PETER NEALEN

Also By Peter Nealen

The Brannigan's Blackhearts Universe

Kill Yuan

The Colonel Has A Plan (Online Short)

Fury in the Gulf

Burmese Crossfire

Enemy Unidentified

Frozen Conflict

High Desert Vengeance

Doctors of Death

Kill or Capture

The Maelstrom Rising Series

Escalation

Holding Action

Crimson Star

Strategic Assets

Thunder Run

SPOTREPS – A Maelstrom Rising Anthology

The American Praetorians Series

Drawing the Line: An American Praetorians Story (Novella)

Task Force Desperate

Hunting in the Shadows

Alone and Unafraid

The Devil You Don't Know

Lex Talionis

The Jed Horn Supernatural Thriller Series

Nightmares

A Silver Cross and a Winchester

The Walker on the Hills

The Canyon of the Lost (Novelette)

Older and Fouler Things

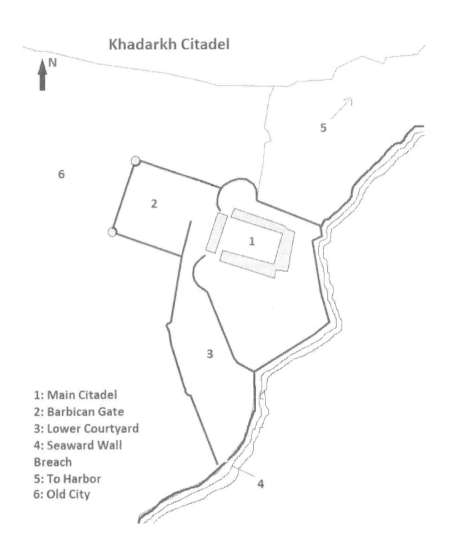

Khadarkh Citadel

N

5

6

2

1

3

1: Main Citadel
2: Barbican Gate
3: Lower Courtyard
4: Seaward Wall
Breach
5: To Harbor
6: Old City

4

CHAPTER 1

The Airbus A319 touched down on Khadarkh International Airport's concrete landing strip with a bounce and a slight squeal of rubber. The engines howled as they reversed, struggling to slow the big plane before it got too close to the end of the runway. Beyond lay only a short strip of desert sand, which quickly fell away to the cliffs that descended steeply into the Persian Gulf, only a few short meters below.

The combination of flaps, airbrakes, ground brakes, and reverse thrust successfully brought the aircraft to the pace of a fast walk, still a good three hundred meters from the end of the strip. The engines still roaring, the twin-engine jet slowly turned onto the taxiway and trundled toward the main terminal and the big cargo hangars that loomed nearby.

Following radio instructions from the tower and signals on the ground, the cargo plane turned in to park in front of the cargo terminal. Airport workers hurried out onto the tarmac, while a white tractor chugged out behind them, towing a rolling ladder that it carefully and precisely snugged up against the airplane's forward hatch.

A Nissan pickup rolled out onto the taxiway behind the tractor and parked next to the ladder. Two uniformed Khadarkhi Customs Officers got out and climbed up the ladder to the hatch, their clipboards under their arms. They were relaxed, chatting in

Arabic. Customs inspections for cargo were generally routine, and nothing to get worked up about.

"It was the most amazing strike I have ever seen, Qasim," Achmed al Qays was saying as they neared the top of the steps. "I was certain the hare had gotten away; it had dashed into the brush and rocks at the edge of the wadi. But when I tried to call the new saker back to my glove, it suddenly dove, passed right between two razor-sharp rocks, and took the hare by the neck. It was amazing!"

Achmed al Qays was a member of the Khadarkhi royal family. A fourth or fifth cousin to the King—the precise genealogy got a little hazy at times, even to him—he wasn't nearly close enough to the King or his immediate relations to merit much more than a cushy slot with Khadarkhi Customs, but he was a generally lazy man, going to fat, who really had no greater ambitions than to live comfortably, with as little effort as possible. Being a Customs officer suited him. He had an easy, unexciting job, he never had to worry about money or stress, he had three wives and good prospects for a fourth, and all he had to do was check lists, accept the occasional *baksheesh*, and go play at falconry after prayer at the mosque on Fridays. Life was good.

He turned away from Qasim al Faroukh, who, as usual, was polite but seemed less than enthralled by his superior's stories, and found himself staring into the barrel of a gun.

Achmed knew nothing about firearms; those were left to his cousins and their soldiers. He only knew that the pistol barrel presently pointed at the bridge of his nose from about fifty centimeters away looked like the mouth of a cannon. He suddenly started to shake, and clenched his buttocks, trying to keep his bowels from letting go.

"Inside," the dark-bearded man with the gun ordered curtly. "Quickly!"

Achmed took his eyes off the pistol's muzzle just long enough to see that they were not alone in the cargo plane's hold. There were at least twenty men standing amidst the various crates and equipment cases secured along the center of the hold, all of them dressed in the same khaki fatigues as the man with the pistol. They were also all wearing some kind of combat gear and carrying

2

evil-looking black rifles, that looked far newer and more dangerous than the shiny, worn weapons that the Khadarkhi Army carried.

"Do exactly what I tell you and you will not be harmed," the bearded man with the pistol said. He spoke Arabic with a strange accent; Achmed was slightly too rattled to notice that the accent was distinctly Persian. He should have noticed; Khadarkh lying in the middle of the Persian Gulf as it does, there was plenty of traffic through the airport from Iran as well as Saudi Arabia, depending on the shifts in the political climate from year to year.

"Wh-What do you want?" Achmed stammered.

"You will sign off on our Customs inspection, and see to it that this aircraft is moved to the front of the queue to enter the cargo terminal," the man said. "No questions asked. Understand this: if I think for a moment that you are attempting to warn the Army, or the police, I will kill both of you."

Achmed nodded jerkily. The thought of resistance never entered his mind. He did not want to die.

He filled out the paperwork hastily, while Qasim watched with hooded eyes. The other man gave no indication of what he thought about the proceedings, though there might have been a faint glint of amusement in his dark eyes at seeing his soft, pampered superior so unmanned. The hard-eyed, bearded man with the pistol never lowered it, keeping that threat as immediate as possible. Once Achmed could show the man the papers, he motioned to one of the others standing behind him, and that one, a broad-shouldered, mustached man, slung his rifle and stepped forward to scribble an illegible signature in the indicated blocks.

As the man with the rifle signed, a thought began to work its way past the bowel-loosening fear in Achmed's mind, and he started to think that there might be a way out of this. If he could convince these men that he had to go back up to the central office in person to clear them into the cargo terminal...

But his hopes were dashed as the bearded man with the pistol motioned to the phone on his belt. "Go ahead," he said, "call the control tower, and get us into that terminal."

His spirits sinking even lower, Achmed took the smartphone out of its holder and called the central office. It took only a few moments to convince the bored dispatcher to move the Airbus up to the front of the line.

Actually getting the aircraft into the terminal took a bit longer; nothing happened quickly on Khadarkh. The dispatcher had to call the crews, get through to the man in charge, who was probably sleeping, and then get them moving. It was nearly an hour later that the tractor finally started pulling the Airbus into the cargo terminal, but the armed men in the plane's hold stood where they were, impassive and silent.

The wait had given Achmed an opportunity to study them, though furtively, as he did not particularly want to attract their attention any more than necessary. They were mostly lean, gaunt men, with a dangerous, hard-edged look about them that frightened him. He had seen pictures and video of such men before, mostly coming from the battlefields of Yemen and Syria.

Finally, the plane was parked in the massive hangar of the cargo terminal, and the gigantic doors slid shut behind it.

"You may go now," the bearded man said. "I suggest that you leave the airport for the rest of the day."

Achmed did not hesitate, but fled as soon as the stairs were replaced. He did not even look back to see if Qasim had followed before he made a beeline for the parking lot.

***

Farshid Esfandiari holstered his Makarov as the fat Arab nearly fell down the stairs in his haste to get away, and grimaced slightly in disgust. The other Customs officer followed somewhat more sedately, but was still obviously in no mood to linger any longer than necessary.

Esfandiari turned to the mustached man next to him as he checked his watch. "We have twenty-seven minutes before the next two aircraft are due, Jahangir," he told his second-in-command, "thanks to these idiots' laziness. Let us make the most of it."

Ardashir Jahangir nodded curtly, and began barking orders in Farsi. The men quickly started moving toward the hatch. They had been ready to deploy for over an hour.

Esfandiari picked up his own Type 03 rifle from where he had left it in the rack, lashed to one of the equipment cases. He had

4

wanted the more visceral, emotional impact of the pistol when he had threatened the Customs officers. Pistols have a certain curious mystique in the Arab world, he suspected largely due to the likes of Saddam Hussein and dozens of other Arab dictators. Rifles were for fighting. But pistols were for executions. Many Arabs, even those who had never lived under such a regime, feared pistols more than the more powerful rifles.

Teams of four men had already secured the entrances and exits to the cargo terminal by the time Esfandiari reached the floor. Jahangir already had the last ten ready to head out toward the main terminal and the control tower.

Esfandiari joined them, just as Jahangir gave the word. The double doors leading to the skywalk between the cargo terminal and the control tower crashed open under a black leather boot, and then the soldiers were rushing through.

There was no security on the skywalk; apparently the Khadarkis had decided that there was no reason to expect a terrorist to try to come in through the cargo terminal. There were two guards at the entrance to the control tower, one fat one and one short, scrawny one, both in the dark green uniforms of the Khadarkhi Army, carrying their M16s slung over their shoulders. As soon as the men in unmarked khaki fatigues burst into the hallway, their Type 03s leveled at the guards, both sets of eyes got wide, and hands were immediately raised, in both cases with the M16s still dangling from their slings. That was when Esfandiari noticed that both rifles were unloaded.

"Secure them," Esfandiari ordered. Two of his men quickly put the two guards on their faces on the floor, ripping their rifles away and slinging them. Meanwhile, Esfandiari took the lead, bounding up the stairs toward the top of the control tower.

The air traffic controllers still had no idea what was happening. They were bent over their consoles, intent on their radios and computer screens. Only when Esfandiari stepped up next to one of them and spoke did any of them actually appear to notice that they were no longer alone in the tower.

"These two aircraft now have priority," Esfandiari said, putting a piece of paper with two flight numbers written on it on the console next to the man in front of him. The controller started,

5

glancing up to see Esfandiari looming over him. Just in case, he had slung his rifle and drawn the Makarov again. The message was not lost on the controller, whose eyes widened before he nodded vigorously, reaching for the paper.

Esfandiari stayed by the man's side while the next two Airbus cargo planes landed and taxied to the front of the terminal. Then, leaving the control tower in Jahangir's able hands, he headed back downstairs to meet the rest of his men.

***

Transportation into Khadarkh City was easy; the Khadarkhi Army might have been lazy and incompetent, but they were well equipped, especially since King Abdullah al Qays had started cozying up to the Saudi apostates almost as soon as his father had died. Esfandiari, along with Vahid Farroukhshad's platoon, had simply climbed into the armored JLTVs stationed at the entrance to the airport and driven away.

Behind them, shots rang out as Jahangir's men began executing the airport guards.

It was a quick drive into the city. While the Khadarkhi Army had no real combat experience, having sat out the fights in Syria and Yemen where both Iran and Saudi Arabia had blooded their own elite forces, though often in disguise—not unlike this operation—they had enough of a high-profile presence on the island itself that the civilian vehicles quickly got out of the way when they saw the big, black-painted armored vehicles roaring down the road in their rear-view mirrors. It took only a matter of minutes to reach their target house, minutes in which Esfandiari could be reasonably certain that the alarm still had not been raised. They had taken the airport too quickly.

General Ali ibn Ahmadi had been the old king's chief of staff, and had continued in the role with the rise of King Abdullah. The young king had at least been smart enough not to change things up *too* much when he'd taken the throne. Esfandiari was hoping that that would make his job that much easier, given the old king's policies, which ibn Ahmadi had enforced willingly enough, according to intelligence.

Ali's house was a four-story mansion, with balconies at each story and several levels of peaked, red-tile roof above the

6

arched windows and fluted columns. The white faux marble of the façade was chased with gilt. The general did not live poorly.

The guards at his gate looked up lazily as the Army JLTVs pulled up in front, apparently not even especially curious as to why a convoy was arriving at the general's residence mid-morning, unannounced. Their bored expressions turned to alarm when Esfandiari and his men piled out. Unmarked khaki uniforms and Chinese rifles did not fit with Khadarkhi Army vehicles. But by the time it registered that something was wrong, they were already being covered by three muzzles apiece, and any thought of resistance was immediately squashed.

While several of Farroukhshad's men secured the outer guards, and took up their positions at the gate, Esfandiari and Farroukhshad led the remainder into the courtyard.

Surprisingly, one of the guards at the door inside was a brave man. He shouted the alarm and swung his M16 off his shoulder. Esfandiari whipped his own rifle to his shoulder and shot him. Pahlavi, Farroukhshad's point man, poured a long burst into the guard's chest at the same moment. The man crumpled to the stone steps, blood soaking his dark green uniform and spattering against the white stone tile behind him.

The dead man's companion had no desire to die a hero. He tossed his rifle on the steps with a crash, raised his hands, and surrendered.

Esfandiari strode through the double doors, four more of his men flanking him. The entryway to General Ali's mansion was even more ornate than the exterior, with gilt columns holding up the vaulted ceiling and expensive tile on the floors. Heavy curtains hung over the windows, to keep the heat of the sun out during the middle of the day.

General Ali appeared at the top of the central staircase. He was a short man, going bald, his remaining hair silver but his mustache still pitch-black. He was developing a paunch, presently mostly uncovered as he was wearing only green trousers and a white t-shirt. He had a Beretta 92 in his hand.

"General Ali," Esfandiari said, stopping at the base of the stairs, "I have need of your authority. If you cooperate, you will not be harmed. Your family will remain unmolested. If you resist, I will be forced to kill you and do the rest of this the hard way."

Ali stared at him for a moment, his face stony, his dark eyes inscrutable. The general's dossier was sketchy before he had come to serve the Khadarkhi royal house. But there was a distinct possibility that he had fought the Soviets in Afghanistan, most of a lifetime ago. Looking into the old man's eyes, Esfandiari believed it. This man was a world away from the soft-bodied amateurs that his men had already gunned down.

"You are Qods Force?" Ali asked.

"We are independent contractors, as the Americans would say," Esfandiari lied. "A simple yes or no, General. That is all I require."

"What do you need of me?" Ali asked. He still had not put the Beretta down, but he had not raised it, either. "You seem to have the situation well in hand."

"As I said, I need your authority," Esfandiari said. "I need you to order the garrison at the Citadel to stand down and surrender. It will save many lives, General."

Ali studied him a moment longer, then nodded wearily. He reversed his pistol in his grip and held it out.

Esfandiari mounted the steps and accepted the weapon. "Thank you, General," he said. He could have some respect for this man, regardless of the fact that he served a vacillating king who drifted back and forth between the Islamic Republic and the apostates, depending on how the wind blew. "We have time for you to get dressed. Transportation is waiting outside."

***

It took even less time to reach the Citadel than it had to drive into the city. With General Ali dressed in his full Khadarkhi Army uniform, it was easy enough to get through the ancient barbican gate, with its twin round towers looming overhead, without even needing to make a move against the guards. Only when the vehicles were parked inside the barbican itself, and Esfandiari's men poured out with their weapons ready, did General Ali address the garrison, instructing them to stand down when the men in khaki came to their posts. It had actually been the General's idea to suggest that the Iranians were simply coming to help, rather

8

than making an initial demand for surrender. Apparently, the chief of staff was less than impressed with his sovereign's choice of allies of late.

Ali's assistance made it a quick matter to have khaki-clad Iranian fighters at every garrison post in the Citadel in a matter of less than thirty minutes. Only then did Esfandiari give the order. "Execute."

Gunfire rattled out across the walls and deep in the Citadel itself, as Esfandiari's men quickly and systematically murdered the Khadarkhi garrison. General Ali did not even flinch as the shots echoed across the ancient fortress. He had to have known that this was coming.

"And what will you do with me now, Commander?" Ali asked, assuming Esfandiari's rank. He was not far off, but Esfandiari was not going to correct him, since he was not on Khadarkh in any *official* capacity from any *official* government.

"As long as you continue to cooperate, General," Esfandiari said, "you have nothing to fear. I do not expect you to pose any threat to us, especially now that the Khadarkhi Army has been effectively eliminated. And you might be able to help me with your 'guests.' Am I to understand that you are as angered by their presence as I am?"

Before Ali could answer, Karim Mehregan, one of the platoon leaders who had arrived on the last flight, blurted out, "Sar-Commander Esfandiari! We should not extend mercy to this willing servant of apostates! Let me execute him, as an example to the entire island!"

"Silence, Mehregan," Esfandiari snapped. "I have promised the General that he will not be harmed, and he will not be. If you are in such need of something to do, take your men and sweep the New City and the harbor. Find any Westerners, round them up, and bring them back to the Citadel. We will need hostages, at least for a few days."

His face tight, Mehregan stiffened to attention and nodded. As he turned to leave, Esfandiari called out to him, "And Mehregan? We want hostages, not corpses. You may execute one or two as examples if need be, but no more. Understood?"

9

The younger man looked as if he had bitten into something sour, but nodded stiffly, before marching out of the room.

Esfandiari watched him leave with narrowed eyes. *I should never have let them saddle me with a thrice-damned Twelver. He will be trouble before this is over; those fanatics always are.* That Esfandiari himself could be classed as a fanatic by some did not bother him.

"Come, General," he said. "Let us go begin our conversation with your guests."

***

Immanuel Ortiz was enjoying his coffee when he heard the first gunshots.

Ortiz was getting fat, knew it, and was no longer of the age or vanity to care much. Heavy jowls framed a salt-and-pepper mustache, and he had developed a permanent squint, below thinning silver hair.

He did, however, care very much about his ship, the *Oceana Metropolis*, and his crew. As the reports sounded in the quiet of the increasingly hot morning, his coffee cup froze just below his lips. "Did anybody else hear that?"

Chris Hild and Mark Tranter were the only other crewmembers on the bridge. It was morning, the *Metropolis* was docked, and nothing ever happened on Khadarkh until at least eleven o'clock. Most of the crew was still sleeping below; even though the island was *technically* a Muslim country, there was plenty of booze to be found if you knew where to look. And a few of his people were extremely resourceful when it came to finding out where to look.

Hild looked up, a confused look on his face. "Hear what?"

Tranter looked out the ports, a frown on his face. "Was that fireworks?"

Ortiz didn't think so. It was the wrong time of day, for one thing. He'd never seen fireworks in a Middle Eastern city in the morning. Plenty at night, for any and all occasions, but not in the morning. He levered himself out of his chair and moved to the windows, peering out at the harbor and the city as best he could. The pier where the *Oceana Metropolis* was moored faced the east

10

and the Strait of Hormuz, so he had to crane his head to see much of the city.

The *pops* were continuing, but there were no fireworks rising over Khadarkh City.

"Wake everybody up," he said quietly. "I think there's trouble."

"What kind of trouble?" Hild asked.

"That's not fireworks, which means it's shooting," Ortiz said. "We need to start getting ready to leave if this turns ugly." He had visions of every revolution and civil war that had torn through the region for the last decade running through his head. He did not want to still be moored in the harbor when the next Yemen or Syria kicked off.

Tranter had immediately gotten on the intercom, and was blaring the warning to get up and get to stations across the ship. Paul Carver, the head of the Poseidon Maritime security contractors, stumbled onto the bridge a couple minutes later, looking bleary and hungover. With the weapons having been tossed overboard before entering Khadarkh Harbor, he and his team had had little to do. "What's up?" he asked.

"I don't know, but somebody's been doing a lot of shooting, somewhere out in town," Ortiz said. He was still scanning out the ports, using his binoculars. The shots had died down by then, and he was starting to wonder if maybe he hadn't overreacted. There wasn't even any smoke rising over the city. Maybe somebody had gotten a little carried away with celebrating something. Celebratory gunfire was not unknown in the Middle East, either.

But the strange timing still nagged at him.

"Bridge, this is Carleoni." Vinnie Carleoni was the only crewman fatter than Ortiz, and he sounded out of breath. "We've got company on the gangway. And, uh, Cap'n? They, uh, look like they mean business."

Ortiz recognized that sinking feeling in his gut. He hadn't moved fast enough. He hadn't overreacted; he'd underreacted. He should have weighed anchor and been five nautical miles offshore by now. Instead, he was about to get wrapped up in the latest wave of political and sectarian violence in the Middle East.

Of course, it wasn't that simple; it takes time to get a tanker underway. But he couldn't help but feel like he'd failed, anyway.

"Don't try to stop them, Vinnie," he said heavily over the intercom. "Let them come aboard." There was no other choice. The Poseidon Maritime guys were unarmed, thanks to the laws applying to any ship that docked in Khadarkh's harbor. Resistance was only going to get all of them killed.

He looked down at the coffee in his cup. He took a quick gulp. It tasted sour. He knew it was his own despair he was tasting; his coffee was good. He'd just lost his taste for it, having a good idea of what was coming.

Boots rattled on the ladder leading up to the bridge. A moment later, five men in khaki, with combat vests on and black rifles in their hands, stormed onto the bridge. Ortiz held his hands up, glancing to either side to make sure that Hild, Tranter, and especially Carver, were doing the same. They were merchant sailors. They weren't in any position to try to fight, especially to try to fight soldiers, and these guys looked like soldiers.

The five men kept them under their guns, but didn't say anything. They seemed to be waiting for something. After a prolonged, awkward silence, a sixth man entered the bridge. Short, dark-haired and bearded, he pushed past the riflemen and looked around the bridge imperiously.

"Who is the Captain?" he asked, in thickly accented English.

"I am," Ortiz immediately answered. "Whatever you want, we won't resist. We'll cooperate."

"Good," the man said. As Ortiz looked the little man in the eyes, he saw a feral glint there that made his blood run cold. He recognized the look. He'd seen it before, in more than one dive bar down harborside. However conciliatory his words might be, this man was eager to kill someone, and was going to take any excuse he could find. A drop of sweat rolled down Ortiz' back. The situation was suddenly far more dangerous than he had feared.

The little man looked from man to man, sizing each of his captives up. His eyes came to rest on Carver, and Ortiz thought his heart had just stopped.

12

"Who are you?" the little man asked Carver. "What do you do on the ship?"

Carver glanced at Ortiz. It was possible that he might manage to bluff that he was just another sailor, but he didn't have the same look. None of his guys did. Most of them had still maintained fairly military physiques; they hadn't had much else to do at sea so far, and the *Oceana Metropolis* had a decent gym, one that the rest of her crew didn't actually use that much.

"I am a security contractor," he said, apparently deciding on the truth.

It was the wrong thing to say. Ortiz could tell that immediately, as the little bearded man looked back at him with a sudden ugly light in his eye and a small half-smile on his face. "Security? Like mercenary?" he asked. His swagger seemed to suddenly become more pronounced, and Ortiz felt his heart sink. The would-be killer had found his convenient target.

"You protect the ship? Protect these men?" the little man asked.

Either Carver didn't see where this was going, or he did and couldn't see a way out. When Ortiz looked at the man's eyes, he saw something close to panic there; Carver knew what was coming. And he knew that there was no escape.

And Ortiz cursed silently as he realized that he couldn't think of a way to head this off, either.

"Yes, that is my job," Carver said quietly.

The little man nodded, satisfied. Then he let his rifle hang on its sling, drew his Makarov, and shot Carver in the head.

The man fell to the deck, blood spattering on the console behind him as he dropped. More poured from the exit wound at the back of his skull, pooling on the deck. He was twitching as his nervous system shut down from the sudden, catastrophic damage to his brain. Hild and Tranter were staring in shock.

"He cannot protect you now," the little man said, satisfied. "Any who resist will die just like him. Understand?"

Ortiz only nodded. "Yes, we understand," he said. He momentarily wanted to protest that he'd already said they wouldn't resist, but he knew that that would be a very, very bad idea. He'd be right there on the deck next to Carver, spilling his blood and

13

brains out on the steel, and there wouldn't be anyone to look after his crew. Leterrier was a good First Mate, but he wasn't made for this kind of situation. He wouldn't do well, trying to keep the crew together, sane, and as safe as possible in captivity, especially not captivity with the immediate threat of violent death.

The little man pointed to him. "You, come with us. Find the rest of your crew."

Ortiz only nodded again, and followed when the man started to leave the bridge. There was nothing else to do.

CHAPTER 2

There was an envelope waiting on the step when John Brannigan came down out of the hills and got to the door of his cabin.

He looked down at it, frowning. He had a PO Box in town, but he rarely checked it, because it was rarely used. He hadn't told many people where he had been going after Rebecca had died. And this envelope wasn't marked. No address, no stamp. Just a plain white envelope, sealed and sitting on his porch. And from the looks of it, it hadn't been there long. It had rained two days before, and the envelope was dry and smooth. It hadn't gotten wet.

He picked up the envelope, opened the door, and walked inside. The cabin was snug, and though he'd been gone for a week, it wasn't that cold inside. He'd made sure that it was well-built. It had been intended to be Rebecca's last house. She had died before he'd finished it.

Levering the heavy pack off his back, he tossed the envelope on the rough-hewn table and started unpacking. He had just shy of a hundred pounds of venison in game bags in the pack, along with the muley's not-inconsiderable rack. There was more hanging on the tree, back up the mountain, and he still had to go get it. But his eye kept straying to the envelope on the table. It bothered him.

His isolation and anonymity had been deliberate. When the Marine Corps had forced him to retire, just before Rebecca had been diagnosed with cancer, he had descended into a bitterness that had eaten away at him. No longer a part of the profession that he had devoted twenty-three years of his life to, and suddenly faced with an invisible enemy that he couldn't fight, couldn't grapple with, couldn't blow up or shoot, he'd been tempted to descend into the bottle, but Rebecca had needed him to stay strong. So he had, and by the time she had eventually died anyway, he hadn't even felt the temptation. He just hadn't wanted to be around people. So, he'd retreated to the woods. Only his son, who was presently halfway across the country, following in his father's footsteps at Camp Lejeune, knew for sure where the cabin was.

Had Hank told someone? That was the only explanation he could think of. Someone had hand-delivered that envelope, and they had to have had precise directions to find the cabin in the first place.

His eyes narrowed. It had to have been important for Hank to have talked. He just couldn't think of what it might be.

Well, there was only one way to find out. He hung the last game bag, stepped to the table, and picked up the envelope.

There was a note inside. It was short and to the point.

Colonel,

I need to see you. It's urgent. I wouldn't have disturbed you if it wasn't. Please meet me at the Rocking K in town at noon on the 22nd.

Chavez

He folded the note and stuffed it in his pocket as he looked around the cabin, already cataloging what he needed to do before he left in his head. That he was going to go had been decided without much in the way of reflection. He recognized Hector Chavez' handwriting, as he was sure the other man had known he would. And if Hector was looking for him, he trusted that it really *was* important. He didn't know why, but he felt something that he hadn't felt in the three years since his forced retirement. It was still vague, more a hope than anything else, but it was there.

Purpose.

He had to go back up the mountain and get the rest of the meat. He wasn't going to leave over half his kill to the bears and the scavengers. But that could easily be done by nightfall. It was the 20th. He could be in town on the morning of the 22nd with ease.

He finished getting the game unloaded and hung, and then shouldered his pack and headed back up.

***

The Rocking K was *the* local diner in tiny Junction City. Mama Taft had run it for years, and newcomers, like Brannigan, learned quick that Mama Taft wasn't anyone to mess with. You addressed her as "Ma'am" when you made your order, and you said "Please" and "Thank you." In return, you got some of the finest cooking in the county, if not the state. It had been an easy adjustment for Brannigan, since a strict upbringing, in addition to twenty-three years in the Marine Corps, had hard-wired such manners into him, at least when dealing with most people. His language tended to change when surrounded by gunfighters, but that was another habit that many men like him developed.

As he strode through the door and took off his hat— another one of Mama Taft's unspoken rules—Ginger Taft, Mama's granddaughter, was at the counter. "Good morning, John!" she said brightly. Ginger was as red-headed as her name suggested, and was one of the single most cheerful people Brannigan thought he'd ever met. She leaned across the counter. "There are a couple men in a booth in back," she confided. "They're looking for you; asked me to point you back there when you got here."

"Thanks, Ginger," he said. "I'll go join 'em. How are you and Mama this morning?"

She dimpled. "We're fine, John. How did the hunt go?"

"Nice twelve-point muley, two days ago," he replied. "I'll bring some of the venison by later. I sure can't eat it all myself."

Ginger cocked an eyebrow skeptically, eyeing him. John Brannigan was six-foot-four, broad-shouldered and narrow-waisted. He could pack away a lot of food when he was hungry, and Ginger knew it. "I doubt that, but we'll be happy to take some of it off your hands," she said. "Shoo, now, those men want to talk to you."

17

Brannigan headed toward the back, a faint smile on his lips. Ginger was about the same age as Hank, and it always cheered him up a little to talk to her. It made the world feel a little bit less bleak and empty, with Rebecca gone and Hank far away, putting his own neck on the line.

Hector Chavez stood up as Brannigan approached the booth, and held out a hand. Brannigan shook it firmly, looking his old friend in the eye.

Hector had been medically retired a year before Brannigan's own forced retirement. He and Brannigan had been peers for many years, though Hector had been within reach of a star before his heart had betrayed him. He was looking a bit heavier these days, accentuated by the suit he was wearing, in marked contrast to just about everyone else in the diner.

As for Brannigan, he knew what Hector saw. The outdoor life had kept him lean and strong. His hair was a little longer, and quite a bit grayer, than it had been the last time his old friend had seen him. His thick, handlebar mustache was new, too, almost blending with the salt-and-pepper stubble from a week in the woods. None of the gray could disguise the hard lines of his angular features, the power still resident in his towering frame, or the renewed, steely glint in his gray eyes.

"I'm glad you could come, John," Hector said. "It took some talking to get Hank to spill the beans as to where you'd gone."

"He's a good son," Brannigan said, as he slid into the booth across from Hector and another man, fatter and balder, and wearing a rather more expensive suit. Brannigan momentarily felt slightly underdressed, as he'd come down in his jeans, boots, and flannel shirt, but shook the thought off. He was here for business, and he was too old to worry about image games. *They* wanted to talk to *him*.

"I'm sorry to bother you, but when this came up, you were the first one I thought of," Hector said. "This is Frederick Tanner. He's a rep for Tannhauser Petroleum." The fat, bald man extended a hand, and Brannigan shook it. Rather as expected, Tanner's handshake was soft, clammy, and somewhat less than impressive. "I take it you haven't been paying much attention to the news?"

"No attention whatsoever," Brannigan replied. "I'm out of the game, so I hunt, fish, and work on my cabin. That's about it."

"We have a...delicate situation in the Persian Gulf," Tanner said. His voice was soft and somewhat breathy. "One of my company's tankers has been taken hostage."

"Hold on," Hector interjected. "Let's back up a moment, and give the Colonel the *full* story." Brannigan kept his face carefully impassive at Chavez' use of his former rank. It was a signal, a quiet message about just why they were there. And he forced that sudden, hopeful feeling in his chest down. He was going to hear them out, and get all the details before he made any decisions.

Chavez looked Brannigan in the eye. "Are you at all familiar with the island of Khadarkh?" he asked.

Brannigan nodded. "We sailed by it on a float or two," he said. "Strategically placed just west of the Strait of Hormuz, technically an independent kingdom, though the royals have played the allies game with both Iran and Saudi Arabia over the last few decades."

"Well, about a week ago," Hector said, "a force of paramilitaries, looking suspiciously like an IRGC Qods Force unit, but without any insignia or markings, seized control of the island. Not a lot of details have gotten out, but it sounds like it went very smoothly. Up until they massacred the surrendered Khadarkhi Army, anyway.

"The king was out of the country, in Riyadh for a meeting with the Saudi royals at the time," he continued. "Needless to say, he's staying there for the moment. These unknowns completely control the island. In the course of the coup, however, they also took hostages."

"One of our tankers, the *Oceana Metropolis*, was docked in Khadarkh Harbor at the time," Tanner explained. "The entire crew was taken hostage, and the leader, a Commander Esfandiari, issued a warning that any sign of American naval presence or aircraft within one hundred nautical miles of the island will result in all of the hostages being executed." He shuddered suddenly. "They already murdered our security contractors. There were pictures."

Brannigan looked at Chavez. "Don't tell me that the Navy's holding off because of terrorist threats," he said.

Chavez looked troubled. "No one is saying anything," he said, "but so far the Navy is holding off, both to the north, near Kuwait, and off the Strait of Hormuz. The word I'm getting from the inside is that it's not just because of the hostages, either."

Brannigan just raised an inquisitive eyebrow.

"The word on the street is that the Saudis got the message through their lobbyists in Washington to certain influential Congressmen and Senators. They want the US to stay out of the Khadarkh situation entirely," Chavez said. "No one knows why, but they appear to have gotten their way. There are negotiators flying into Dubai and Bahrain, but the Navy is presently in a holding pattern."

Brannigan frowned. That was unusual. Especially in the last couple of decades, the Navy had come down on pirates like a ton of bricks, the *Maersk Alabama* mission being one of the most high-profile such incidents. It really made no sense that they wouldn't move on terrorists, simply because they had hostages.

"The tanker can be written off," Tanner said, "but the longer our people are in those terrorists' hands, the worse this could get. I've tried talking to anyone in Washington who might listen, and so far, all they've offered are the same canned platitudes about negotiations. But the terrorists haven't made any demands. They've only warned everyone to stay away, or else they'll start killing the hostages."

He wrung his hands in front of him. "After getting stonewalled for three days, I started to look for other options," he explained. "Mr. Chavez was the first one I managed to make contact with."

"I'm running a maritime security concern of my own, now," Chavez said when Brannigan glanced at him. "They're good boys, but not really cut out for hostage rescue. Not to mention that we're far too high-profile to pull off an Operation HOTFOOT." He was referring to Ross Perot's 1979 rescue of two of his employees from Tehran. "That was when I thought about you. I know you've been off-grid for a while, but I also know that you know people, you've got a well-deserved rep for pulling off the impossible through sheer guts and audacity, and that it wouldn't take you long to get back in the zone." He gave his old friend an appraising glance. "From the looks of things, even less time than I'd expected."

Brannigan had a host of questions and concerns, but the gears were already turning in his mind. "This is one hell of a risky op you've got in mind," he said, "not only in terms of possible opposition." He looked at Tanner. "Legal authorities don't tend to like private military forces crossing international borders and conducting unilateral operations, you know."

"Tannhauser has a small army of lawyers," Tanner replied. "If anything goes wrong on the legal front, we will cover you as best we can. You have my promise on that."

Brannigan eyed him. "Under the circumstances, you'll understand that I don't know you well enough to know if your promise is good in that regard," he said quietly. "This is some heavy stuff we're talking about. Lifetime in Leavenworth level heavy."

And yet, even as he said it, he knew he was going to take the job. It was an opportunity, regardless of the risks involved.

"Mr. Brannigan...*Colonel* Brannigan," Tanner said earnestly, "I fully understand the risk I'm asking you to take. Really, I do. But you know as well as I do, deep in my gut, that negotiators aren't going to solve this. And if the military waits too long..."

"Then the hostages are dead," Brannigan finished for him. He took a deep breath, then looked at Hector. "If I do this, it won't be cheap, you know that? I'm going to have to find men, good men, set up logistics, get in, and get out."

"How much are you thinking?" Chavez asked. Brannigan took a pen out of his pocket, grabbed one of the paper napkins on the table, thought for a moment, then scribbled a figure on the napkin and shoved it across the table.

Chavez's eyebrows climbed a little, and he whistled softly, but then he got a thoughtful look on his face, as he started to run the numbers in his own head. Chavez was no fool, and he knew the costs involved as well as Brannigan did. Maybe even better. Tanner just stared at the number blankly, then nodded.

"Consider it done," he said. He pulled a checkbook out of the inside of his suit. "How much will you need up-front?"

Brannigan held up a hand. "Doesn't work that way," he said. "Hector?"

"I can get a shell company set up in fairly short order," Chavez said. "All transactions—all 'white' transactions, anyway, can go through that."

"Get me the info by the end of the day, if you can," Brannigan said. He was already fully in planning mode, building a mental checklist of things he would need to do, and men he needed to recruit. "What kind of a timeline are we talking, here?"

"As soon as possible," Chavez said, before Tanner could say anything. "You know as well as I do that the hostages are living on borrowed time, especially since the bad guys have already killed five people, not counting Khadarkhis."

"How many in the crew?" he asked.

"Fifteen," Tanner replied. Brannigan was already taking brief, almost indecipherable notes on another napkin.

"There are unconfirmed reports that the terrorists might be holding as many as thirty to forty American hostages," Chavez put in. "The *Oceana Metropolis'* crew were not the only Americans on the island."

Brannigan nodded. "I'll need as complete an intel breakdown as possible, as soon as possible," he said.

"I'll have a comprehensive intel dump put together and delivered to your cabin by eight o'clock tomorrow night," Chavez said.

"Send it to my PO Box," Brannigan replied. "I'll probably be out of town at that time. There are some guys I'm going to have to go find personally." He already had three men in mind. He'd need more, but at least one of them was going to have recruits of his own in mind, as well. "Crap. I'm going to have to get a cell phone for this." Brannigan hadn't owned a phone in over a year. "One other thing," he said, spearing Chavez with a look. "I'm going to need as up-to-the-minute reports on what the Navy's doing as you can get me. If the Navy starts moving in, the op is off. I am *not* getting caught in the crossfire, and I am *not* getting rolled up for an illegal military operation. Fair enough?"

"I'll see what I can do," Chavez said. "I've still got a few friends in high places, who might be willing to bend the law a bit to help out an old friend." He chuckled dryly. "They've done it before, and for far lesser causes."

Brannigan nodded again. His mind was already far away from the table, the diner, or even Mama Taft's cooking. Planning details and considerations were flying through his head. There was a lot to get done.

Most importantly, after three years, he suddenly felt more alive than he had since that fateful night on the African coast, when he'd defied the ROEs to save another group of hostages. That had been the end of one career. Fitting, perhaps, that another hostage rescue could be the beginning of another.

He stood up. "If I'm going to make this happen," he said, "I'm going to have to get moving. Hector, is your phone number still the same?" Chavez nodded, though he looked slightly nonplused that Brannigan apparently remembered it. "Good. I'll pick up a couple of burners today, and hit you up with the primary's number. In the meantime, gentlemen, I have a lot of work to do. I'll be in touch."

He didn't notice Ginger's eyes on him as he strode out the door. She noticed the change in him, though. While John Brannigan had always had a considerable presence, the man who had just left the diner had a new drive and purpose in his step.

John Brannigan was going back to war. And he couldn't wait.

CHAPTER 3

Carlo Santelli figured that he was probably the last man in America who actually went out to his fence to get the morning paper anymore. Everyone else just read the news online, or skimmed the headlines and got angry. Which, of course, was part of why he only read the local paper. It was mostly meaningless, but still far more applicable to his own life than the slanted ramblings of a major national news outlet, trying to get him outraged about things he couldn't control or alter in any way.

Carlo would never be the image of athleticism, and he had gotten slightly rounder since his retirement. He still ran twenty miles a week, more out of deeply ingrained habit than anything else, but he didn't look it. He looked like a clerk, or maybe a baker. It took a second look to see past the belly, the round face, and the glasses, to see that his shape was closer to the barrel torso of a powerlifter, his hands were broad, thick, and scarred, and that his nose had been broken several times. The Eagle, Globe, and Anchor tattoo on his shoulder was usually hidden by his shirt.

He was presently dressed in his pajamas and a t-shirt as he stepped out onto his porch. Melissa was still asleep; she probably wouldn't stir for another half hour. Which was fine with him. He loved her well enough, but she liked to talk, and sometimes Santelli just wanted some quiet.

With a wide stretch, he sauntered down to the picket fence and retrieved the paper. As he looked around, he shook his head. The old suburb wasn't what it used to be. There was trash in the gutters now, and while most of the houses were still fairly well kept-up, a few were noticeably decaying. The wealthier folks had all moved away. It wasn't the ghetto, not yet, but it was getting a little run-down.

Picking up the paper, he scanned the headlines, seeing nothing particularly of interest, and wandered back inside. He'd go for his morning run in a few minutes, after his coffee. But when he stepped inside, Melissa was standing in the doorway, her hair a mess, holding up his cell phone. "It's for you," she said blearily.

"Thanks, doll," he said, taking the phone from her. "Sorry it woke you up, I don't know who would be calling at this hour." The sun wasn't even all the way up. Melissa mumbled something sleepily and shuffled back toward the bedroom. Santelli lifted the phone to his ear. "Yeah?" he said, his nasal Boston accent suddenly slightly more pronounced.

"Hello, Carlo," a familiar voice rumbled over the phone.

A broad grin spread across Santelli's face. "Hot damn, Colonel, it's good to hear from you. What's the job?"

He could almost see Brannigan's frown over the phone. "Carlo, we haven't talked in two years. I don't even own a phone. How do you know I've got a job?"

"Because that's the only thing I can think of that would have brought you back into the modern world, sir," Santelli laughed. "Plus, I might have been waiting most of that two years for you to call me with a mission. You know me. I've been retired for two and a half years, and I still don't know what the hell I'm supposed to do."

"Plenty of jobs out there for a retired Sergeant Major," Brannigan pointed out.

"Yeah, and most of them are either pushing paper or babysitting," Santelli replied, sitting down at his kitchen table. "I did plenty of that during my last eight years in the Corps. So come on, sir, spill it. I know you wouldn't come down off the mountain for just any old contracting gig."

"Not over the phone," Brannigan replied. "At least no details. But it's a rescue mission, in the Middle East. Pay's good, too."

"I'm in," Santelli said. "Where are we meeting up?"

"Damn, Carlo, you didn't even hesitate."

"Of course not," Santelli snorted. "Not when you're asking. Where? And do I need to scrounge anyone up?"

"I've got two more names in mind, but I think we'll need eight men, at a bare minimum," Brannigan said. "I'm going after Hancock and Villareal."

"Villareal's going to be a hard sell," Santelli warned.

"I know it," Brannigan replied grimly. "But if you've got a better combat doc in mind, I'd like to hear it."

Santelli blew a deep breath toward the ceiling. "No, I don't. Good luck, though. You're gonna need it." He thought for a second. "I've got one or two guys in mind. I'll see if I can dig them up."

"You sure about this, Carlo?" Brannigan asked. "I called you because I had to, but Hector told me you've settled in a bit. Even have a lady friend."

"Yeah, but I think she's getting tired of me, anyway," Santelli replied. "Come on, sir. You know I'm not the settling down type. I've tried it, and it ain't working out for me too good. I'll go find a couple guys, and we'll meet up."

"Good to have you aboard, Carlo," Brannigan said. "I feel better about this already."

***

Brannigan walked down the beach, breathing deeply of the cool, salt air. He'd had to leave early to make sure he got to California while it was still morning, which was why it had still been dark when he'd called Carlo Santelli, out in Boston. He was already tired, from a combination of the early wakeup, the flight, and the drive up the California coast. It had been a while since he'd had to negotiate California traffic, and he did not have fond memories of it. That morning had already confirmed that those memories were understating the case.

Tammy Hancock had told him where he could find Roger in the morning. The man was doing pretty well for himself and his

27

family, having been a canny investor during his Marine Corps career. From what Brannigan had managed to find out, Hancock didn't really need to work anymore. He worked as a firearms and skydiving instructor more for something to do than for the sake of income.

With any other man, that would have immediately scratched Hancock off the list. Well-to-do, comfortable men with families didn't usually go haring off on dangerous mercenary missions in the Third World. But Brannigan knew Hancock. If anything, he was banking on the man's current comfort to be his primary selling point.

The beach wasn't crowded; it was a Monday morning. The only people in sight were the usual beach bums and surfers, mostly affluent locals who, like Roger, didn't really need to work. At least half a dozen surfers were visible out on the waves.

He stopped and folded his arms, as he watched the man with the black-and-white surfboard suddenly turn in toward shore. The swell of the next wave set was rising behind him, and began to break as he hopped up to his feet. Expertly maintaining his balance, the man rode the edge of the wave almost clear in to shore, weaving beneath the crest, always staying just barely ahead of getting hammered into the ocean floor by the wall of water behind him. As the wave finally broke in a cascade of white foam, the man slid off the side, dropping back down onto his board and paddling in toward shore.

Brannigan walked down to the waterline to meet him. Roger Hancock was still fit, his sharp, angular features perhaps more lined than they had been, his hair close-cropped. He really didn't look that different from the last time Brannigan had seen him, when he'd been Gunny Hancock.

"Holy shit," Hancock said, as he waded ashore, gathering his board under his arm. He stuck out his hand, and Brannigan shook it, both men's grips like vises. "What brings you down the mountain, John?"

"Something I think you'd be interested in, Roger," Brannigan said. "Somewhere we can talk for a minute?"

"Sure," Hancock said, motioning up the beach. "Let's go up by my truck. I was done for this morning, anyway."

28

The two men, Branningan standing almost a head taller than Hancock, headed up the sandy strand to where Hancock's big dually was parked. Hancock slid his board into the open bed, then grabbed a towel off the back seat and started rubbing the saltwater off of himself as he unzipped his wetsuit. "So, give me the rundown," he said.

Brannigan explained the mission briefly, making sure to stress the fact that, as far as he knew, it was an entirely off-the-books, unofficial op. He wanted Hancock, but he wanted the man to go in with both eyes open.

Roger listened without comment, nodding once or twice. "Who else is on board?" he asked.

"Santelli, so far," Brannigan said.

"Well, I'm in," Hancock said. "And I know another guy who would be perfect, if we can find him."

"What about Tammy?" Brannigan asked. "Don't you need to discuss this with her?"

"Tammy will understand," Hancock replied. "Honestly, she's been worried about me for a while. She doesn't talk about it very often, but I'm bored, and she can tell. Did you talk to her already?"

"Only to ask where you were," Brannigan answered.

"Then she already knows something's up," Hancock said. "She's no dummy. And I know she knows you just well enough to be reassured that I'll have a good chance of coming back in one piece."

Brannigan eyed his old subordinate skeptically, then shrugged. "You know her better than I do, so I'll take your word for it. Make sure you do what you can to put her mind at ease, though. It's never easy to go back to deploying, once you've gotten comfortable at home."

"I will, but she'll be fine," Hancock said. "I'm assuming you drove here?"

"Yeah," Brannigan said, jerking a thumb at the rental sedan. Hancock looked at it, looked at Brannigan's towering frame, and grinned.

"Really? How do you fit in that thing?"

"With difficulty," Brannigan growled. "Are you done?"

29

Hancock laughed. "Come on, follow me to the house. I've got to get changed and make a couple of calls if we're going to go raise hell in the Persian Gulf for a few weeks. And you can help ease Tammy's mind while I do."

***

Sam Childress got out of his truck and trudged toward the temp office. He paused in front of the glass doors. "I hate my life," he muttered, then pulled the door open and went into the lobby.

"Over here, Sam," Julie Keating called. She was at her desk in the corner, apparently waiting specifically for him, since there were several other people there ahead of him, sitting and waiting to be called, while the other three receptionists were busy. Trying to ignore the looks he was getting from the other temp workers, he walked over and sank into the chair across from Keating's desk. His too-long arms and legs dangled from the chair, and his dark, flyaway hair looked like it hadn't seen a comb in a month, even though he'd tried to smooth it just before he'd come through the door.

"Sam, you have got to learn to go along to get along," Julie said. She was a pretty woman, either around Childress' age or a little younger, with shiny blond hair pulled back in a ponytail and an enormous diamond on her left ring finger. Sam had looked rather wistfully at that rock a few times, rather envying whoever had his shit together enough to have afforded that ring, to give to that woman. His own last girlfriend had suddenly wanted nothing to do with him as soon as he'd gotten fired from his first civilian job.

"He was going to get people hurt, Julie!" Sam protested. "I had to say something!"

Keating sighed. "Look, Sam, nobody's telling you not to say something if you see something wrong," she said, a note of exasperation working into her voice. "But there are polite ways of saying these things, that won't get you a black mark from one of our client companies. This is the second client who's told us not to send you back! If you get a third, we won't be able to find work for you anymore!" She put a hand to her forehead. "You've got to work on a better filter between your brain and your mouth, Sam."

"Childress with a filter?" a voice with a heavy Boston accent said from behind him. "That'll be the day."

Sam twisted around in surprise. He knew that voice. "Sergeant Major Santelli?" He instinctively scrambled to his feet. "What are you doing here?"

"Looking for you," the short, stocky Italian replied. "Can I borrow Sam for a few minutes, Ma'am?" he asked Keating.

"I'm trying to get him some work for today," she said.

"Well," Santelli replied, as he put a meaty hand on Childress' shoulder and started to steer him toward the door, "I might just have a solution to that problem. If not, I promise I'll send him back." Without waiting for Keating to answer, he kept propelling Childress toward the door.

"I'm sorry, Julie," Childress called over his shoulder, giving her an apologetic look. "I'll be back in a minute."

Once they were out in the parking lot, Santelli turned and folded his arms, shaking his head as he looked Childress over. "It's been a merry chase, tracking you down, Childress," he said disapprovingly. "At least six *former* employers, that I've had to follow like breadcrumbs ever since I went looking for you at the job your mother *thinks* you're still working at. Still haven't learned to keep your mouth under control, have you?"

Childress stared at the horizon past Santelli's shoulder, remembering more than one previous such conversation happening in the Sergeant Major's office, on a couple of occasions that had gone past the First Sergeant's office. Neither man was still in uniform, but when it came to Sergeant Major Santelli, some habits died hard, even for Childress.

"I guess not, Sergeant Major," was all he said.

"Well, it's a good thing for you that I really don't have to give a damn about your mind-to-mouth filter, or lack thereof, anymore," Santelli said. "I only care about your abilities and your loyalty. The latter I already know is more than sufficient. You look like you've kept in shape. How soon do you think you could knock the rust off your combat skills?"

Childress snapped his eyes down to meet the former Sergeant Major's. "You mean…?"

The shorter man nodded. "Colonel Brannigan's got a job. High-risk, combat zone sort of stuff. Strictly off the books. I thought of you first thing. Are you in?"

Childress never thought he'd feel so grateful to Sergeant Major Santelli, the man who had signed off on not one but two Battalion-level Non-Judicial Punishments for insubordination that had busted him back down a rank. But the man had just offered him a lifeline.

"Fucking A right, I'm in, Sergeant Major," he said. "When do we leave?"

***

Doctor Juan Villareal was taking a much-needed break, sitting down for the first time in six hours. He had just lifted the coffee cup to his lips when there was a knock at the break room door.

"The door's open," he called out, frowning slightly. None of the other doctors or nurses would have hesitated to just walk in the door; the break room was for everybody in the ER. But when the door swung open, he suddenly understood the reason for the knock. He put the coffee cup on the table and stood up, holding out his hand to the towering, broad-shouldered man in the doorway.

"Holy hell, John," he said, shaking Brannigan's hand. "What are you doing here, half an hour after midnight?"

"Looking for you, Doc," Brannigan said, shutting the door behind him and waving Villareal back to his seat. He grabbed another one of the metal and plastic chairs, flipped it around, and sat down, his forearms resting on the back. "I've got a proposition for you."

Villareal gave him a sharp glance. The young MD was thinner than most of his colleagues, still just as rangy as he had been as a young Navy Corpsman, almost ten years before. His hawk-like features were starting to show a few lines, though they paled in comparison to the deeper look of weariness that only a few who knew him could ever see in his eyes. His hair was as black as it ever had been. "What kind of proposition?" he asked warily.

Brannigan looked him in the eye. "I need a medic for a job," he said levelly. "A rescue mission."

Villareal's black eyes narrowed. "What kind of a rescue mission?"

Brannigan glanced meaningfully at the ceiling. "There's CCTV over just about every inch of this hospital," Villareal said, a deeper feeling of dread forming in the pit of his stomach. "But there's no audio. You can talk."

Brannigan laid out the mission that Chavez had told him about. Villareal's face got drawn, and the old, haunted expression came into his eyes. He shook his head.

"I swore off all of that when I went to med school, John," he said. "And you know damned well why."

"And I also know damned well that none of that was your fault, Doc," Brannigan retorted. "As do you, if you'd disengage your damned emotions from it for a moment and looked at it clearly."

"Clearly?" Villareal demanded, leaning forward and clenching a fist on the tabletop. "It was clear enough, John. 'The best medicine is lead downrange,' wasn't that the line we all parroted? But it turned out that it wasn't all bad guys downrange, was it?"

"And you had no way of knowing that, Doc," Brannigan replied, with a weariness that suggested that both of them were simply repeating a conversation they had had before. Which they were. "We all saw the fire coming from that reed line."

"Doesn't matter," Villareal said, as he slumped back in his chair. "The fact remains that I pulled the trigger, and afterward there were three dead kids in the ditch, and none of them had weapons."

"They didn't have weapons when we found 'em," Brannigan replied tiredly. "But you know as well as I do that the bad guys regularly took the weapons after an engagement."

Villareal shook his head. "They were kids, John. That's all that matters to me. That's why I haven't touched a gun since I got out, and why I went to med school and took the Hippocratic Oath. I won't carry a weapon again. You need someone else."

Someone who doesn't have a problem with spilling blood went unspoken.

"I need a doctor," Brannigan replied, a hard edge in his voice. "And you were the best field medic I ever had, before or since. If you can't carry a weapon in good conscience, fine. I can work around that. Medics didn't carry for a long time. But I need you. The boys I'm going to be taking in there need you. Hell, in all likelihood, those hostages are going to need you."

Villareal looked Brannigan in the eye, and felt his resolve weakening. Brannigan had been one of the best combat leaders he'd ever served under, and despite his own doubts, misgivings, and the demons that visited him at night, he suddenly felt a powerful urge to say yes. Not because of some mystical leadership ability of Brannigan's, that magically inspired men to follow him. He didn't believe in any such thing, any more than Brannigan did. No, this was simply because, despite his own bitterness, Brannigan had won his loyalty a long time before the incident that had scarred his soul for life, and, his own ghosts notwithstanding, it felt like turning the man down, especially when he sincerely said he was needed, would feel like a betrayal.

Juan Villareal, MD, was a fundamentally moral man. He had become even more so ever since the fight in Afghanistan that had nearly broken him. Betrayal wasn't in him.

He looked down at the table, his lips thinned, a frown creasing his brow. When he looked up at Brannigan again, there was a pained look in his eyes. "It would be a lot easier to say, 'No,' if I could convince myself that you were being manipulative," he said. He sighed. "Unfortunately, I know you too well, John, even if it has been nine years. Why can't you be as cynical and hollow as all the other officers I knew?"

"It's not in my nature, Doc," Brannigan said. "And I won't apologize for that fact working in my favor now. Are you in?"

"I've got patients here," Villareal protested, trying one last tack. "I've got a work schedule, people who are counting on me."

Brannigan chuckled darkly. "Do you really think I came in here without doing my homework, Doc?" he asked. "I know you've got two *months'* worth of leave that you're about to lose if you don't take it."

Defeated, Villareal nodded. "When and where?" he asked.

Brannigan pulled a card with a set of directions out of his pocket and shoved it across the table before standing. "Here, in two days," he said.

Villareal shoved the card in his pocket and reached for his coffee. He didn't look up again as Brannigan left the room.

***

Joe Flanagan easily whipped the fly in a big figure eight above his head, then, with a practiced swing, expertly dropped the nymph just upstream of the bank. The brightly-colored bit of thread and feather drifted downstream, then suddenly vanished. Flanagan lifted the rod tip upward, setting the hook before the trout could figure out that the fly wasn't nearly as edible as it looked. In a moment, he was working the fish in toward shore, pulling it in with a side-to-side give-and-take, slowly reeling the fish in as it tired. Finally, he reached down and scooped a good-sized German Brown up out of the water.

"You've gotten good at this," Roger Hancock said, farther up the bank. Flanagan looked up at his old Platoon Sergeant and cracked a lopsided smile, but said nothing as he removed the hook from the fish's mouth and laid it in his creel.

Hancock looked around at the surrounding cottonwoods and the slow-moving river as he descended the bank. "I've got to hand it to you though, Joe. You sure can find some good spots."

"It's quiet, and not too many of the tourists know about this stretch of river," Flanagan said, as he climbed up to meet Hancock. The two men shook hands, turning it into a one-armed bear hug. "If this gets into some 'fly fishing guide,' I'm going to have to find somewhere else." He set his rod down. "So, what brings you so far inland, that you couldn't talk about over the phone?"

"Brannigan's coming out of retirement," Hancock said. "He's got a job; a hostage rescue mission on an island in the Persian Gulf. Officially unknown adversary, but suspected to be Iranian. He's putting a small team together. You were the first one I thought of."

Flanagan cocked an eyebrow. Middling height, broad-shouldered, and dark-haired, his green eyes were bright in a deeply tanned face above a beard so black it almost looked blue. "I've been out of the game for a bit," he pointed out.

"We all have," Hancock replied. "And I know you. How many days a week are you still PTing?"

"Five or six," Flanagan admitted.

"You've got a good mind for tactics, Joe, and I know you too well to think that you've lost your edge," Hancock continued. "Come on. You're itching for this. Don't try to bullshit me."

Flanagan just smiled slightly, shrugged, and dug a phone out of his pack. He punched a contact and held it to his ear. Hancock just shook his head and smiled. He'd won. Flanagan didn't often say much, and a lot of people could be somewhat weirded out by it. But Hancock had gotten close enough to the quiet man to understand what he was thinking, even when he didn't say anything at all.

"Iggy?" Flanagan said. "It's Joe. Yeah. Don't know. Maybe a couple weeks, maybe a couple months. Good deal. Thanks, Iggy. Later." He hung up the phone. "Okay. I'm free for a while," he said.

"That's how you tell your boss that you're leaving?" Hancock asked with a laugh.

Flanagan shrugged again. "He's an old vet, himself. We've talked about it. He's cool."

As they gathered up Flanagan's fishing gear and headed up the bank toward Flanagan's Jeep and Hancock's rental car, Hancock asked, "Are you going to call Mary and tell her you're leaving for a while, too? Or do we need to stop by?"

"Mary and I broke up about a month ago," Flanagan replied. "Didn't work out. It's fine. It was amicable."

"I'm sure Kev has read you the riot act over that," Hancock observed as he opened his car door. "Or does he know yet?"

"You think I'd tell *him*?" Flanagan retorted. "He wouldn't leave me alone for *months*."

Hancock laughed. "So, where is he?"

"It'll be a few hours," Flanagan said as he climbed behind the wheel. "Let's go drop that rental off. I'll drive."

***

Santelli was just reaching for the doorknob when the door swung open. He hastily stepped out of the way as the thin, dark-haired woman with dark-rimmed glasses stormed out of the office in a huff, pausing just long enough to shoot the short, stocky retired Sergeant Major a somewhat imperious glare before stalking away down the hallway, managing to radiate pure, self-righteous fury with every stomping step.

Santelli watched her go for a moment, unsure if that was a good sign or a warning.

When he stepped through the door and closed it behind him, he asked, "What was that all about?"

The slender, hatchet-faced man with a small patch of beard on the tip of his chin looked up from his desk. "Who wants to know?" he demanded. His accent was decidedly Midwestern, though he looked like he'd be right at home on the streets of Baghdad or Amman.

"You David Aziz?" Santelli asked, dropping into the chair across the desk from the younger man.

"*Professor* Aziz," was the reply. "Who are you? I don't have any appointments, and don't take this the wrong way, but at this hour of the day, I'd only be accepting appointments with hot coeds, anyway."

Santelli laughed. "Is that why that chick was so pissed off?" he asked. "If that's your definition of 'hot coed,' I might have to doubt your credentials a bit."

Aziz snorted derisively. "Shannon? No, she's another professor. And just like the rest of the dipshits running around this place with PhDs, she doesn't like to hear the truth about the real world, outside the ivory tower bubble."

Santelli just eyed Aziz with heavy-lidded eyes, his well-practiced bored look on his face. It was the look he had often used on young officers just before he cut them off at the knees. So far, he was decidedly unimpressed with David Aziz' attitude. He sincerely hoped that the word he'd gotten about the man's ability was on the level, because he was getting short on time.

"My name's Santelli," he said. "I'm putting together some names for a job, overseas. A job more along the lines of your previous profession." Aziz' eyes suddenly focused on Santelli a little more sharply. "Fact is, I need an Arabic speaker who is also well-versed in the local culture in the vicinity of the Persian Gulf, and since my first choice turned me down flat, he gave me your name."

Aziz leaned back in his chair, a sneer of disgust on his face. "I'm not in the terp business, sorry," he said.

"Not looking for a terp," Santelli grunted. "This is too small an operation for that kind of specialization." He passed over Villareal; he already knew the Doc's conditions, and had warned Brannigan about them beforehand. That was the Colonel's call. "I'm looking for a shooter who can interact with the locals, seamlessly."

Aziz' eyes narrowed. "Who told you I might be the candidate for that?" he asked.

Santelli snorted. "Does it matter? You've worn your veteran status on your sleeve ever since you went into graduate school. Don't act like you've kept it some kind of deep, dark secret. I'm ninety-percent sure that part of why that woman stormed out just before I came in here had to do with you rubbing it in her face."

Aziz leaned back again, watching Santelli more thoughtfully. "You're very well-informed, Mr. Santelli," he said.

"I make it my business to be," Santelli replied, "especially when I'm recruiting. When I couldn't get the guy I wanted, and he suggested you, I grilled him pretty hard. This is going to be a small team. I can't afford to get sloppy."

"What's the job?" Aziz asked. Despite his air of lazy superiority, his interest was piqued.

"Hostage rescue mission. Private contract, on the island of Khadarkh," Santelli said. "It'll be high-risk, but the pay's commensurate."

Aziz was thinking about it, even as he tried to smooth his face into a look of studied boredom. "I don't know," he said. "I've always hated the Middle East. Not sure I really want to go back."

"Yeah, yeah, I know, that's why you changed your name from Daoud to David," Santelli said. "Rocky told me."

"Rocky sent you to me?" Aziz asked. Santelli could see the uncertainty in the man's eyes. His sense of superiority was getting rocked, the more Santelli revealed that he knew about his past. And Rocky had told Santelli a few things about Aziz, things that had strengthened Santelli's own misgivings about the man, but that also could be useful on the op.

Frankly, from what Rocky had told him, Aziz could be a massive pain in the ass, in no large part because he was too smart for his own good, and knew it.

Aziz looked up at the ceiling. Santelli sighed. He was increasingly convinced that the man was milking the theatrics for all they were worth. He stood up. "I don't have a lot of time," he said. He put a card with the directions Brannigan had given him on the desk. "Be here by noon on the 25th if you're in." He turned and left.

Aziz hadn't said, "yes," but he hadn't said "no," either. Santelli knew that they were getting really short on time to find another Arabic speaker, but all the same, he wasn't sure if he wanted Aziz to come along or not.

***

"Finally!" Kevin Curtis whooped, as he looked up from the table to see the two men approaching the booth. "Took you long enough to finally get your ass out here to civilization, Joe!" He had a muscular, ebony arm around each of the stunning women sitting on either side of him, a platinum blond on his left, and an olive-skinned woman whose dark, smoldering eyes almost took away from the plunging neckline of her blouse. Both women overtopped him by a couple of inches. "Come on, sit down! Welcome to the fleshpots!" He grinned, perfectly straight, white teeth flashing in his dark face as he looked at Hancock. "What did you do to finally bring Silent Joe in out of the cold, Rog?"

"We're not here to party, Kev," Flanagan said as he sat down. "Which means, ladies, that I'm sorry, but you're going to have to shove off for a bit. We've got to talk some business with Kevin, here."

The blond pouted. The brunette gave Flanagan a sultry stare. "We're interested in business," she said.

"Not this kind, darlin'," Flanagan said. "Sorry. Beat it."

The brunette sighed, then kissed Curtis on the cheek. "We'll see you later, baby," she said. "Don't keep us waiting too long."

The women slid out of the booth, and Curtis watched them go wistfully. Then he turned to his old friends.

"See, Joe, this is why you were single for so long," he said. The short, stocky man seemed to almost bounce with energy. "I'm surprised even Mary's put up with you."

"He and Mary broke up," Hancock put in helpfully, smiling as Flanagan turned a glare on him.

"What?!" Curtis exclaimed. "When did this happen?"

"A few weeks ago," Flanagan said. "Can we get to the business at hand?"

"A few weeks?!" Curtis was almost beside himself. "You've been single for that long, and you didn't come here to let Uncle Kevin hook you up with a Vegas beauty? What the hell is wrong with you, Joe? There are hundreds, *hundreds* of gorgeous women who would be all over you in a minute, if you weren't such a…"

"We're not here to talk women, Kev," Flanagan said, trying to head things off before Curtis really built up a head of steam.

"There is *always* time to talk women," Curtis replied. "You should know this by now."

"I take it you've been having a good run?" Hancock asked.

Curtis grinned widely. "Easiest job in the damn world, brother!" he said. "You would be amazed at how many people in this city have somehow learned how to lose at poker. Even Joe here could clean up, with his flat, dead face."

Flanagan looked at Hancock tiredly. "Do you want to tell him about the job? Because he doesn't seem to want to listen to me."

"Wait, job?" Curtis asked, his voice suddenly comparatively hushed, as he leaned forward. "What job?"

"If you'd shut up about poker and booty calls for ten seconds…"

"Brannigan's got a hostage rescue mission laid on," Hancock said, before Flanagan could get going in turn. "Short fuse, high-risk, strictly hush-hush."

"Are you going?" Curtis asked Flanagan. The bigger man nodded. "Then of course I'm in," Curtis said. "What have we got for firepower?"

"Still at the recruiting stage right now," Hancock said. "Though I'm sure the Colonel has a few things in mind already."

"Give me an hour...make that two hours, to say my goodbyes," Curtis said. Flanagan rolled his eyes. "Then we'll get on the road. After all, somebody's got to keep an eye on Closemouthed Joe, here."

"Are you sure we can't leave him behind?" Flanagan asked, as he and Hancock got up.

"Don't lie," Curtis said. "I was the first one you thought of. 'I've got to get Kev,' you thought. 'I can't go into a war zone without Kev.'"

Hancock just chuckled and shook his head as he headed for the door. They had a long drive ahead.

CHAPTER 4

There was very little detail that could be discerned about the room from the video. The place looked dark, except for the bright work lights that had been set up, focused on the twenty-five figures in various modes of dress kneeling on the floor, their hands tied behind their backs. Unlike many other such videos that had been circulated over the years, there was no flag against the wall; there was only bare, white stone, though there might have been a hint of dark mosaics along the top of the screen. Armed men in plain khaki fatigues, carrying what the practiced eye could identify as Chinese Type 03 rifles, stood on either side of the frame, in front of what might have been thick, marble columns.

Five corpses were lying on the floor in front of the hostages.

Another man, clad in the same khaki uniform as the guards stepped forward. His hair was close-cropped and his lean face was half covered by a neatly-trimmed, black beard. His dark eyes bored into the camera.

"These five men behind me are dead for one reason," the man said, in precise, only slightly accented English. "To ensure that you know that we will not hesitate. They were unarmed, and did not resist. We killed them anyway. The same fate awaits the other twenty-five behind me, should any American aircraft or

43

warship come within the Strait of Hormuz, or pass closer to this island than Bahrain."

He squared his shoulders. "We now control the Strait. The Western powers and their apostate allies in the so-called 'Kingdom' of Saudi Arabia no longer have a place in the Persian Gulf. Accept this as a fact, or watch these men die. I assure you, their deaths will be far slower and less merciful than those their colleagues faced."

The video ended.

"That's who we're up against," Brannigan said. The eight of them were gathered in his living room. A fire was burning in the fireplace, and the early afternoon sun was starting to peek through the trees to the east, throwing dappled shadows through the windows. "Chavez doesn't have an ID on him, aside from a name: Esfandiari. No other details about him are available; whoever he is, he's not a major player in any of the Shi'a groups that State or CIA is aware of. I think that narrows things down a bit."

"Qods Force?" Flanagan asked.

Brannigan nodded. "I don't think there's any doubt. They're being *somewhat* sneaky about it, refusing to identify themselves as such. But from what we know about the op so far, the way they handle themselves and their weapons…unless there's some Shi'a secret society somewhere that's paralleling the IRGC Qods Force in organization and training, the list of candidates gets pretty short."

"They don't really think that they can drag this out for very long, do they?" Santelli asked. "Hostages or not, nobody's going to let them shut down the Strait of Hormuz indefinitely. Eventually, those hostages are going to be written off as 'acceptable casualties.'"

"There will probably be a rescue attempt sooner or later," Brannigan agreed, "but our employer is afraid that this guy is going to be true to his word, and murk the hostages as soon as the helos show up on radar. Reports are that they've got control of the airport and the harbor, as well as the citadel. So, we are going in to get the hostages out *before* that happens. Coincidentally opening this guy up to a full-scale assault."

"How many are there?" Hancock asked.

"Unknown," was the reply. "But considering they managed to neutralize the entire Khadarkhi Army—which, admittedly, was little more than a tiny parade-ground army in the first place—we can't assume any less than a company reinforced."

Aziz looked around at the little group, a skeptical grimace on his face. "And we're supposed to do this with…eight guns?"

"Seven, actually," Brannigan said. *May as well get it out in the open and get the bitching over with.* "Doc Villareal is going to be a non-combatant."

"What?" several voices chorused.

"What, Doc can't be bothered to get his hands dirty?" Childress demanded.

"He's an MD who took the Hippocratic Oath," Brannigan said, a note of warning in his voice, before Villareal could say anything. "He takes it seriously. I've accepted that."

"That's fine, for a Stateside hospital," Aziz put in, apparently not catching the warning in Brannigan's voice, or else disregarding it. "We can't exactly afford dead weight, not with this few shooters."

"And if Doc was dead weight, I'd take that under advisement," Brannigan said coldly, fixing Aziz with an icy stare. "But I know Doc Villareal, I trust him with my life, and with all of yours. I can always find more shooters. I can't always find the best combat medic I've ever seen."

That time, Aziz got the point, and subsided, though there was still a bit of an *I can't believe this* look on his face.

"As much as I hate to say it, sir," Flanagan put in, "Aziz does make a good point. Seven shooters against a company plus, or more? How the hell are we supposed to pull that off?"

"Pure firepower isn't going to do the trick," Brannigan agreed. "So, we will have to rely on stealth, maneuver, deception, and guile." He fixed Aziz with another stare. "That's actually where you come in, Aziz."

Their Arabic speaker blinked. "Me?"

"Have you ever been to Khadarkh?" Santelli asked. He'd been a close part of Brannigan's initial planning.

"I might have," Aziz answered.

45

"It's a yes or no question, Aziz," Brannigan growled.

"Yeah, I was there with my dad, about sixteen years ago," he said, apparently deciding he'd pressed his luck with the towering, broad-shouldered Colonel enough. Brannigan was getting a bit irritated with their professor, not least because he was a last-minute addition, an unknown to any of them.

"How much of the local atmospherics do you remember?" Brannigan pressed.

"Enough to blend in after a bit of observation," Aziz replied. "Oh, hell, I'm going to have to go mix and press the flesh with the fucking camel jockeys, aren't I?"

"Uh, dude," Curtis pointed out, "you're an Arab. Aren't you?"

"My dad was an Arab," Aziz replied. "My mom was an Arab. I'm an American. I fucking hate Arabs."

"Aziz' self-loathing racism aside," Brannigan continued, "it seems that the local Sunni population, much of which belongs to the same Al Qays tribe as the royal family, isn't terribly happy with their new overlords. There have been several reports of regular protests. Most of them have still remained relatively peaceful, mainly due to the disparity of firepower between the demonstrators and the Iranians."

"And we don't want the demonstrations to *stay* peaceful." Aziz was nodding his understanding. He sighed. "It's going to suck ass, but I think I can make that happen."

Brannigan nodded. "You're going to head into the city as soon as we make landfall," he said. "The rest of us will lay up for the first day, unless circumstances on the ground mean we have to push in sooner." He unrolled a printout. "Judging by that video, this is going to be our target: the Citadel."

***

They planned, chalk-talked, scrapped plans, got onto several wild tangents that had to be reined in, and slowly hammered out a basic plan. Many of the finer details were going to have to depend on the situation they found on the ground.

"Dubai is our best bet for a staging area," Santelli said. "It's not even seventy-five nautical miles from the island, and it's crawling with gangsters and black marketeers. Any gear that we need, and can't get in legally, we should be able to purchase from the locals."

"Does anybody in this group actually have underworld connections?" Flanagan asked. "I doubt that international arms dealers are going to have billboards up."

"There are ways," Brannigan said quietly. "I'm working on that part." It did worry him a bit, but he had feelers out through Chavez, and already had a good idea of where to start looking, and discreetly asking, from having done some investigating of his own.

The truth was, they were way out on a limb on this operation. They could count on no international support if things went sideways. And with only seven shooters, there were innumerable ways that it could go sideways.

He was as exhilarated as he was worried.

"What can we take in with us?" Curtis asked.

"Anything not on any ITAR lists," Santelli replied. International Traffic in Arms Regulations were nothing to screw around with. Get caught in an international port with the wrong equipment, munitions, or weapons, without the requisite paperwork—which this crew didn't have a snowball's chance in hell of obtaining—and you would be looking at a very long stay in a very unpleasant place. "Clothes, minimal combat gear—though I'd suggest keeping that *minimal*, both because we don't know what we're going to wind up with, weapons-wise, and to keep things on the down-low. Airport security can get nosy."

"We should be able to get consumables in Dubai," Hancock said. "Food, water, batteries, that sort of thing. Shouldn't attract too much attention."

"I'll get as much in the way of medical supplies as we can carry while we're still Stateside," Villareal said quietly. "Those will rarely get messed with, and I don't want to trust anything we might get in Dubai. There's enough sketchy stuff going on around that city that I wouldn't be surprised that half of what we got was placebos and tissue paper."

"That could certainly suck."

"Especially if that's all Doc's going to be carrying, instead of ammo."

"Knock that shit off," Santelli snapped. His Boston accent was suddenly not quite as pronounced. "If you've got a problem with Doc, we can go out to the woodline and deal with it. This ain't the fucking New Corps."

"Fine," Aziz muttered, not much louder than his earlier imprecation. "I'll shut up."

***

About an hour later, they were getting punchy. Brannigan could tell it was about time to wrap things up. And he had a long, hard day planned for the next day.

"Let's knock off for tonight," he said. "Everybody up and ready for some field exercise no later than 0630 tomorrow."

There were a couple of muffled groans, mainly from Curtis and Aziz. Curtis suddenly spoke up.

"Before we quit, there's one more thing," he said. "Vitally important. This team needs a name."

"No, it does not," Flanagan said, raising his voice a little.

"Can't use GI Joe," Curtis continued, ignoring his laconic teammate. "It's already taken, and even if it wasn't, somebody would probably think it meant Mopey Joe over there," he pointed to Flanagan, "was in charge." He brightened suddenly. "I got it! The Liberators!"

"No," Flanagan repeated.

"Oh, come on, Joe!" Curtis snapped, exasperated. The muscular little man looked like he was about to stamp his foot. "It ain't gonna kill you to be just a *little* bit moto, once in a while!"

Flanagan looked at Hancock. "Can't we just, I don't know, sew his mouth shut until the op is over?"

Hancock smirked. "You seemed to consider bringing him along to be a foregone conclusion when I met up with you," he said. "You only started bitching once he was within earshot."

"Ha!" Curtis exclaimed, jumping up and pointing a triumphant finger. "I knew it! I fuckin' knew it!"

"Shut the fuck up!" Santelli bellowed. "Meeting's over for today. Go get some shut-eye. Otherwise you're gonna be regretting it from sunup to sundown tomorrow. We've got a lot of prep work to stuff into a few days."

With more muttering and a few jibes, the meeting broke up. Santelli turned to Hancock. "You really couldn't resist pushing that button, could you?" he asked.

Hancock grinned. "No, I could not."

***

The sun still wasn't all the way up when they gathered out behind Brannigan's cabin the next morning. As Brannigan had instructed, they were all wearing some sort of fatigues and boots, though they had turned out in a motley assemblage of old Marine digis, khakis, greens, and a few British desert tiger stripes. Each man also had a rucksack on his back and a climbing rope with carabiner slung around his chest and shoulders.

Most were still blinking sleep out of their eyes. Curtis especially looked like he hadn't seen the near side of nine in the morning for some time.

Santelli stepped out in front. "Since the Colonel is only going to be with us for today, I'll be taking charge of training," he announced. "As I said last night, we've got a lot to cram into a few days, so get ready for the suck. Just bear in mind, it will be infinitely worse if we get on the ground on Khadarkh and we're not ready for it. Now, let's go."

He turned and started off at a stiff jog, heading out toward the road. The rest followed, Brannigan in the lead.

They didn't keep much of a formation, but more of a loose file. These were all men who had done their fair share of formation runs, and no longer felt the need for the kind of strict regimentation that younger soldiers require. They might all have been out of the game for a while, but at their core, they were professionals, who could be expected to do their job with as little supervision as possible. Brannigan wouldn't have recruited them, otherwise.

He glanced back at Aziz, who was keeping an easy pace, about two paces behind Childress. Aziz was the question mark. One or another of the core team all knew each other. Aziz had been a last-minute addition, and he was already demonstrating a bit of an attitude problem. Brannigan wasn't worried about that because of any self-regard for his no-longer-effective rank. He was worried about it because an ego has no place in a small team deep in enemy territory.

49

Aziz would bear watching. Fortunately, he knew that Santelli was more than equal to the job. Carlo had announced that he'd gone the First Sergeant to Sergeant Major route, rather than Master Sergeant to Master Gunnery Sergeant, because he was lazy and didn't want to work. Brannigan had always suspected that it had been a far tougher choice for the little fireplug of a man than he'd ever let on. He was as passionate about training as he was about taking care of his Marines. He'd chosen the disciplinary route because the latter had won out. Probably by the margin of a coin toss.

The short, fat-looking Italian steadily increased his speed as they hit the paved road, until they were moving at a stiff seven-and-a-half-minute mile pace. Curtis was already starting to breathe hard, his shorter legs pumping as he tried to keep up. Hancock and Villareal were keeping pace with Curtis, while Flanagan and Childress didn't look like they were hurting at all.

Abruptly, Santelli turned off the road and plunged into the woods. There was no trail, and his route led them over multiple fallen trees, down into steep draws, and back up over towering boulders and cliffs. It was a run coupled with a lot of climbing, and it was a smoker. By the time they had gone five miles, Brannigan was huffing and soaked in sweat. Curtis wasn't looking too good, and neither was Villareal.

They finally stopped under a good-sized cliff. Santelli turned and bellowed hoarsely, "Walk it off for a minute. Just don't get too comfortable; we're just getting started."

"I thought this was a snatch-and-grab, not a movement to contact mission," Aziz bitched, leaning down and putting his hands on his knees.

"You ever been in an extended, close-quarters fight, Aziz?" Santelli demanded. The former Sergeant Major was red in the face and breathing pretty hard, himself. "It's a smoker. We don't have time to find a place in the desert to train, so we're making do. Cardio is a must. Being able to climb over things is also a must. And this," he continued, jerking a thumb at the cliffside looming over them, "is going to have to make do for simulating going over the Citadel wall. Attacking the front gate is probably going to be a non-starter, so we're going to practice getting up a sheer rock wall for the next three hours, until we can do it in a matter of seconds, or we start falling off the cliff from exhaustion."

***

The rest of the day was a continuous parade of pain, sweat, and misery. Once Santelli was grudgingly satisfied with their times getting up the cliff, they started the run back toward the cabin, stopping several times to practice break-contact drills, or ambushes, or even stalking, wherever Santelli could find a stretch of ground with minimal ground cover. They were bruised, exhausted, and hurting by the time they got back to the cabin.

They weren't done, though. After a brief, spare meal, Brannigan opened up his gun safe, and they drew out an assortment of rifles. There was a fairly open stretch of land behind and below the cabin that Brannigan often used for a range; he had several steel targets permanently set out there at various yard lines, clear to the next ridge over, about eight hundred yards away.

"Since we don't know for sure what we're going to end up with for weapons," Brannigan said, "we're going to practice with a variety. Ultimately, marksmanship is marksmanship. I'm going to try to get something in the AK family; they are common enough in the region that they should be easy to obtain. I'm sure everyone's used 'em, but I've got two that we can practice on." The rest of the rifles consisted of a pair of ARs, three FALs, a PTR-91, and a SIG SG550.

They commenced three more hours of shooting drills, from up close to as far as Brannigan's most distant steel. They started with simple marksmanship and familiarization—or re-familiarization, as the case may be—with each rifle type. Then Santelli worked them up to break contact drills, fire and maneuver drills, and even some CQB practice, using some hastily set up paper targets and an L-shaped "room" set against the hillside.

"I sure hope you're getting reimbursed for us shooting all of your ammo, John," Hancock said at one point, between drills.

"Don't worry," Brannigan replied. "I'll take it out of Tanner's hide if I'm not."

***

After the shooting practice, it was Doc's turn. He hadn't participated in the weapons drills, which had drawn some not-so-friendly glances from Childress and Aziz. But he'd been hastily putting his own training schedule together.

"I'm sure this is just going to be a refresher for all of you," Villareal said, "but we need to go over it anyway. Tee-Triple Cee. Tactical Combat Casualty Care. I wish I could have some pigs or goats here to work on, but we don't have the time or the funds right now. So, we're all going to be each other's meat puppets. First things first; tourniquets."

For the next four hours, he went into detail on treatment for the most common battlefield wounds, ranging from gunshot wounds, to traumatic amputations, to blast injuries. The basics were always the same. Win the fight, stop the bleeding, get the casualty to cover, then assess and treat as you go.

If they were hoping to be done after Villareal's medical class, Santelli wasn't having it. "On your feet!" he roared. "Some of you have been getting soft in the fleshpots!" Brannigan stifled a chuckle; he knew Santelli well enough to see that the other man was hurting just as badly as any of the rest of the team. "So we're going to be doing two-a-days for the rest of the training cycle, just to try to catch up!"

There was a chorus of groans and curses. But Santelli led out at another stiff jog, heading back out to the road, even as the sun was going down.

***

Brannigan hadn't put on the one suit he owned since Rebecca's funeral. But it still fit fine. He was glad of that; there really wasn't time to get it tailored again, and he didn't want to have to get a new one, either.

He stepped out of the rental car outside of the offices of Taylor and Tailor. Hector Chavez had given him the name of the shipping company after some careful investigation, not all of it entirely aboveboard. While Hector's company dealt primarily in maritime security and counter-piracy, he had close contacts in the cyber security realm, and a few of those guys resided in a sort of murky, ethical gray area, where it was probably best not to inquire too closely as to how they had obtained the information they provided.

There was no evidence that Taylor and Tailor was actually involved in any black-market dealings. But in the new reality of globalization, the lines between licit and illicit networks were often very hard to see, and there *was* information that suggested that, with the right questions being asked, Taylor and Tailor could provide contacts that might or might not be on the darker side of gray.

Brannigan strode in through the double glass doors, his back straight and his head up, even though he was feeling every minute of the previous day's exertions. His outdoor lifestyle since Rebecca's death had kept him in good shape, but Santelli's training program was downright brutal. He momentarily felt for the guys back at the cabin, going through the same grueling routine, this time with some boat work down at the lake thirty miles away. But he put his game face on and approached the receptionist.

"Good morning," the pretty brunette said brightly as he stepped up to the desk. "Can I help you?'

"I hope so," Brannigan replied. He hadn't had time to trim his hair, but he'd shaved and trimmed his graying handlebar. "My name is Gunnar Zebrowski," he said. Corporal Gunnar Zebrowksi had died under his command, in a motorcycle accident. "I have an appointment with Mr. Daniel Taylor."

The girl looked down at her monitor. "Oh, yes, I see you, Mr. Zebrowksi," she said, in the same bright, cheery tone of voice. "I think Mr. Taylor is about to get out of a meeting. If you'd like to have a seat, I'll call you when he's ready."

"Thank you," Brannigan said with a smile. The brunette returned it dazzlingly. Brannigan momentarily had to remind himself that she was probably young enough to be his daughter.

Taylor didn't keep him waiting for long. He'd barely sat down and opened a magazine, something banal about investing, that seemed to be full of ads for *very* expensive rich kid's toys, when the receptionist called his alias. "Mr. Zebrowski? Mr. Taylor is ready to meet with you now."

He stood up, to see a short, clean-shaven man with brown hair and wearing a suit that probably cost as much as Brannigan's truck walking out into the lobby. "Mr. Zebrowski?" the man said, holding out his hand. "I'm Daniel Taylor." Taylor had a firm grip, but there was something in his eyes when he met Brannigan's gaze that he didn't like. "Come this way, and hopefully we can do some business today."

He led the way to the elevator, and up to the sixth floor. Ushering Brannigan out into the richly appointed hallway, he led him to a conference room, with a deep pile carpet, what looked like a real wood conference table, and a view of the city through giant, plate-glass windows.

Taylor motioned Brannigan to a seat, and took a chair across the table from him, leaning forward and clasping his hands together on the tabletop. "So, what can we do for you today, Mr. Zebrowski?" he asked.

"I represent a security company that is looking to expand our operations into the Persian Gulf," Brannigan said carefully. "We're strictly private at this point, no government contracts. We're having some…difficulties with obtaining all the equipment we need to secure our clients in the region, between the threats of terrorism, kidnapping, and piracy. I was told by a Mr. Vernon that you might have some contacts that could help us with our difficulties."

Taylor's eyes had flickered, ever so slightly, at the mention of "Mr. Vernon." Brannigan frankly had no idea if it was the name of a real person, or a code phrase. Hector's people hadn't been able to find that out. Just that "Mr. Vernon" seemed to be in some way connected with Taylor and Tailor's *possible* underworld ties.

Taylor straightened and leaned back in his chair, studying Brannigan impassively. "That is a touchy subject, Mr. Zebrowski," he said. "ITAR can be difficult to navigate, especially in that region. While we are not in the same business, security is, of course, vital to our operations, so we are somewhat familiar with the problems that you are describing."

He leaned forward again, slightly, resting his elbows on the table and tapping his forefingers together under his nose. Brannigan watched him, noting the curious light feeling in his chest as he mentally prepared to go over the table and plunge the pen that was resting in his breast pocket into the other man's jugular. He didn't like this kind of subterfuge; he had been a warrior his entire life, and preferred the messy certainty of combat to the soft-clothed, duplicitous back-room dealing that this man exemplified, especially if Chavez' information was correct.

"I might be able to help you, Mr. Zebrowski," Taylor said finally. "We have often had to make certain…local arrangements when passing through that area, and there are some local contacts who can offer certain…services for far cheaper than any regular Western company." By which he meant either the security equivalent of sweat-shops, companies that paid their contractors pennies on the dollar, more than likely for the sake of "getting a foot in the door," or outright illegal protection rackets. Brannigan's money was on the latter. "I can provide you with a couple of these contacts, if you are going to be going that way soon. The question is, however, what does my company get out of it?"

Brannigan spread his hands. "You have me at something of a disadvantage," he admitted. "We're still little more than a startup. But I think I can guarantee that, if you provide us with this little favor, I can offer you the chance to hire some top-notch security contractors in that region, all genuine US combat vets, for considerably below market price."

Taylor pursed his lips, in what had to be a practiced "thoughtful" look. Brannigan was beginning to wonder if the man had a soul at all, or if he was just a carefully put together collection of mannerisms and buzzwords. "That is certainly an option to take under consideration," he said, "considering the quality of many of the local security contractors in the area." He thought some more, though as Brannigan looked into the other man's dead eyes, he thought that the decision had already been made. This was theater.

It had always been a possibility that Chavez' information had been wrong, and that his inquiry would only prompt a call to the FBI, followed by his arrest and the end of the entire operation. But he didn't think so, and watching the suited man across from him, he was fairly certain that the "Mr. Vernon" code had, in fact, gotten him in the door. It was still possible that Taylor was simply stringing him along until the local FBI office could get agents there, but if that happened, he'd just have to deal with the situation as it developed.

Finally, Taylor reached into his pocket, drew out a business card, and scribbled something on the back. When he slid it precisely halfway across the table, leaving one finger pinning it to the wood, he said, "Contact this email. It belongs to a facilitator, of sorts, whom we have had certain dealings with. He can help you out with what you need."

Brannigan reached over and pulled the card out from under Taylor's finger. Taylor had kept the pressure on the card, but Brannigan drew it out easily. Taylor smiled suddenly, showing a line of even, perfect teeth, and stood up, holding out his hand. "It has been a pleasure, Mr. Zebrowski," he said. "I hope that this is the beginning of a long and fruitful business relationship."

I'm sure it won't be. Brannigan shook the man's hand. "Here's hoping," he said, instead of what he was thinking.

As he left the building, he felt like he desperately needed a shower. But they had a contact. He checked his watch. He still needed to get tickets purchased for the team to fly to Dubai, preferably by several different airlines, traveling from different airports. There was still a lot to get done before they even left the country.

CHAPTER 5

After the mountains and woods of the Intermountain West, Dubai was mercilessly hot.

"You'd think that with all the shit in the air," Childress griped quietly, "it wouldn't be so hot. All the dust and smog should filter some of the sunlight out."

"You'd think," Brannigan replied. "You'd be wrong, though."

Childress snorted.

It was a bad day, even so. The smog was so thick that much of the city's distinctive skyline, including the towering, needle-like Burj Khalifa, was only visible as little more than shadows in the brownish haze. A haboob had come through not long before, and the wind was down, so the dust and industrial smog just sat over the city, adding its own unpleasantness to the blazing, blast-furnace heat.

Fortunately, the air conditioner in their car was still working, though Brannigan wasn't sure how much longer that was going to last. The temperature inside the car was rising as they waited outside the Karama Collective offices, just a few blocks from the Dubai docks and associated warehouses. He expected the AC was going to quit within another hour.

Taylor's "facilitator" had put them in contact with the Karama Collective. Some of Chavez' contacts suspected that the Collective was, in fact, a front for the Suleiman Syndicate, a relatively new but fast-growing Pan-Arab organized crime network that had started in Egypt and was spreading across the Middle East. It made sense. If anyone was going to have black market arms and military equipment for sale, it was going to be the mafia, of one stripe or another.

Brannigan was sweating this a bit. They didn't have much in the way of weapons; flying into Dubai with even pistols had been a non-starter. Even pocket knives had been impossible; Flanagan and Childress had both tried, only to have them confiscated at Customs. There had been a considerable delay as they had been questioned by the UAE police. Both men had kept their cool and managed to get by with only a warning, but it had been a near thing.

So here they were, getting ready to meet with a bunch of transnational criminals, with little more than their hands, rolls of change in their pockets, and a couple of other sundries as weapons. And the criminals probably already knew that they were expats looking for highly illegal military hardware.

The number of ways the entire thing could go wrong was staggering.

The two men lapsed into silence again as they waited. Brannigan's phone vibrated, and he checked it. It was a brand-new smartphone, with a worldwide plan and several commercial apps installed that allowed for text messages with end-to-end encryption. It wasn't perfect; he would have preferred something put together a bit more in-house, but it would do. It was unlikely that anyone in Dubai had the encryption cracked.

The screen had a message from Santelli. "In position. Have eyes on you."

"Rgr," Brannigan typed in reply, then left the phone on his lap. Once the meeting started, he'd have it back in his pocket, but he wanted it close at hand, so that he could open a call to Santelli just before they got out of the car. Carlo, along with the rest of the team, would be able to listen in on the entirety of the meeting, and would be standing by to move in if things went haywire.

Three very shiny, silver Land Rovers pulled up to the curb. A moment later, a small coterie of Arabs in suits stepped out of the offices, followed by several glowering specimens in polo shirts and cargo pants, who had to be the muscle.

"Holy shit," Childress muttered. "Are the Arabs doing the 'security contractor starter kit' now, too?"

"Looks like it," Brannigan said. "Easy way for them to differentiate who's important and who's a knee-breaker. Not so great if you're trying to keep a low profile, though."

"Isn't this, like, the organized crime capitol of the Middle East, though?" Childress asked.

"Yep," Brannigan replied, as he saw the lead man of the entourage, a short guy with slicked hair and a line-thin, sharply pointed beard, look over at their dusty rental car with a barely veiled sneer. "Between here and Bahrain, it's something of a tossup, though I'd say this place tops the island. This is the city that organized crime built, after all. The Burj Khalifa? Russian Mafiya using mostly Filipino indentured workers." He opened the door and swung his feet out, even as he opened the call to Santelli. "So, yeah, I doubt these guys are all that worried about keeping a low profile."

He stepped out of the car and straightened up. The brutal heat felt like it was scorching every inch of his skin, and the pollution made the back of his throat smart. He shut the door as he slipped the phone back into the inside pocket of his sports coat, and started around the hood toward the pointy-bearded Arab and his entourage, who were still standing on the sidewalk.

"Mr. Al Fulani?" he asked.

The bearded man watched him with hooded eyes, while the bodyguards stepped forward to put themselves between Brannigan and their principal. They might have been somewhat impressive specimens among most of the Arab population of Dubai, but Brannigan towered a head taller than the biggest of them. He obligingly spread his arms when the gimlet-eyed man in the black polo shirt motioned for him to do so, and submitted to the sloppy pat-down, hoping that the thug didn't attempt to investigate his phone too closely.

He didn't. He was looking for guns or knives. He stepped back and nodded to the man with the pointy beard. His colleague had just finished with Childress.

Holy hell, if we'd had weapons we could have gotten a veritable arsenal past these clowns. The search had been cursory at best. Either the Suleiman Syndicate's soldiers were really confident about the UAE police keeping expats unarmed, or they were just that lazy and untrained.

The short man didn't step forward, but looked Brannigan in the eye, with that sort of machismo look that suggested he considered himself far superior to the tall American, who was doubtless too stupid to understand what he was getting himself into. "I am Qasim Al Fulani," he said. "You are Mr. Zebrowski?"

"I am," Brannigan confirmed. "I was hoping we could do a little business."

"Not here," Al Fulani said. "Get in your car and follow us." He and his entourage proceeded to get into the three Land Rovers, while the wannabe gorillas gave the two Americans the stink-eye.

Together, Childress and Brannigan went back to the car and got in. Brannigan started the engine and had to floor the accelerator to follow the trio of vehicles, which quickly roared away from the curb, heading northeast.

"We're with you," Santelli said, his voice tinny through the phone's speaker. Brannigan did not reply, but kept his attention on the road and the vehicles they were supposed to be following.

He had a bad feeling about this. He really wanted a gun on his hip. Not only were these guys criminals, but he knew enough about the underground to be reasonably certain that they also did plenty of business with various jihadi groups around the Middle East. Groups that would love to get their hands on a couple of Amriki and saw their heads off on the Internet.

They followed the three Land Rovers, weaving through the very modern streets of Dubai. They were soon passing the airport and continuing northeast, until they were moving into the suburb of Sharjah, passing the artificial lakes near the sea shore.

"Where the hell are we going?" Childress muttered.

"I'm guessing the Sharjah docks," Brannigan replied. "There should be plenty of places to do shady business up there, in between the warehouses and stacks of containers."

Childress looked over at him. "Have you been here before?"

"Once or twice," Brannigan said, "though I was only passing through. I have an idea of where we're going because I studied the maps and imagery on the plane. Didn't you?"

Childress looked out the window. "I looked at 'em," he said, "but I've got to actually spend time on the ground before I can really translate the image into a solid idea of where I'm at."

"No worries," Brannigan said. "We'd have to follow these clowns, anyway."

The little convoy finally turned northwest, confirming Brannigan's suspicions that they were heading for the docks. While it *was* a natural choice of place to do this sort of thing, presuming the thugs had paid off the local cops and port authority to look the other way when they went about their business, it was also a great place for an ambush, and they had no guns.

"If this goes south," he told Childress, speaking loudly enough that Santelli could hear him over the phone in his pocket at the same time, "and they're out of reach, don't try to be a hero. Get to cover, and let the rest of the boys take out their exterior security. If they are within reach…"

"Then they'll wish they weren't," Childress finished. While neither man had a knife, they each had aluminum pens, a couple of rolls of Dirhams, and, in Childress' case, a bike lock, stuffed in various pockets. Easily passed over by men looking for guns or knives, every one of those things were expedient weapons; potentially deadly ones, so long as the man wielding them was within arm's reach of his adversary.

The Land Rovers led the way through an open gate in the concertina-topped cyclone fence around the dockyards, not far from the domed port authority building. Through another gate, then a right turn, and they were rolling up the long, artificial peninsula that formed the Sharjah harbor.

When the Land Rovers stopped at a large set of warehouses, Brannigan breathed a little bit easier. Warehouses would lessen the chance of snipers, which would make things moderately easier. Only moderately, though. He still wasn't going to relax, and neither was Childress. They were walking into the lion's den, and they both knew it.

Qasim Al Fulani stepped out of the middle Land Rover, looked back at them, and beckoned before going inside. His entourage and his thugs followed, though the drivers stayed out in the vehicles.

"Here goes," Brannigan said. "Let's hope they actually want to do business."

"With us," Childress added. "And not with AQAP or somebody."

The younger man might be a bit of a hillbilly, but that didn't mean he was dumb.

The two of them got out of the car and followed the group into the warehouse. The sudden darkness inside was momentarily blinding, and they both whipped their sunglasses off as soon as they crossed the threshold, each man instinctively checking the corners to their left and right as they moved, looking for ambushers.

As his eyes adjusted, Brannigan could see that the warehouse was about two-thirds empty, with most of the pallets stacked toward the far end. There was enough stuff back there to conceal a platoon, if he was judging the space right. That wasn't encouraging, especially since Al Fulani and his goons were standing in the middle of the empty part of the floor.

The two of them walked forward to meet them, surreptitiously scanning for any overwatch that might be positioned above. There didn't seem to be any catwalks, fortunately; there was no place for snipers to be sitting above them. So, all they had to worry about were the thugs in front of them and anyone who might be hiding back behind the pallets.

Unfortunately, Brannigan couldn't check with Santelli as to the status of the rest of the team. They had gotten a few updates on the way, so he knew they were close, but how close and how quickly they could go into action was presently unknown. So, he'd have to play this carefully, to give the rest of them time to get into position, just in case.

"So, here it is nice and quiet, no listening ears," Al Fulani said. Maybe it was his fine-edged paranoia, but Brannigan thought he could hear a note of triumphant gloating in the other man's words. "We can do business. You want weapons?"

"Yes," Brannigan said. "At least fifty rifles, with ammunition and magazines. Maybe some explosives."

"Explosives?" Al Fulani asked, poorly feigning surprise. "What do you need explosives for?"

"In the event of a pirate attack, if we cannot repel it outright, we might have to breach a hatch to clear the ship," Brannigan explained, keeping to the cover story that they were a security company looking for equipment. He really didn't owe this thug any explanation, and he doubted that the man really cared, anyway.

"How much money did you bring?" al Fulani asked. Maybe they were getting somewhere, after all. Greed is an eternal motivator.

"We have a quarter million dirhams," Brannigan said. "In cash."

The man smiled widely. There was no friendliness in the expression. "Good. It will be a nice addition to whatever the Brothers give us for you."

Well, shit. Looks like my suspicions were right. "You son of a bitch," he snarled, loudly enough that his voice echoed off the far end of the warehouse. Hopefully, the rest of the team was close enough to act on the signal.

The Arabs only grinned, the polo-shirted thugs drawing pistols from their waists and moving toward the two of them. Even as Brannigan glared at the short man who had sprung the trap, he looked aside at Childress, giving him the briefest of glances, warning him not to jump the gun.

Childress was just watching the advancing gangsters, his hands held loosely down at his sides. He looked gawky and awkward, deliberately so. It was kind of easy for him; Childress was long and skinny, with a beak of a nose and a slightly receding chin. He didn't look nearly as imposing as Brannigan did. Both men were counting on that fact to give them an advantage, however slight.

The nearest gunman, with that same sly, arrogant smile on his face, reached out and took hold of Brannigan's arm with his off hand. In the same instant, about three things happened at once.

There was a sudden commotion at the back of the warehouse. It wasn't loud until a single shot rang out, echoing thunderously through the nearly-empty warehouse. A moment later, there was a hammering storm of gunfire back behind the pallets. Even as every eye involuntarily twitched toward the noise, Brannigan and Childress both moved.

Brannigan took a single step forward, planting his foot between the gunman's legs and grabbing the wrist of the man's gun hand with a crushing, vice-like grip. There weren't many men who could stand that grip without wincing; the Arab wasn't nearly as tough as he thought he was, and nearly crumpled as Brannigan's fingers ground the bones of his wrist together. In the same instant, Brannigan wrenched his other arm free of a suddenly slack hand, and landed a short, wicked hook to the joint of the man's jaw. There was a sharp *crack* at the impact, and the man let out a slurred howl of pain.

Then he was moving back, twisting the gunman's body around to shield himself, one brawny arm still clutching the gunman's wrist, across his neck and shoulder. With his free hand, which ached a little more than it should have from the punch, he plucked the gun, an old Tokarev with most of the bluing worn off, out of the man's hand.

Childress had handled his antagonist almost as neatly, though that one was of slightly less utility as a human shield. He was out like a light, presuming that Childress hadn't actually killed him. The gawky hillbilly was still holding the man up by the throat, his Glock leveled over his shoulder.

All of the Suleiman gunmen were now leveling their own weapons at them, though so far, they were reticent to shoot, probably for fear of hitting their buddies. Brannigan and Childress had moved quickly enough that they were now outside the slow-moving semicircle of thugs, backing up toward the walls to keep their flanks clear.

Without a word, Brannigan started to drift off to the left, dragging his generally inadequate human shield with him.

64

Childress started moving to the right a moment later, having glanced over and seen what the Colonel was doing. There were still bad guys in the vehicles outside, behind them.

"It didn't need to come to this," Brannigan said loudly. "We just wanted to do business. Instead, you wanted to play games. So, we'll play games."

Behind the Suleiman entourage, figures were starting to come out from behind the boxes. Footsteps sounded on the concrete floor. Al Fulani was regaining some of his composure. He glared at Brannigan. "What do you think this will gain you?" he asked. "I have men all around this warehouse. Now we will simply have to kill you."

"You *had* men around the warehouse," Brannigan corrected, glancing at the men who were advancing from the far end of the warehouse. Santelli and Hancock were in the lead, each one carrying an AKS-74U, leveled at the Suleiman gangsters. "Look behind you."

Two of the gunmen glanced over their shoulders. One of them started, and swung around, trying to bring his TMP to bear. It was a mistake.

Hancock drilled the man with a short burst, the short-barreled AK spitting flame in the dim light of the warehouse and the reports roaring thunderously against concrete floor and sheet metal walls. In a moment, all hell broke loose.

The thin-bearded Suleiman chief grabbed for his own belt line, and Brannigan shot him. The Tokarev's bark seemed muted compared to the hammering reports of the AKS-74Us, but the 7.62x25 was still plenty powerful enough. Brannigan didn't take the chance that the little man was wearing body armor. It was only twenty feet, so he just shot him in the face. The man's head jerked back with a spray of red, and he spun to the concrete floor.

Brannigan was still dragging his captive off to one side, trying to stay out of Santelli's and Hancock's lines of fire. He shifted to another gunman, who momentarily seemed frozen, uncertain which way to point his gun, and dropped him with a quick pair of shots. The first round tore through the man's throat, the second blew a chunk out of the back of his skull as he fell. That little 7.62x25mm was a hot, fast-moving round.

Then it was all over but the echoes. All of the Suleiman Syndicate thugs except for Brannigan's and Childress' meat shields were down and either dead or bleeding out. Hancock and Santelli moved from body to body, kicking weapons away from clutching hands. One didn't let go, and Hancock put a single round through the man's skull, just to make sure.

Childress let his hostage fall, and the man hit the concrete with a bonelessness that suggested to Brannigan that the wiry backwoodsman had hit him hard enough that he wasn't ever going to wake up again. As for his own captive, he let go of the man's wrist and kicked him in the back of the knee, forcing him down to the floor, before stepping back and levelling the Tokarev at his head.

"Where are the rest?" he asked Santelli. He was still deciding what to do about this last survivor. Brannigan wasn't one to shoot a defenseless man, but at the same time, they weren't exactly in a position where they could afford to take prisoners, either.

"Aziz is covering the back," Santelli replied, finishing his last dead check. "Flanagan and Curtis are securing the vehicles."

"You," Brannigan said to the man kneeling in front of him, who was staring in shock at the corpses on the warehouse floor, "do you speak English?"

When the man didn't reply, Brannigan reached over and smacked him on the head with an open palm. "English, asshole!" he barked. *"Inglizi?"*

"La, la," the man insisted, flinching away from the blow. He might have been a tough guy with a gun in his hand and a lot of buddies at his back, facing two unarmed men, but now he was a cringing, frightened animal.

"Get Aziz in here," Brannigan said, staring at his captive. "I want to talk to this son of a bitch."

"I'll get him," Childress said, as he bent over the body of the man he'd disabled, digging a single spare Glock mag out of his pockets. He shook his head. "Fuckers didn't even have enough ammo on 'em." Without another word, he jogged toward the back of the warehouse.

Brannigan kept his basilisk glare on the prisoner while they waited, saying nothing, but tapping the barrel of the Tokarev against his leg. He was careful to keep his finger well away from the trigger; the Tok didn't have an external safety, and it wouldn't do to accidentally shoot himself in the leg while trying to intimidate a captive.

Finally, Aziz came out from behind the pallets, carrying an AKMS. Brannigan looked up at him and his eyes narrowed. "Does Childress have a long gun?" he asked as Aziz walked up to them.

Aziz shrugged. "There might have been another one back there," he said.

Brannigan maintained his stare. Aziz started to look a little uncomfortable. "So, the one man we have on rear security only has a Glock and one reload?" he asked quietly.

Aziz swallowed. Hancock was pointedly keeping an eye on their surroundings, but both Brannigan and Santelli now had the other man pinned with identical glares. "I'll...I'll go trade with him," he said lamely, after a minute.

"You do that," Brannigan said, keeping his voice low. "Hurry up."

Aziz turned and jogged back toward the far end of the warehouse, disappearing behind the pallets. Santelli shook his head. "I really wish I could have gotten Rocky," he muttered.

"We got who we could," Brannigan said. "He'll work out or he won't. Too late for 'might have beens' now. We've got to make it work."

Hancock said nothing. His own silence spoke volumes about his opinion.

Aziz came back in, carrying the Glock, pointedly avoiding looking directly at either Brannigan or Santelli. Brannigan decided to let it slide, for the moment. They had more pressing matters to attend to.

"Ask him where the weapons are," he said.

Aziz translated in to Arabic, and got a frantic, stammered answer in reply. "He says he doesn't know."

"Were there any weapons or gear in the first place?" Brannigan asked, continuing to stare down at the prisoner, death in his eyes. "Or was this all a setup from the get-go?"

The prisoner looked up at him as Aziz translated, then started yammering rapidly in Arabic, shaking his head emphatically. "He says that it wasn't, it never was a setup," Aziz translated, contempt dripping from his voice. "He's lying. He's full of shit."

Brannigan glanced up at him. "What makes you say that?" he asked. He didn't necessarily disbelieve Aziz, but he wanted to know the other man's reasons for saying so.

"He's a fucking Arab," Aziz snapped. "He'll tell you whatever he thinks you want to hear, *especially* when he's at this kind of a disadvantage. He wants to save his own skin, and you've got a pistol in your hand."

"Then press him," Brannigan said, turning his cold eyes back on their captive.

Aziz barked at the man in Arabic. He apparently was not impressed with the reply he got, because he raised the Glock as if to pistol-whip the man. The captive cringed away, speaking rapidly and frantically.

"He doesn't know," Aziz finally said. "He thinks maybe there were some weapons, but Al Fulani didn't tell him anything. He was just there to do his job."

"Really?" Brannigan asked skeptically. "Somehow, I find that difficult to believe, given that he and his buddies were well-prepared to try to snatch us." He glanced at his watch. "Are we going to get anything else out of him?"

"Short of hooking his nuts up to a car battery?" Aziz asked. When Brannigan gave him a look that was considerably less than amused, he hastened to say, "No, I don't think so. He's muscle, nothing more. I really don't think Al Fulani told him shit."

Brannigan nodded. "Tie him up and drag him back into the pallets back there," he said. "Carlo and I will gather up the rest of the weapons and head out to the vehicles. Once you've got him stashed, grab Childress and get out front. I don't think we've got a lot of time left to linger around here."

Aziz nodded, and stepped forward to grab the prisoner by the arm. When the man started to let out a wail, Aziz rapped him on the head with the butt of his pistol. The plastic of the Glock didn't have as much impact as if he'd full-on pistol-whipped the man, but the guy got the point, and shut up.

A quick search of the bodies produced a couple of FN FiveSevens, a Steyr TMP, and two more Glocks. There really wasn't enough ammo to go around, but it was more than they'd had to begin with.

Brannigan exchanged his Tokarev for one of the FiveSevens, then stripped the expensive sport coat off of Al Fulani's corpse and used it as a sack for the rest of the weapons and ammo. Hancock sent a piercing wolf-whistle toward the back of the warehouse to let Childress and Aziz know it was time to move, and then they were heading back out the way they'd come, Brannigan carrying the coat full of weapons over his shoulder.

Flanagan and Curtis were already behind the wheels of two of the Land Rovers. The previous drivers were stuffed into the back seat of the other one, piled on top of each other, tied and gagged. Brannigan didn't know where they had found the materials, but he knew that both men were resourceful. It looked like the gangsters had been tied up with bailing wire, and they'd probably been gagged with their own socks.

"Doc's already on his way back to the hotel," Flanagan said as Brannigan and Hancock got into his Land Rover. "We got the cash out of the car, too. Didn't think we wanted to leave that behind."

"Good," Brannigan replied. He turned to Santelli, who was staying next to his door, the AKS-74U still in his hands, watching for Aziz and Childress to come back out of the warehouse. "Once we get clear," Brannigan said to Santelli, "we'll split up. Take as long and roundabout a route back as possible; if the local cops get wind of this, I don't want them following us back to the hotel."

Santelli nodded, as the last two men came running out of the warehouse, Childress still carrying the AKMS. "And make damned good and sure those weapons are hidden before anyone goes back inside," Brannigan added.

"Common sense, sir," Santelli replied. "We'll see you back at the barn."

The two Land Rovers peeled out of the warehouse district and headed north into Sharjah, even as the wail of UAE police sirens filled the mid-morning air.

CHAPTER 6

The room where the hostages were being kept had once been some kind of meeting or banquet hall, Ortiz thought. It was spacious and surprisingly chilly for the region; he could only assume that the thickness of the ancient stone walls was keeping most of the heat out. The Iranians were not furnishing their hostages with much in the way of blankets or bedding; they slept on the floor, waking shivering and stiff from the hard marble tiles.

Ortiz had just awakened from another fitful night's sleep. Morning light was coming in the arched windows high in the wall. It was the only light that ever entered the room; their captors did not provide them with lamps or turn on the chandeliers overhead, either.

Finding his little scrap of rock that he'd managed to palm, Ortiz turned to the wall behind him and scratched another faint mark on the tile. Fifteen days had passed since the fanatics had stormed aboard the *Oceana Metropolis* and murdered Carver and his fellow contractors. So far, the rest of them had managed to survive. It seemed that the Iranians were satisfied with keeping them as human shields. At least for the moment.

He remembered the look in that little man's eyes as he'd shot Carver in the head. It had been over two weeks, but the scene was just as vivid in his memory when he closed his eyes as it had been while he'd watched it happen. He doubted that it would ever really fade. But that look haunted him more than the violence.

That little man wanted to kill more of them. And it was only going to be a matter of time before he found an excuse.

Slowly and carefully, as much because of his own stiffness as to avoid alarming the guards stationed at the single entrance to the hall, Ortiz stood and stretched. He had to keep his worries to himself; while some of his crew might be able to handle the situation, not all of the American hostages were members of his crew, and the tourists especially had *not* been in any way mentally prepared for this. Ortiz had had some training; Tannhauser Petroleum and the companies that shipped their oil had mandated hijack survival classes. These people had not.

It had taken a great deal of effort and patience to get the wealthy, forty-something woman in the white sundress to calm down after she had been manhandled and dragged into the Citadel. She had been nearly hysterical.

Fifteen days. How much longer could they hold out? When was the Navy coming?

Ortiz didn't doubt that they would come. There was no way that the US could just leave them in captivity. The United States did not negotiate with terrorists. That was government policy. He knew it was.

But several past incidents involving the Iranians nagged at him. The original Iran Hostage Crisis had dragged on for four hundred forty-four days. That Navy gunboat that had been captured by the Iranians had finally been liberated by a cash payment, not by Navy SEALs.

He had to assure himself that this was different. Americans were dead. *Somebody* had to do *something* about that.

The doors banged open suddenly. Several of the hostages who were still sleeping, many of them trying desperately to escape the misery of their circumstances in unconsciousness, started awake, more than one with a faint cry. Ortiz peered into the shadows near the door, and his heart sank.

The man called Esfandiari was stalking into the hall, flanked by six more of his shooters. And the same little man who had murdered Carver was walking next to him, with that same eager, murderous look on his face.

"Everyone get up!" Esfandiari bellowed, his voice echoing around the hall. "Now!" The shooters started chivvying the hostages to their feet and herding them into a corner, behind the massy pillars that held up the tiled ceiling. Esfandiari waited, his arms folded, watching with implacable black eyes.

Once the hostages were up and gathered in a tight knot, Esfandiari walked up to them. He looked at Ortiz. "Come out here, Captain," he said mildly.

There really was no other choice. Ortiz advanced out of the group, coming to stand in front of Esfandiari.

"Despite our warnings, an American Navy aircraft overflew this island early this morning," Esfandiari said, in the same mild tone of voice. "Unfortunately, I think you know what that means." He turned to the short man beside him. "Mehregan!" he barked. The little man snapped to attention. Esfandiari gave a brief command in Farsi. A vicious little smile creased Mehregan's face, and the man stalked over to the group of hostages.

Another command was given, and soon the guards had all of the hostages line up against one wall of the great hall. Mehregan, evidently enjoying himself immensely, walked down the line, pausing in front of each hostage for a moment and studying them before moving on.

"Commander, this is unnecessary," Ortiz tried to protest. He got a rifle butt to the stomach for his troubles, and sank to his knees, wheezing in pain.

"Unfortunately, it is entirely necessary," Esfandiari replied, almost regretfully. "Although, I will admit, that Mehregan's theatrics are somewhat…excessive." He barked at the smaller man in Farsi, and Mehregan stopped, taking a deep, angry breath, before grabbing one of the hostages—Ortiz was momentarily thankful that it wasn't one of his crew, then cursed himself for thinking it—and dragging the middle-aged man into the center of the room.

Ortiz knew what was coming. It became even more obvious to the rest when one of Esfandiari's soldiers drew out a video camera and turned it on.

"No! No, no, no!" a half-dozen voiced chorused. The middle-aged woman in the sundress was the loudest; the chosen victim was her husband.

"*Silence!*" Esfandiari shouted. "Your own country has brought this upon you. They were warned, and they chose to disregard that warning. Now you must pay the price." He turned on his heel and marched to the hostage's side, where the balding man was down on his knees, shaking, his head bowed, with Mehregan's fist clenched in the back of his shirt.

Esfandiari took a deep breath, then turned to the soldier holding the camera and nodded. The soldier signaled that he was ready, and Esfandiari began to speak.

"This morning, at 0455 local time, a US Navy aircraft overflew the island of Khadarkh," he said, his English precise. "To the President of the United States and the commander of the US Navy task force who sent the aircraft, I must ask, did you not think that I was serious? Did you think that your decades of imperialism in the Middle East meant that you could ignore my warning with impunity? You chose to disregard it, and now this man must pay the price." He turned and looked down at the hostage. "What is your name? Tell your countrymen, so that they know whom they have killed by their arrogance."

The man just knelt there and shook. Mehregan kicked him in the ribs and he nearly fell over. Esfandiari glanced sharply at the smaller man and shook his head. "Answer me," he said, almost gently.

"M-my name is Trevor Ulrich," the man said, in a small, frightened voice.

"Trevor Ulrich," Esfandiari said, turning back to the camera. "That is the name of the man you have killed. Trevor Ulrich has paid the price for your transgression." He turned and nodded to Mehregan.

The little man drew the Makarov from his belt, placed the muzzle to Ulrich's temple, and pulled the trigger.

Ortiz could not help but flinch at the sharp report, as blood, bone, and brain matter spattered out of the side of Ulrich's skull. The man flopped on the floor, twitching slightly. The sudden odor of blood and excrement filled the room, as his bowels loosened in death.

Esfandiari looked at the camera. "This time it was one," he intoned. "Next time, two will die. After that, three. Keep your ships and aircraft beyond the limits I set last time, or you condemn more of your countrymen to death."

A couple of the hostages vomited as the soldier turned off the camera. Mehregan stalked over to the lineup, and picked out two more, pointing to Ulrich's corpse. "Carry him out," he ordered.

None of the selectees thought of resisting. They had just seen what would happen if they tried. And there was still an ugly light in Mehregan's eyes. He would welcome the opportunity to add to the pile of American corpses.

The two that he had picked out shuffled over and gingerly picked up Ulrich's corpse. It was difficult going; even after fifteen days of relative privation, Ulrich had still been a heavy man. And dead weight is always harder to move. They lost their grip on the body twice before reaching the door, the corpse flopping obscenely on the floor each time, the ruin of Ulrich's skull leaving bloody splotches on the floor.

Esfandiari left with Mehregan and his guards, without a backward glance.

Ortiz sank to the floor against the wall, nursing his bruised midsection, and prayed that, somehow, rescue would come. Because they were never going to survive if it didn't.

***

They didn't have a lot in the way of comms back Stateside, but Brannigan had brought a small, ultralight laptop and a satellite internet puck, both of which he had bought with funds from the shell company that Chavez had set up. He needed some kind of connection, if only to get updates from Chavez, who was maintaining that level of involvement, if no more. If asked, he was simply emailing updates on a situation of some interest to an old friend.

The morning after the incident with the Suleiman Syndicate, Brannigan found an email waiting for him. And it wasn't pretty.

"Everybody bring it in," he called, turning the laptop so that everyone in the suite could see the screen. "We've got an update. Apparently, the Navy tried probing Khadarkhi airspace last night. This was the response." He played the video.

The men watched in grim silence as Trevor Urlich was cold-bloodedly murdered while he knelt on the stone floor.

When the video ended, Brannigan leaned back against the side of the desk and folded his arms. "Clock's ticking, gents," he said. "Right now, I'm told that between the Saudi lobbyists and the imminent threat to the hostages—including the reluctance of the politicians in charge to risk having those hostages' blood on their hands—the Navy is going to be held back for a bit. I don't know if the negotiators are here in Dubai, or in Abu Dhabi, but they are reportedly on the ground."

"Have they made contact with the Iranians on the island?" Flanagan asked.

"From what Hector's telling me, they're getting the cold shoulder," Brannigan replied. "They've tried talking, and the Iranians aren't interested. Which has just about everyone stumped."

"Yeah, how do you negotiate for the release of hostages when the terrorists ain't interested in negotiating?" Childress asked.

"You can't," Curtis said.

"It was a rhetorical question!" Flanagan said, exasperated.

"How do you know?" Curtis demanded. "You didn't ask it!"

"Enough!" Brannigan said. "With the Suleiman deal going bad, we're back to square one, and now we're going to have even less time to prep once we finally do find a contact that can get us what we need. On top of that, the clock is also ticking for us, because the gangsters we didn't kill will probably have provided the police with descriptions, along with some detailed bullshit story about what happened. Which means we have a limited amount of time to get what we need and get the hell out of Dubai before the police come after us."

"And that's probably a *very* limited window," Aziz put in. "The UAE police have some serious high-tech toys for tracking people. And their street patrol cars here in Dubai are all Lamborghinis. There won't be any running if they do find us."

"I've got a meeting with our 'facilitator' this afternoon," Santelli said. "I'm going to mix things up a bit, since you were front and center on that last deal, John. Hopefully he doesn't screw us again, but we're going to have to be ready if he tries."

"Curtis, Aziz, and I will be running backstop on the meet," Flanagan said. "We've got enough pistols to go around if things go sour this time, though our ammo supply leaves something to be desired."

Brannigan nodded. "Hancock and I will go see about getting some boats for insert. That was supposed to happen today, anyway, and I think we can rely on boat sellers *not* being an ambush, especially with the amount of tourism around here."

"Have we got transport to get us closer to the island before launching?" Villareal asked from the back of the room. He'd had very little to say during the preparations, outside of his medical classes.

"Working on that, too," Brannigan answered. "Given that we'd be moving in the direction of Khadarkh, where nobody wants to go right now, that might have to be on our facilitator." Santelli nodded, making a mental note.

"All right, let's get this done," Brannigan said. "Keep your heads down and try not to look suspicious. As Aziz said, it's only a matter of time before the local cops come looking for us, so let's not move that timeline up any more than we have to."

***

The meeting was in the Armani-Hashi restaurant in the Burj Khalifa itself. Santelli didn't know if the contact, whom he only knew as "Mr. Green," was the actual facilitator or simply an intermediary. Given the tangled web of licit and illicit networks that formed the weave of the tapestry that was Dubai, either one was a possibility, though Santelli's money was on Mr. Green being an intermediary contact.

The restaurant was not busy, and Green had apparently flashed enough dirhams at the staff to get an entire corner blocked off for his use. Not exactly as low-profile as Santelli would have liked, but it would give them some privacy, provided there weren't half a dozen laser mikes already zeroed in on the window.

"Mr. Green?" Santelli asked as he came to the table. "I'm an associate of Mr. Zebrowski's."

The man called Mr. Green looked up. He was enormously fat, with a dark complexion and completely bald head. He was dressed in Arab casual, with dark slacks and a dark sports coat, open, a white shirt, and no tie. His eyes were brown, and he could easily have hailed from any Mediterranean country, whether north or south. When he spoke, he had no appreciable accent that Santelli could identify.

"Ah, yes, have a seat," he said. "And how is Mr. Zebrowski?"

"Surprisingly well," Santelli said, pulling back a chair and sitting down. "Considering that the last contacts you gave us didn't work out so hot."

"Yes, I heard about a bit of an altercation up in Sharjah," Mr. Green said, apparently completely unfazed. "The police are eager to find out who killed several of the Suleiman Syndicate without them knowing about it."

Santelli studied the man in front of him. There was little doubt in his mind that he was dealing with a sociopath; most men didn't become underworld facilitators otherwise. Which, to him, made Green ultimately unpredictable. He didn't know what all was going on under the surface, what kind of tides of information and money were going to decide for Mr. Green, or whoever he worked for, whether it was lucrative to do business with Brannigan and his men, or to turn them over to someone else, either the police or the Suleiman Syndicate, which would doubtless be looking for revenge after Al Fulani's death.

If anything, Santelli liked this kind of thing even less than Brannigan would have. There were realms of endeavor that Carlo Santelli was very good at. Soldiering was one of them. Reading between the lines of money, power, and criminality was not. And when he wasn't good at something, it tended to make him angry. Fortunately, a lifetime of discipline and professionalism had enabled him to detach his anger from his words and actions.

So, he watched and waited while Mr. Green examined the menu, peripherally aware that Flanagan, Curtis, and Aziz had slipped into the restaurant behind him, and were spreading out around the room, taking up positions where they could cover the doors as well as Green himself.

Green put the menu down on the table and finally looked levelly at Santelli. "I am honestly unsure, at this point, just how wise continued business with you and your people really is," he said. "Piles of corpses, in Dubai, of all places, is not conducive to my work, or that of most of the groups in whose circles I move. I am not suggesting," he continued, raising a finger, "that I will turn you in to the authorities. That would not be good for business, either. But if more of this kind of violence is in the offing, here on what is, ostensibly, safe turf, I might have to distance myself and my operation."

Which could be disastrous, Santelli knew. They had no other contacts, and if Green pulled out completely, any other *potential* contacts were probably going to disappear, as well. Which would leave them stuck, less than a hundred miles from their objective, having to slink back home with their tails between their legs and leave the hostages to their fates, unable to procure weapons or insert.

"I am curious, however," Green said, "as to just how you managed to turn the tables on the Suleiman Syndicate so thoroughly, especially considering the unlikelihood of your getting weapons into this city beforehand."

Santelli leaned back in his chair. It creaked a little under him; the restaurant might have been fancy, but the furniture was a little chintzy up close. Which fit with most of the Middle East. "You'd be surprised what can be accomplished with a combination of speed, surprise, a few two-foot lengths of rebar, and a complacent opposition." Not to mention a fist-sized rock launched into the one rear guard's head with the speed and accuracy of a fastball. Hancock had a hell of an arm.

Green cracked a faint smile, one that never reached his eyes. "Interesting," he said. He pursed his lips as if thinking, though Santelli was sure it was an act. Whatever course of action the man had decided on had been determined long before this meeting had begun.

"While I have certain misgivings," he said, leaning forward and placing his elbows on the table, making the entire thing tilt toward him, "there is one more possibility that I might have for you. Time is of the essence, of course. Your welcome in Dubai is waning fast. Whether you manage to make a deal with these people or not, you had best be on your way out of the city within the next twenty-four hours. And I would not suggest returning within another year, at least."

That was going to affect their extract plans, but there was another port not far away, in Abu Dhabi. That might work.

Green reached into his coat and pulled out a small, folded piece of notepaper, placing it on the table in front of him. "If you are at this location, between the hours of eight-thirty and nine this evening, carrying a white plastic bag with the emblem of the Dubai Mall, you could make contact with some individuals who might be able to help you."

Santelli reached for the menu, palming the note as he did so. "Who are these 'individuals?'" he asked, as he scanned the menu.

Green shrugged. "They are business associates," he replied unhelpfully. "The one I have spoken with the most goes by the name Dmitri."

"Russian Mafiya," Santelli said.

"Perhaps," Green said. "Perhaps not. Does it matter, as long as you obtain the supplies and equipment that you are looking for?"

"That depends," Santelli replied. "Considering the way the last meeting you set up went. Of course, we've got a bit more in the way of, shall we say, 'contingency planning' available to us this time."

For the first time, something close to expression actually flickered in Green's eyes. It might even have been nervousness. His gaze flicked to one side, and Santelli thought that he'd just noticed either Flanagan or Curtis, and put two and two together.

"Just try to avoid leaving a bloodbath behind," Green said, his voice still composed, sounding almost bored. "It is bad for

81

business, and if it happens again, I might *have* to report on certain contacts I've had with aggressive Westerners to the police, if only to cover my own ass."

"We'll be nice," Santelli assured him as the waiter, who had been hovering at a distance during their conversation, finally approached the table at a faint nod from Green. "Until it's time not to be nice."

He doubted the underworld facilitator would get the reference.

CHAPTER 7

Roger Hancock was relaxed as he stood in the parking lot near the Royal Arms Hotel, looking like just about any other Westerner in Dubai on vacation or business, waiting for a taxi. The shopping bag in his hands, bearing the Dubai Mall crest in gold on its white plastic, was filled with various and sundry knickknacks, along with a box of baklava. He wasn't carrying a firearm, himself. That was left to Flanagan and Childress, who were shadowing him in one of the Land Rovers from the previous day, with the captured AKMS and one of the AKS-74Us next to each of them.

Hancock had been comfortable with danger for a long time. Whether it was the dangers of training and combat, or the dangers inherent in dealing with rough men who had passed into the gray areas where many former soldiers and Marines walked, Hancock had become familiar enough with them to be comfortable. He was still alert, every sense honed to a fine edge, but he was not frightened.

Maybe it meant that he'd been out in that gray area himself for too long, he mused. But he didn't consider it complacency. Complacency would have meant treating this meeting like another tourist lark, and he was far from doing that. He was aware of everything around him, aware with a keenness that only adrenaline made possible. That was probably why he surfed, and skydived, and did all the other wild stuff that he did when he was at home. He wasn't looking for a high, unlike so many others who took up such hobbies. He was trying to maintain that edge; to keep his adrenaline levels up to where he could really *see*.

He was a little surprised when the gleaming, black Hummer H2 pulled up beside him and a faintly accented voice from the rolled-down window said, "Get in."

He'd been expecting something a little less ostentatious. But then, it was Dubai. Conspicuous displays of wealth were the norm, to the point that they no longer *were* conspicuous.

The door swung open and he got in, pointedly avoiding looking over at the Land Rover behind him. He knew Childress and Flanagan were watching, and that they'd be discreet when they followed. They were pros. He'd known Flanagan for a long time, and from what he'd seen of Childress so far, the other man wasn't far behind his taciturn old friend.

He slid onto the leather seat and pulled the door shut behind him. The overhead light had not turned on when the door had opened; his hosts didn't want their faces seen, at least not yet. The other man in the back seat, who was little more than a silhouette, a few details of a flat, pugnacious face limned in the faint glow of the streetlights and the blazing neon in front of the Royal Arms, tapped on the driver's shoulder, and they pulled out of the parking lot. The Hummer had barely stopped long enough for Hancock to climb in.

"We can talk," the other man said. "My name is Dmitri."

"Roger," was Hancock's reply. His first name would give no one much information.

"I am not going to search you, Roger," Dmitri said, a faint note of amusement in his voice. "Call it a show of trust. I know what you did to those Suleiman Syndicate fools. That is part of why we are meeting now. I admire that sort of ingenuity and ruthlessness. I wanted to meet you and your associates, if only because of what you did to them."

"We must have hurt them more than we thought," Hancock said blithely, "if you're so happy about it."

The other man laughed. "Indeed, they have been a thorn in our side," he said. "Arrogant goat-fuckers. Bunch of rich upstart sons of rich oil sheiks want to muscle in on the *Bratva*'s turf." He sounded like he wanted to spit, though in the shifting lights from outside the vehicle's windows, he had a hard, amused look on his face. "It is always good to see them get their comeuppance."

He lit a cigarette, the flare of the lighter momentarily giving Hancock a clear look at him, as well as the driver. Dmitri was of medium height, medium build, with a mashed nose that looked like it had been broken a *lot*, and brown hair slicked back over his boxy skull. The driver, who had not made a sound, was a mountainous shaved gorilla, his traps nearly reaching the base of his scarred, stubbled skull.

"So," Dmitri said, as he blew out a cloud of harsh, noxious smoke, "you are looking for small arms, explosives, ammunition, combat gear, and transportation."

If the other man was looking for a reaction to his extensive knowledge, Hancock did not oblige him. All the same, it was worrying that this Russian gangster knew so much about their operation, and their shopping list. Hell, he didn't think that transpo had even been discussed with the facilitator.

Dmitri grinned in the dim, orange light of his cigarette as he took another drag, the coal glinting in his eyes as he studied Hancock. "Oh, yes, we know all kinds of things," he said merrily. "Though some of it was more a matter of 'putting two and two together,' as you Americans say." He took another drag. The cab was getting hazy with the foul smoke. Those Russian cigs were really bottom of the barrel. Hancock momentarily wished he'd brought some American cigarettes along just so that he could have offered the man one, if only to get him to put that rotgut cancer stick out.

"Several Americans try to make a deal with the Suleiman Syndicate for small arms, ammunition, and explosives, preferably both Semtex and grenades," Dmitri continued. "Interestingly enough, this deal happens to coincide with a certain hostage situation involving Americans not far from Dubai, on the island of Khadarkh. A hostage situation that presently appears to have the American Navy paralyzed, probably to avoid harming the hostages." He shrugged, a vague movement in the darkness. "It was not actually all that difficult to figure out."

Hancock leaned back in the seat, eyeing the dark form of his companion. "So, that raises another question," he said contemplatively. "Aren't the Iranians Russian allies? I've heard a few things about the *Bratva*'s Russian patriotism from time to time. Why would you help a bunch of Americans against an Iranian op?"

Teeth flashed in the dimness. "Ah, but Tehran has not claimed responsibility for anything happening on Khadarkh," Dmitri pointed out. "So, technically, even if we were not transnational outlaws, there would be no harm to Russian-Iranian relations from the *Bratva* making a bit of extra profit on the side."

Hancock got the message. The Mafiya might occasionally work with the MGB when they saw it as being in their interests, but greed is the eternal motivator. However they had decided, this particular clan of the Russian mob had come to the conclusion that there was no patriotic reason to go along with the Iranian hostage takers. That was, of course, assuming that this wasn't another setup.

Either that, or they simply didn't imagine the American mercs had a prayer of actually pulling a rescue off, and figured they may as well make a few extra bucks "helping."

"So," Dmitri continued, "what do you need?"

"Fifty rifles, with fifteen magazines and a full combat load of five hundred rounds apiece," Hancock said. They didn't actually have a use for that many weapons, but at this point, the less an observer could tell about their operation from supply numbers, the better. Besides, Brannigan had expected that they might well get a lot of non-functional weapons mixed in with good ones. Ordering fifty for seven men made the odds better that they'd have plenty of working weapons when the time came. "Fifty pistols, with four magazines each, and ammunition. Two machineguns, with two thousand rounds per. One hundred frag grenades, and one hundred concussion grenades. Fifteen satchels of Semtex, with detonators, blasting caps, time fuse, and shock tube. Fifty combat vests, desert tan, for the rifles, and two machinegun chest rigs for the MGs. Fifty sets of night vision goggles—the best that can be found, not the fifteen-year-old Russian models."

Dmitri hadn't taken notes, but he was nodding. "That is a considerable order," he said, "but one that I believe we should be able to fulfill, and even on short notice." In other words, they had gotten word, probably through spies, as to generally what the Suleiman Syndicate had been hired to provide, and had already made arrangements to poach the deal. Whether they had intended to move on the Syndicate before or after the Americans made some sort of deal, Hancock didn't know, nor did he particularly care.

"You will need transport to the island, as well, will you not?" Dmitri asked.

"We are getting boats," Hancock said.

Dmitri laughed. "Rubber dinghies, I am guessing?" He shook his head. "No good, my friend, not for seventy-five nautical miles across the Gulf." He took another long drag on the cigarette, which was almost burned down to his knuckles, then rolled the window down just far enough to toss the butt out into the night. "We have a dhow that can get you within five nautical miles of Khadarkh without raising suspicions. This Commander Esfandiari is looking for American Navy ships, not ancient, creaky Arab dhows."

"How much more will the use of the dhow cost us?" Hancock asked.

"Not much," Dmitri assured him, in a tone of voice that nevertheless said, *A lot*. "Another…five hundred thousand dirhams?"

Which, given what they were already prepared to pay, was going to mean nearly a million dollars' worth of dirhams going into the mafiya's pockets in a single night.

Brannigan had assured him that whatever they ended up having to pay, as long as it was within the limits of the cash they had brought with them, he would lean on Tannhauser to make sure they all still got paid. Expenses and pay were two separate animals, and Brannigan was going to make sure that their employers understood that. Even so, it was a good-sized chunk of their cash on hand, and they would still need more to get out once the job was done.

"That's pretty steep," Hancock said. "Two hundred fifty thousand."

"This is a negotiation, not a souk bargaining party," Dmitri said, his voice suddenly cold. "Do not insult me. Four hundred thousand, or you can try to make that seventy-five nautical miles in rubber dinghies."

Which would be a long shot, at best, Hancock knew. The boats that Brannigan had procured had limited legs, even more so since they had only managed to get one fuel bladder for each boat. Trying to cross from Dubai to Khadarkh that way was probably not going to work.

Hancock made a show of considering it, but Brannigan had already given him the go-ahead to procure transportation from the Russians. He just didn't want to give Dmitri the satisfaction of knowing that.

"Four hundred thousand it is, then," he said. He reached out a hand, and the Russian shook it firmly.

"Good," Dmitri said. "We will have your weapons and equipment aboard the dhow. Meet me at the marina on the tip of Al Mamzar, this time tomorrow night. We will board a yacht and sail out to the dhow; it is rather too old and run-down for most places around Dubai itself, at least if you want to avoid being spotted by the Syndicate again. They have people all over the main docks, and they are going to be hungry for blood for some time, after you killed Al Fulani."

"Al Mamzar," Hancock repeated. "Looking forward to it."

"As am I, my friend." Dmitri grinned, then pointed out the window. "Here is your stop. Tomorrow night. Be sure to bring the money."

Hancock got out, and the Hummer rolled away down the street. He watched it retreat with narrowed eyes, then turned and started walking in the opposite direction. They had made a large loop, and he was now only about four blocks from the Royal Arms. He stepped into a shadowed side street, and a few moments later, Flanagan and Childress pulled up in the Land Rover.

"We're going to have to ditch this vehicle pretty soon," Flanagan commented, as Hancock got in and pulled the door shut. They had barely stopped at all. "Somebody's going to notice that it looks an awful lot like one of Al Fulani's vehicles."

"There are a ton of Land Rovers around this city," Hancock replied. "And we already switched the license plates." That had been an interesting bit of skullduggery, as they'd had to slip out to Kizad in the middle of the night after the debacle in the warehouse, and swap plates with a couple of hopefully still-unknowing Kia van owners.

"Still," Flanagan said. "Good fieldcraft, and all that."

"Did we get a deal?" Childress asked.

"We got a deal," Hancock replied. "We'll just have to be even more prepared for a double-cross this time."

***

By the time they pulled up to the marina the next night, both Land Rovers had been carefully wiped down for prints, and every man was wearing black nitrile gloves, pulled from spares that Doc Villareal had in his massive trauma kit. He had the big pack stuffed inside a rolling suitcase. He could draw the pack out once they were away from prying eyes.

The AKS-74Us were loaded and ready in backpacks, pistols were similarly concealed around the men's persons. Brannigan had the AKMS broken down in his own pack, which was, fortunately, just big enough to contain it. They had little enough ammo for any of the weapons, but hopefully it would be enough, if things went sideways.

If the entire deal was an ambush, they were probably dead. There would be no way to get the rifles out and into action fast enough on the pier. They'd make the Russians pay in blood, but they would still probably all go down before it was over.

Dmitri was waiting on the quay, next to a yacht that was probably extremely expensive, but was still somehow only vaguely middle-of-the-road in Dubai. It wouldn't attract much attention, either from being too ostentatious or too poor.

Hancock led the way, since he'd been Dmitri's point of contact. Brannigan and Curtis hovered just behind him, hands never far from the FiveSeven pistols in their waistbands. But Dmitri only shook Hancock's hand with a grin, waved to the rest of them, and led the way onto the yacht.

The rest of the mercenaries followed cautiously, checking their corners as they went through hatchways and carefully watching the Russian crew of three.

"Is this all?" Dmitri asked, a jocular note in his voice. "I thought you wanted enough for fifty men."

"We do," Hancock said. "Don't worry about it. You're still getting paid."

Dmitri grinned again. "Yes, about that…"

Santelli swung the big duffel down off his shoulder and unzipped it. He pulled back the flap to show the tops of stacks of pink, blue, and tan 1000-dirham notes. Dmitri nodded again, apparently pleased, and barked an order at the crew in Russian. Moments later, the engine purred to life, and they were pulling away from the quay.

The yacht motored out into the channel, and headed out past Al Mamzar Park, which was a low, dark line of trees on the horizon, pricked by the glowing bulbs of the path lights in the night. In moments, they were out past the mouth of the channel and heading out into the Gulf.

No one talked. The mercenaries had nothing to say that they wanted the Russians to hear. The Russians weren't being chatty, either. Even Dmitri seemed to have suddenly become all business.

Slowly, the lights of Dubai receded behind them, though they still formed a brilliant splash against the horizon to the southeast. Ahead lay only the darkness of the ocean and the night.

Then a light flickered to life in the darkness, a few hundred meters in front of the yacht. The radio crackled with a voice speaking Russian, and Dmitri answered. A minute later, they were pulling alongside the most ancient, rattletrap-looking dhow Brannigan had ever seen. And he'd spent some time in the Middle East.

It was a big one, with a large cabin at the rear. Paint was peeling off the hull, and even the dim light from the yacht, it was hard to tell where paint ended and rust began. Bumpers were put out as the yacht pulled up alongside the dhow, and a ladder was lowered. The ladder, at least, seemed to be in decent repair. The Russians just wanted the dhow to *look* like it was about to fall apart.

"We have dinghies," Dmitri said, as they climbed up over the dhow's gunwale. "Since our means of getting out here precluded loading your own."

But Brannigan shook his head. "After your meeting with Roger, here, we had them delivered to the Khalid Port, Sharjah," he said. "If we can sail up there, we can pick them up and load them. Will that be a problem?"

Dmitri shrugged. "As you said, we are still being paid. Smart thinking, though. The Suleiman gangsters will be looking for you on shore, not coming in from the Gulf." He chuckled. "And this dhow will not stand out so much in Sharjah."

He went up to the pilot house to give orders, and then another Russian, a sallow, beak-nosed man in a tracksuit, beckoned them to follow him. Hands still hovering close to pistols, they complied.

He led the way down a rickety ladder into the hold. The hold stank of open bilges, and it was pitch-black until the Russian flicked on a fluorescent lantern. Wordlessly, he pointed to the crates and equipment cases strapped down in the center of the hold.

With Curtis and Aziz hanging back to watch the Russian, Brannigan led the way and started to open the first crate.

True to Dmitri's word, everything that Hancock had asked for was there. Fifty AK-12s, the newest Russian service rifle, were packed in two crates, with seven hundred fifty magazines in another. There were even fifty PKU-2 red dot sights, with batteries for same. The requested pistols turned out to be Bulgarian Makarovs, and about a third of the magazines were badly rusted. Two PKP machineguns were stuffed in another crate. Still more crates held ammunition and explosives. The NVGs weren't the latest, contrary to Hancock's specifications; the PNV-57Es had been developed in the '80s, but they would do for what the mercs needed them for. Hopefully. Other cases held the chest rigs and combat vests.

Flanagan was pulling some of the weapons out, grimacing slightly as he handled the Russian rifles. Flanagan was something of a patriot when it came to firearms; he'd always preferred American firepower to "Communist, stamped-metal crap."

"Looks like we're in business, boys," Brannigan said, hefting one of the AK-12s and checking it over, keeping one eye on the Russian, who was still standing back by the ladderwell. It certainly seemed like Dmitri and his *brodyagi* had come through, but that didn't mean they were going to start letting their guard down.

The mercenaries would be "in the red" until after the hostages were rescued, and they were back Stateside.

***

Getting to the port and loading the rubber boats was another production, and all of the mercenaries were just as tense as before. On the pretense of being ready for a Suleiman Syndicate ambush, all of them had broken out and loaded AK-12s, though they hadn't had a chance to zero, or even test fire them yet. That would have to happen en route to their insert point, off the coast of Khadarkh.

Once Brannigan made contact with the Arab seller who was making delivery, and ensured both that the goods were there and that the last of the payment was handed over, loading became simply a matter of hard work and some time. They threw their all into it, getting the boats loaded and stowed in near-record time. All of them were acutely conscious of just how little darkness they had left, and none of them wanted to spend an extra day and night with the Russians aboard the dhow, though as midnight came and went, Brannigan was starting to think they might have to. Making landfall in daylight was not going to be a good idea.

With the boats loaded, they put Dubai behind them once again, and motored out into the Gulf.

***

Test firing and zeroing took longer than anyone would have liked. The Russian optics weren't quite as easy to get used to as their American equivalents, and not all of them worked. When Hancock pointed this out to Dmitri, the Russian only shrugged and grinned.

"That is why you asked for fifty, *nyet*?" he said. "If you had fifty men, then you might have more reason to complain."

Flanagan had shot the man a glower, that seemed to have no effect on the gangster. He had his money.

Finally, the last of the red dots were zeroed, the best-working NVGs had been selected, the PKPs had been checked and tested, magazines were loaded, and gear was packed and ready to go. Unfortunately, the sun was starting to rise by then.

"We're going to need to go to ground for the day," Brannigan said, hating to say it.

"That greedy Russian bastard is going to want more money," Hancock pointed out.

"I'm sure he will," Brannigan answered grimly. "I'm sure he'll also realize that at this point, our mission is more important than maintaining good relations with the Russian mob." He glanced up at where Dmitri was standing in the pilot house. "If we have to kill all of them and take the dhow, then we can, and we will."

***

There turned out to be no need to take the dhow by force. Dmitri didn't even argue that hard. They dropped anchor off the coast of Sir Bu Nair and prepared to wait out the day.

CHAPTER 8

The lights of Khadarkh City cast a faint glow against the sky on the other side of the looming, black escarpment that formed the southern tip of the island. Brannigan was briefly surprised that they were still on, given everything that had happened on the island, but then decided that it was probably in the Iranians' best interest not to stir up the populace unnecessarily. From Chavez' intel reports, the loyalists were not happy that their King was in exile in Saudi Arabia while the Iranians held the island by force of arms. Turning off the power would only exacerbate the unrest.

He turned his attention back to the task at hand. Launching the boats was proving more difficult than anticipated. While launching from a larger dhow like the Russians' was certainly doable—Somali pirates did it all the time—with the outboard motors and the fuel bladders it became somewhat more difficult. And the dhow didn't have a crane that could swing the boats out over the side and lower them to the water, either.

The course of action they had decided on while they'd waited and baked in the sun off the coast of Sir Bu Nair was kind of messy, but it was the best they could come up with, given the resources at hand.

"One, two, three!" With a shove, Curtis and Santelli sent the rubber boat sliding over the gunwale. Brannigan, already in his combat vest, heavy with loaded mags, grenades, and med kit, his AK-12 slung across his chest, watched the boat hit the water bow-first. Fortunately, it was at such an angle that it slid down onto its keel instead of flipping over. That would have meant more work to get it righted, though since the commercial dinghy was considerably lighter than the Zodiac Combat Rubber Raiding Craft that most of them had trained on, many moons ago, that wouldn't have been as difficult as it could be.

With the boat in the water, both Curtis and Santelli climbed over the gunwale and hung on for a moment, looking down at the water to make sure they weren't about to hit the boat itself. Santelli let go first, dropping out of sight. Curtis hung on for a second longer, grimacing, then vanished. A moment later there was a splash, then the two men were clambering aboard the dark green boat.

Brannigan could hear Curtis complaining. "Why the hell did I let myself get talked into a fuckin' amphibious operation?" he was muttering. "I hate the fuckin' ocean. Fuckin' sharks and shit."

Santelli hissed at him to shut up, and then they were paddling the boat closer to the side of the dhow, while Brannigan and Villareal hoisted the outboard motor up to the gunwale.

This wasn't going to be easy. Flanagan and Hancock were both holding onto the rope that they'd gotten from the Russians and tied around the motor, and Brannigan and Villareal were going to lower the outboard slowly, but it was still likely to swing, and possibly clang against the side of the ship. The noise wouldn't necessarily be catastrophic, as far out in the Gulf as they were. They were still fifteen nautical miles from shore, and hadn't seen any sign of Iranian patrol boats. But Brannigan wasn't about to let himself start thinking that that meant there weren't any. Quiet would be the rule from there on out.

Slowly, a few inches at a time, they lowered the motor over the side. Flanagan and Hancock moved toward the side, inch by inch, lowering the motor by the rope. The rope creaked, and a faint gonging sound rang through the hull as the motor brushed the side. But finally, the rope went slack, and Santelli stage-whispered up that they had it.

With one boat in the water, the second boat went next. Brannigan didn't want to risk reducing the number of hands on deck any more than necessary before all of their gear was in the water. The Russians hadn't made any hostile moves or even looked as if they were plotting any more than normal, but it didn't pay to take any of that for granted. So he wanted to keep Aziz and Childress on security until both boats were in the water, with motors and fuel bladders, and they were ready to go.

Santelli and Curtis had time to get their boat out of the way while Brannigan, Villareal, Flanagan, and Hancock manhandled the second boat to the side. With four of them working at it, it went over easily. Unfortunately, it went over at a steep enough angle that it struck the water bow-first, teetered for a moment, then dropped, hitting the water with a *slap*, its keel pointed toward the sky.

"Hey, Joe," Curtis hissed up from the first boat, "it's upside-down!"

"Thank you, Captain Obvious," Flanagan replied through clenched teeth. "Shut up before you bring the whole Iranian Navy down on our heads."

"Get a line on that boat," Brannigan instructed. "Don't let it float away. We'll get the rest of the gear down, then we'll worry about righting it."

Santelli steered the first boat over, and Curtis, not without a certain amount of grumbling, got a line lashed to the bow tie-down. Then the men still up on the dhow started manhandling the next boat over the side.

Finally, after a lot of grunting, cursing, and struggling, there were four boats in the water, loosely connected into a sort of pontoon raft, with four outboards, fuel bladders, and fuel lines sitting in them. One boat had to hold two sets, since the second one was still capsized. Only then did Brannigan and the rest begin to descend the ladder to get in the boats.

Brannigan himself turned to Dmitri, who was watching from the bow. "Can we trust you to be back here for pickup?" he asked bluntly.

"Of course, my friend," the Russian replied, sounding wounded. "We accepted your money. The deal was made. We will come back here at the same time for the next three nights." Even Brannigan had to admit that if they didn't make it back out in three nights, they probably weren't going to make it at all.

"Glad to hear it," Brannigan said, in a tone of voice that said, louder than words, that he'd believe it when he saw it. He was far too old to believe in honor among thieves, and the Russians were definitely thieves, among other things.

Hell, if there had been honor among thieves, the Russians probably would never have made the deal in the first place.

He clambered down the ladder, swinging off and into the nearest boat, which Santelli was holding somewhat steady with a paddle. He was the last one off the dhow, so Santelli reached out with the paddle and shoved the boats away from the side. Dmitri waved from the gunwale above them, and then the dhow's engines started to rumble more deeply, white water beginning to gather at the bow as she surged away. The Russians weren't going to stick around until it was time for pickup.

As the dark shape of the dhow dwindled into the night, the mercenaries set about getting the second boat righted. That meant Villareal clambered over to get on top of the upturned keel, while Childress lowered himself into the water and grabbed ahold of the handles on the gunwales.

Villareal took hold of the righting line that ran down the length of the keel, stood up, and leaned backward. The boat creaked and bent, then flipped back over handily, Villareal going in the drink while Childress sprawled across the top of the gunwales. The lanky hillbilly hurried to get the paddles out and untie the bow line, lest the twisted rope cause more problems. Villareal clambered back aboard, hauling himself and his gear over the gunwale, against the pull of the salt water now weighing down his clothes and boots.

After that, it was a matter of getting all of the outboards distributed, mounted, and started up. It took longer than Brannigan had hoped, but not as long as they had planned for. They could still make it to shore a good four hours before daylight. Finally, all the gear stowed, the old Russian NVGs hauled out of their waterproof bags and strapped to their heads, they got ready to move in, two men per boat. One would drive, the other would sit in the bow, AK-12 ready to engage if need be.

Four boats might have seemed slightly excessive for only eight men, but they were going to need the space for the hostages on the way out. Even then, with possibly as many as thirty hostages, it was going to be a tight fit, and it would not be a fast or comfortable ride.

They could worry about that part once they had the hostages in hand. Until then, their focus was on getting ashore undetected, and in one piece.

The outboards purred as they made their way over the waves, the jagged escarpment looming larger and larger in front of them. No one said anything; even if they hadn't been trying to stay stealthy, the noise of the motors and the hiss and slap of the water against the hulls would have made it difficult to talk. The fact that, as always, the men in the bows were getting hammered, bounced off the rubber gunwales with every wave, only made them that much less interested in conversation.

It took a long time, but they finally came to the edge of the surf zone, a little more than a hundred yards offshore. Brannigan, in the lead boat, eased off the throttle and brought the craft to a faintly drifting halt, rocking on the waves.

It was very quiet, out there on the water with the motors throttled back. He scanned the shore in the green-scale glow of the NVGs, hoping against hope that the ancient Russian optics weren't going to crap out from the salt spray at any minute.

Waves crashed against the rocky shore, whitecaps hitting with a dull, rhythmic roar in the quiet of the night. There was otherwise no movement on the dark line of terrain ahead.

There was also no good site to land the boats; the cliff was only a few feet high, but it was still a sheer cliff. They needed to find an actual beach.

Turning the tiller, Brannigan twisted the throttle slightly, steering the boat against the current, moving to the west. He kept it slow, scanning the dark cliffs for a likely spot. The other three boats followed. Comms would make noise they wanted to avoid, and there was little to say anyway; they'd just have to stick together until he found a Boat Landing Site.

There. It was shallow, and the sandy, rocky ground rose steeply not too far inland, but there was a stretch of beach just ahead. He just hoped, as he turned in toward it, that it was unoccupied. The likelihood of tourists being out at night while Iranian soldiers held the island by force was low, but he'd spent enough time in the war-torn Middle East to have seen stranger things.

Opening the throttle a little wider, so that the boat would have enough momentum to beach properly, he aimed the bows for the narrow shingle. A couple of minutes later, they were there, the nearness of the beach announced by the harsh grinding of the outboard's boom scraping on the bottom.

Hastily killing the motor, hoping that the props hadn't been badly damaged, Brannigan hauled the motor up out of the water. Their momentum was dead, however, and he and Aziz had to hop out and drag the boat the rest of the way up onto the beach, wading from knee-deep water and then slogging up onto the sand. The other three boats had done better, the motors coming up out of the water before impact, allowing the boats to glide ashore, getting higher up the beach on momentum alone.

"Thanks for the warning that we were getting to the shallows," Brannigan snarled quietly to Aziz.

"I couldn't see shit!" the other man protested weakly.

"That's funny," Brannigan said. "The rest managed it." He stepped closer to Aziz, dropping his voice still further. "Listen up, Aziz. I don't think it's quite sunk in for you yet, just how far out in the cold we really are on this job. There are eight of us, with no support except for some Russian mobsters who might or might not be back for us tomorrow night. You need to lose the attitude and start pulling your damned weight, or you're not getting off this island. I'll make sure of it. *Comprende?*"

Aziz was a blurry impression in the green image of the NVGs, but there was no mistaking his nervous gulp. "Understood, Colonel," he replied in a whisper.

"Good." They finished making sure the boat was high enough that it shouldn't float away at high tide, and gathered with the rest up on the higher ground. Brannigan was last, having first scanned their surroundings, looking for signs of human activity.

They couldn't afford to leave a watch on the boats, and if this was somebody's tryst spot, they were screwed. But there was none of the trash and detritus that usually marked such places in the region. This spot appeared to have been left alone for a long time.

Boots crunched on the dirt and gravel as they climbed the slope beyond the beach. Flanagan and Hancock were already in the prone at the crest, AKs pointed north, toward the interior of the island. Curtis joined them a moment later, setting up his PKP on its bipods and scanning the ground ahead of them.

"All right," Brannigan whispered. "We're going to move up to the planned patrol base. Keep together; it might be a smaller footprint if we scattered and moved in pairs, but we can't afford to break comm silence if something goes wrong."

There were all sorts of other little details that he could have gone into; in fact, he knew quite a few officers with far less experience than he who would have. But he knew that these men were pros, and didn't need the reminder. They knew how to patrol. So, he pointed to Childress, who nodded and led out.

***

It was not a walk in the park. The entire island was basically a dusty, sandy rock pile in the middle of the Gulf, and there didn't seem to be a level spot wider than a couple of yards to be found anywhere. Brannigan had read that the airport had needed to be blasted level, in some places knocking down ten-meter tall hills just to create a straight enough strip of ground to land aircraft.

Every step seemed to find a jagged rock, and footing was treacherous, especially carrying as much ammo as they were, along with assault packs full of explosives, batteries, water, and just enough chow for three days. It felt like half the rocks on the island were loose, just waiting to slip or turn under an unwary foot.

They'd barely gone three hundred meters from the beach, and Brannigan was already feeling it. The fact that each rifleman was carrying twelve loaded AK-12 magazines, in addition to the mag in his weapon, didn't help anything. Despite his still above average conditioning, between the difficult footing, trying to see through the old Russian night vision, the heat, the humidity, sand and salt abrading skin already softened by seawater, and the weight of their loads, Brannigan was breathing hard, soaked in sweat, and thoroughly miserable before Childress suddenly sank to a knee ahead of him, holding up a fist.

Brannigan dropped immediately, as did the rest. He scanned all around, having to crane his neck backward just enough to be uncomfortable in order to see. The NVGs just wouldn't sit *quite* right, not on the Russian mounts.

He didn't see any movement, or lights. But Childress had stopped for a reason. Slowly, rolling his feet so as to make as little noise as possible, he rose into a half crouch and crept forward until he could take a knee next to the point man.

"Got a road," Childress whispered, the breathed words barely audible over the sound of the surf, already well behind them.

"Let's check it out," Brannigan said, looking back to make sure Hancock was watching them. He gave the signal for "Linear Danger Area," then tapped Childress on the shoulder.

Together, the two of them moved up to the edge of the road. It wasn't paved; it was only a packed earth and gravel track through the desert. And in the less-than-ideal image of the NVGs, it was impossible to see if there were fresh vehicle tracks in the dust.

Even if it was unused, they would have to get across it quickly and back into the rolling, rocky hinterlands. A road was a bad place to be, especially since they still didn't know what kind of patrols the Iranians might have out. He looked back, got Hancock's attention again, and signaled that they would cross by twos. "Let's go," he murmured to Childress, and the two of them rose and scurried across the road, pushing up a couple of meters into the rocks on the far side before crouching back down and pointing their weapons up and down the road. They might not have practiced it together much, but the drills were old ones, and the habits were still solid.

By twos, the rest of the team quickly crossed the road and moved into the hinterland. Once the last man was across, Brannigan and Childress moved back up to the head of the formation, and they continued inland.

***

They were north of the escarpment now, and more of the island was becoming visible. The airport was a blaze of lights, seemingly far too close for comfort. Brannigan felt horrifically exposed on the open, rocky ground, a niggling fear in the back of his mind that they had to be clearly visible in the bright sodium glow of the airport's lights. The rotating green and white beacon sweeping its beams across the landscape only made things worse.

When he saw Childress flinch lower as the white beam of the beacon swung overhead, he knew that he was not alone.

Childress began to angle to the east, trying to keep their distance from the airport itself. So far, Brannigan hadn't seen any patrols around the airport, though he knew that they had to be there. He kept one eye, as best he could, on the splash of lights, watching for any sign that they had been detected.

They still had to get past the airport, and they were going to have to go closer; the end of the runway was a bare four hundred meters from the eastern shore. So, reluctantly, Childress started to move north again as they neared the eastern end of the airport.

Brannigan wanted to tell him to slow down, but trusted that his pointman knew his business. They had all studied the same imagery, and he was pretty sure that Childress would remember the checkpoint on the coastal road, placed to shut off any traffic when an aircraft was landing or taking off.

But after another hundred yards, Brannigan was starting to have his doubts. Childress wasn't slowing down or showing appreciably more caution, the closer they got to the spot where he was sure the checkpoint was set up. He was about to stop the other man when Childress halted, once again sinking to a knee and raising a hand to signal the rest to stop.

Through the grainy green of the NVGs, Brannigan could just see the roof of the little guard shack at the checkpoint, as well as the red-and-white striped pole of the swing-arm, presently raised and pointing at the starry sky. There was no sign of guards, but they wouldn't be within line of sight, anyway, given the low pile of jagged rock between them and the checkpoint.

Childress looked back at him, and signaled with a curved hand that he planned on sneaking by the checkpoint to the northwest. Then he put a finger to his lips, as if to signal *Quiet*.

No shit, son.

Brannigan just passed the signals back, noting in the process that they had needed to get a lot closer together just to be able to discern the hand and arm signals. He swore that if he ever took a job like this again, he was going to find a way to get better night vision.

And not do business with organized crime, he added in his head. Not that they would always have the option. He was under no illusions about what kind of compromises had to be made in mercenary work, no matter how justified the ends might be.

Childress was fiddling with his AK. He finally figured out what he was trying to do, and dropped down to all fours, then began crawling forward, carefully placing each hand and knee, his AK across his hands. He wasn't moving fast, but he was being very quiet.

With an inaudible sigh, Brannigan followed suit. This was going to hurt; even aside from the sharpness of the rocks, and the likelihood of running into scorpions out there, his knees weren't all they used to be. But it was better to have sore and bleeding knees than to get shot through the skull.

In a winding, slow-moving line, they crept around to the northwest of the checkpoint, never going far without turning to look back toward the shack and the swing-arm. They were closer than any of them would have liked, but that had been necessitated by the need to keep their distance from the runway. Get too close, out on that level, clear ground, and get accidentally illuminated by one of the runway lights, and it would be all over.

Voices speaking in Farsi sounded in the night. Brannigan froze, wanting to hiss at Childress, who was still slowly moving forward. But the other man must have heard something anyway, because he stopped, sinking to his belly on the ground.

Not a moment too soon; headlights blazed on the coastal road in front of them, sweeping brilliant white illumination across the rocky ground and the eight mercenaries. All eight were already hugging the rocks, trying to become one with the dust. They weren't seen; no gunshots split the night, no cries of alarm rang out across the barren plain.

A truck rolled up to the checkpoint, stopping with a crunch of tires on gravel that they could hear clearly from where they lay.

Doors slammed, and more voices spoke in Farsi. The guard was being changed at the checkpoint.

It certainly confirmed the intel reports, Brannigan mused as he tried not to breathe in too much of the dust, his face pressed against the jagged rocks beneath him. The Khadarkhi Army spoke Arabic; the Iranians were obviously in full control of the entire island and all of its infrastructure, if they were stationing guards on the checkpoints at the airport.

It also said something about how many of them there were, if they could spare the manpower to set rotating shifts at checkpoints that far from the city. This was not going to be easy.

There were more raised voices, their tone sounding fairly jocular, then the doors slammed again, and the truck was turning, gravel crunching beneath the tires before it trundled off back to the north, its brake lights blazing bright red in the dark.

Someone was chatting down by the checkpoint. The Iranians did not seem overly concerned; even if someone had seen the dhow loitering near the southern end of the island, it had not been classed as a reason for any kind of serious alert. These were soldiers doing a boring, unpleasant task, and doing as much joking about it as they could.

Footsteps crunched on the rocks, not far away. Brannigan risked lifting his head just enough to see, hoping that he could bring his AK-12 to bear quickly enough if they were spotted. Someone was walking around the perimeter of the checkpoint, examining the lay of the land. Making sure everything really was secure.

Just our luck that one of these bastards turns out to be a professional.

He could see the man's silhouette against the starry sky before he could bring his NVGs in line, a dark shape with a rifle slung over its shoulder. In the green glow, he could see a man of medium height, wearing what looked like khakis and combat gear not unlike their own, a cap on his head, with no NVGs, just scanning the rocks with his naked eyes. After a moment, the man unzipped his fly and took a piss on the rocks, before turning and sauntering back down to the checkpoint.

Brannigan let out a breath he hadn't quite realized he had been holding. He suddenly braced himself again, hoping that

Curtis could resist the urge to make a wisecrack. But the little machinegunner stayed silent.

They lay there for a few more interminable minutes, waiting for the checkpoint to settle down into boring, sleepy routine, no longer fully alert, unlikely to react to the faint rustling of crawling men out in the dark.

The entire time, the tension in Brannigan's chest was winding tighter. Not because of the nearness of their enemy, but because of the time they were wasting. The urgency of their mission was eating at him, silently screaming at him that they couldn't afford to stay there, that they had to move if they were going to get to the hostages in time. They had no way of knowing if another one had been executed since Trevor had been shot. How much time did any of them have?

But Brannigan had been soldiering for a long, long time, and he knew to shut that part of his emotions off. They would do the hostages no good if they were discovered and killed before they could even get close to the Citadel. So he lay there, and waited, and listened, until Childress was satisfied that they had waited long enough, and recommenced his forward crawl.

***

It still took a long, long time to get far enough past the checkpoint that they could no longer hear the voices of the guards. Only then was Childress comfortable with getting up and moving forward on foot.

***

The eastern sky was beginning to brighten by the time they finally reached their chosen lay-up site. It had been impossible to select a precise site just going off of the imagery; one pile of rocks looks much the same as any other on a LANDSAT image. Brannigan even knew of one instance where Marines had gone looking for a series of apparently artificial hills in Iraq, only to find that the images had in fact been of pits in the ground, not hills. So, they'd picked a general area, far enough away from roads, buildings, or the outskirts of Khadarkh City, and decided that they would find a good spot there.

At first, there hadn't seemed to *be* a good spot. The entire area seemed to be nothing but a solid stretch of dusty rock, without a depression or elevation of more than a few inches. They had to push farther north, closer to the now-looming Citadel, before Childress found a depression, part of a shallow wadi leading down toward the shore, probably a channel cut by runoff on the rare occasions that it ever rained on the island.

The eight of them crammed themselves down into the crack, huddling against the rocks as much as possible, wishing for more in the way of camouflage, and prepared to wait out the day.

CHAPTER 9

Aziz wasn't the kind of man who could ever really mentally blend in in the Middle East. Oh, he could certainly play the part; he had the mannerisms and the dialects down, better than he would ever admit. He'd never wanted to be a HUMINT guy, and he'd gone to great lengths to hide the fact that he had a certain talent for it. He'd been a good enough mimic that he'd even dallied with going into theater as a kid, as much as his father had been adamantly against it. Only joining the Army had changed that, and when they'd tried to put him in Intelligence instead of the Infantry, he'd really come to understand just how much he hated the idea of immersing himself in his heritage to that extent. So he'd fought tooth and nail, failed every test they shoved at him, been as bigoted and self-loathing an anti-Arab racist as he could be, until they finally sent him to the Infantry.

He hadn't been any great shakes as a shooter. He knew it, deep down, but he clung to the identity of a grunt and a doorkicker like a lifeline, anyway. Shooters were tough guys. Shooters hated Arabs. He fit right in. And he didn't have to act like an Arab.

He could never really articulate his antipathy for his heritage. It had far less to do with 9/11 and the wars to follow as it did with a fundamental rebellion against his very traditional

Muslim parents. He liked booze, and he liked women, and that was about where his thought processes on the matter ended.

And yet, here he was, wearing a man-dress and keffiyeh, walking the streets of Khadarkh City in the early afternoon, looking for a tea shop or hookah bar, the specific kind of place where he might find the kind of people he was looking for. The kind of people that he really, deep down, didn't want to find.

He hadn't spoken to anyone since slipping into the outskirts of town, pulling the man-dress on over his khakis. He felt naked with only his knife, Makarov, and a couple of spare magazines on him, though the man-dress was good for concealing both weapons. He just wished that Brannigan, in his infinite wisdom, had seen fit to send backup.

No, send the dirty Arab to mingle with his dirty Arab cousins all alone. If he was being honest with himself, he knew that the thought was a lie. He was the only one who had any hope of blending in in Khadarkh City, especially given the fact that the Iranians had already swept through and rounded up any Americans, and presently had them under the gun in the Citadel. But Aziz rarely bothered with introspection when simple resentment would work. Brannigan had been an officer. That was enough for him.

He stopped in front of a café on the outskirts of the souk, just outside the crumbling wall of the Old City. Expressionless, he scanned the clientele. They were almost all younger men, most of them bearded. It was a familiar beard, too, covering the jaw and chin, with the upper lip shaved. It was generally known as the "Wahhabi Beard." These guys weren't on Khadarkh just for work. No one wearing that beard ever went anywhere just for work.

The sheer number of Wahhabi Beards beneath glaring, sullen eyes told him that he'd come to the right place. None of these men were going to be friends of the Iranians. Hell, these fanatics considered the Shi'a to be worse than the infidels, even the Jews.

He sat down at a table by himself, acutely conscious that his own facial hair was not in keeping with the rest, which would make this more difficult. But then, not all of the "Brothers" could afford to appear to be Wahhabi, so he mentally prepared to play that role. He certainly knew enough of the verbal cues to pass himself off as even more of a frothing lunatic than these idiots, as much as he might hate himself for every word that came out of his mouth.

He silently vowed that he'd demand a bonus, just for this. Not for the risk of being found out, tortured, and beheaded. They were all running that risk. No, he was going to demand more money for having to dirty himself by spouting Al Qaeda bullshit.

He got his chai and sipped it. Like every other place in this wretched part of the world, it was more sugar than tea. Of course, if it hadn't had enough sugar, he would have bitched about that, too. Aziz was in the habit of complaining, even if only in the silence of his own mind.

After a long silence, one of the wiry Wahhabis came and sat across the table from him. "*As salaamu aleikum*," the man said. His face was lean and hard, his eyes dead flecks of black with no soul behind them.

"*Wa aleikum as salaam*," Aziz replied, taking another sip of his tea.

"Are we brothers?" the other man asked, coldly. "I do not know you, nor do I remember seeing you in Al Jubail."

"I came by another route," Aziz replied. "Until two days ago, I was killing Houthis north of Sana'a."

No expression disturbed that dark, cold visage. "Indeed? A worthy cause," the other man said, his voice as flat as his eyes. "What brings you here?"

"The Council determined that my skills were best used here," Aziz replied. "The apostates' boldness is more dangerous here than even in the Yemen."

"Indeed," the other man replied, though whether or not he agreed was impossible to say. "What are your skills?"

"Who is asking?" Aziz demanded.

"I am Abu Sayf," the man said.

Aziz felt his hackles rise. He'd heard that name, despite his professed indifference to Middle Eastern affairs. Abu Sayf had popped up in Yemen a few years before, quickly making a name for himself through a combination of unrestrained brutality and sadistic cruelty. He had not been seen or heard of for some time, though a few people had suspected that he had gone to join the

111

growing ISIS insurgency in northern Iraq and Syria, following the fall of Mosul to the combined Kurdish and Iraqi forces. That he was here on Khadarkh was not a good sign.

Or perhaps it *was* a good sign, as far as their mission went. If there were that many Al Qaeda bad guys on Khadarkh, then trouble and chaos was brewing, regardless. Aziz just wasn't sure it was a good sign as far as his personal survival went, and he ranked that rather higher than the mission.

"I am Abdul Rahman al Ramadi," he said in reply, picking the name of an AQI terrorist whom he knew for a fact was dead. He'd seen the corpse. He was just hoping that Abu Sayf didn't know the same fact, at least not with the same certainty.

"I thought you were dead," Abu Sayf said, in the same low, dead voice, that probably would have sounded threatening even if he had just been ordering tea.

"Which is precisely what we wanted the Amriki to think," Aziz answered coolly. "I had to go into hiding for a while."

He tried not to hold his breath while he waited to see if the black-eyed psycho in front of him was going to buy it, or call the alarm and get him killed. He wished, not for the first time, that the man-dress had a slit in the front that he could reach the Makarov through. He was still determined to put a 9mm through Abu Sayf's skull before he died, however he had to get at the gun.

But the terrorist seemed to be satisfied. "Welcome, Abdul Rahman al Ramadi," he said. "You are just in time."

Aziz cocked an eyebrow. "We already have enough people in place to move?"

Abu Sayf nodded. "There are enough to begin. We have waited too long as it is. The first steps will be taken tonight, before the demonstrations disperse." He smiled coldly. "Though our friends have made sure that the demonstrators are staying later and later."

That was no surprise. Toward the end, before Yemen had descended into all-out war, the demonstrations and unrest had gone from mid-afternoon affairs to a constant, background roar. Aziz had done enough research to backstop his paper-thin cover to know that much.

"The assets are being put in place to strike at two of the apostates' patrols here in the city tonight," Abu Sayf continued. "Several of the Al Qays loyalists will doubtless be killed in the process."

Which would provide the Al Qaeda operatives with more resentment and outrage to feed. This island was more of a powder keg than they'd realized when they'd first taken the job.

Under other circumstances, that would be a matter of more than a little concern, and Aziz' reflex was to further resent having taken the job in the first place. The analytical part of his mind, however, recognized the potential advantage for what it was. If this particular Sunni-Shi'a flashpoint was about to blow, it could potentially create enough chaos for them to get in and out under cover of the fighting. It would still be risky, certainly. Doing anything in the middle of a firefight usually is. But he was already thinking ahead to what he would have to do to make sure that things *didn't* calm down after the bombings.

It also meant that he had very little time in which to prepare and act. He'd have to find a way to disengage from the Al Qaeda terrorists long enough to get back to the rest of the team and report.

"We could certainly use your help, Abdul Rahman," Abu Sayf was saying. "A brother of your experience, having fought the infidels in the name of Allah for so long, should surely have some advice to give, particularly to our younger fighters."

"Surely," Aziz agreed, taking another sip of his tea even as his guts twisted. He should have picked a more obscure kunyah. He hadn't realized that Abu Sayf would hold Abdul Rahman al Ramadi in such respect as to want to immediately include him in the chain of command and the planning process. Though, when he looked in the other man's cold, dead eyes, he thought suddenly that Abu Sayf's obsequiousness was not driven by respect at all, but rather suspicion. He felt a chill. He was in this deeper than he'd expected; if he slipped, even a little, in the next few hours, he was going to be killed. And Abu Sayf would not make it quick or merciful.

Well, I'll just have to make sure I shoot you in the face as soon as it looks like the game is up, won't I?

"Come, my brother," Abu Sayf said, standing up. "There are many places to go before the night's attack. We have dispersed the brothers in cells throughout the city, to avoid the watchful gaze of the apostates. You should meet with some of the more important ones."

Aziz rose to join him, feeling like he had a heavy, cold lump of lead in his stomach. *If I live through this, I'm never doing recon in an Arab city ever, ever again.*

***

"He's still not back," Santelli whispered. "He's overdue."

"Do we go looking for him?" Childress asked.

Brannigan shook his head. "He's a big boy," he said. "And we knew that he might not be able to disengage on the set timeline if he got deep enough. His job is to sow chaos; we'll give him some time to sow chaos. Besides, if a bunch of palefaces show up in town too close to his arrival, it just might *get* him killed."

"Presuming he's not dead already," Hancock said ominously.

"Which was always the risk taken," Brannigan pointed out. "And we've got on-the-ground recon to do, ourselves. We'll keep our ears to the ground. If he makes it back, we're good. If he doesn't, we'll have to improvise."

Despite his words, Aziz' absence was bothering Brannigan a lot, not least because it was highlighting just how thin a thread the entire operation was hanging from. If the least thing went wrong, with the numbers they had, the entire show could go entirely to crap in a heartbeat. Then they'd all be dead, and the hostages right along with them.

But we're the best chance they've got. How many more will that bearded psychopath murder before the powers that be get their thumbs out?

"Keep an eye out for him," he instructed. "If he manages to get a duress signal out, then we can see about going in after him." They had at least arranged such a signal, though whether or not Aziz would get a chance to use it was unknown. They'd brought four of the burner phones from Dubai, and Aziz had one. If he sent a text that looked like a random mishmash of letters, numbers, and symbols—but in a pattern that had been, in fact, determined beforehand—then he was in trouble and needed help.

They didn't have the facilities to keep the phones charged, not out in the rocks, so they were turning one on every thirty minutes, top and bottom of the hour. So far, there was nothing. So, either Aziz was on mission, or he was dead. Those were pretty much the only options.

"Let's go," Brannigan whispered to Childress. He would have taken Flanagan, but Childress had proved to have a slightly better skillset when it came to moving silently through the dark. Flanagan might have disputed it, but Brannigan had made the call, based on the gawky man's performance on point the first night. Recon would be him and Childress. Flanagan would have plenty to do once they commenced the assault.

Slowly and silently, the two of them climbed out of the narrow channel, clambering over the rocks until they were back up on the higher ground, and started moving toward the dark silhouette of the Citadel. The sun had been down for half an hour; there was still some light lingering on the western horizon, but it was dark enough that they could move with some confidence that they wouldn't be spotted.

Unless the opposition had NVGs or thermals. So far, they hadn't seen any indication that the enemy had such equipment, at least not the checkpoint troops, but it never paid to assume. Hope for the best, prepare for the worst. That had been Brannigan's planning mantra for what felt like ages, and it had never let him down.

They had less than a mile to cover to get to a good vantage point to observe the Citadel. They had to cross the coastal road once more, but fortunately there was no traffic on it at the time they reached it, so a quick dash sufficed to get them to cover on the other side without incident.

The ground was getting steeper and rockier as they got closer, as the island rose toward the hill where the Citadel loomed. Childress slowed, picking his way through the rocks, looking for a spot with a good field of view while at the same time offering enough microterrain that the two of them could hide from prying eyes that might be watching for them.

He finally found a spot, less than a kilometer from the outer curtain wall, atop a small, rocky hillock, only a few meters from the water. The rocks were broken enough that they could get flat and blend into the terrain, and the constant noise of the waves would mask any sounds they made getting settled. They were still close enough to the Citadel that they crawled the last hundred yards, staying low and moving slowly. Scanning carefully for any movement near them, the two men settled down in the prone amidst the boulders, and Brannigan drew out the binoculars that had been among the short list of equipment they'd been able to bring from the States without raising eyebrows in Dubai.

The ancient stone edifice had been built on a rising escarpment that loomed above a sheer cliff that plunged down to the waters of the Gulf on the eastern coast of the island. An outer wall appeared to encircle the lower half of the hill, while the primary buildings of the Citadel stood amidst an inner curtain wall on the rocky promontory itself. A round tower bulked large against the sky, standing slightly taller than the blocky, U-shaped building that formed the main keep. Two more towers were visible on the barbican gate that thrust its way out into the Old City. There were lights on in the Citadel, though not many. Most gleamed from narrow windows in the keep, high above the lights of the city below.

There was enough illumination that Brannigan could see a decent amount of the top of the wall. He was looking for observation points, heavy weapons, and sentries. He spotted what looked like a sentry point on top of the round tower above the keep immediately, two men silhouetted against the dark blue of the sky. The binoculars were high-quality glass, even though they did not provide the same level of magnification that a good spotting scope would have. He carefully braced them against the boulder in front of him and cupped his hands around the ocular lenses, breathing carefully to lessen the jiggle of the image.

He couldn't make out a lot of detail, even after several minutes' study. But he was fairly sure that he could see a long tube leaning against the crenellations, just barely visible as the end sticking up over the battlements. Up that high, the only thing that could be was a MANPAD, a shoulder-fired Surface to Air Missile.

116

So, even if they'd been able to bring helicopters, getting in that way would have been a bad idea.

He continued to scan the walls. There appeared to be several static sentry positions, though they were dark and hard to see; he couldn't be sure he wasn't missing one or two, at least on the south side. He wished he could get a good look at the entirety of the walls, but time was an issue. They'd have to hope that Aziz had gotten a good enough look at the city side of the Citadel to be able to fill in some of the gaps.

While they had certainly trained to climb the walls, the more he was able to study the real-world Citadel, the less that looked like a good idea. They didn't have sniper rifles to take out those static positions, and they appeared to be pretty well-fortified against small arms fire from below. Not only that...he thought he saw movement, and tried to focus in on it. Yes, there were several roughly man-shaped dark specks moving along the top of the outer curtain wall. They had rovers, too. With time, they could determine the schedule for the rovers' patrol routes, so they could be avoided, but the commotion of taking out the static sentries would doubtless bring the rovers running.

He kept thinking as he continued to slowly and carefully scan the wall. He hoped and prayed that Aziz hadn't been rolled up and killed; the more he looked at their objective, the more he was convinced that starting a Sunni riot out in town was the only way they were going to have a hope in hell of getting in there. And even then, it was going to be a roll of the dice.

He briefly considered calling it quits and heading back out to the boats. The money wasn't the object, even for the poorer mercs. He could help take care of them. He just had too few men to really be comfortable with this setup.

He stopped his scan. *What is that?*

The lower curtain wall took a sharp turn to follow the cliff back toward the main escarpment. And there, about twenty meters from the corner tower, he thought he saw a gap.

It took several minutes of study, during which he was alternately convinced that he was seeing things, and that there was, in fact, a sizeable breach in the wall. Finally, he handed the binoculars over to Childress. "Look just to the right of that closest

117

tower, on the lower wall," he instructed. "Does it look like there's a break in the wall, just over the cliff, to you?"

Childress took the binoculars and settled in, bracing his elbows on the rocks and cupping the binos with his hands. After a moment, which seemed a lot shorter than the time Brannigan had taken, he said, "Yep, there's a breach in the wall, just about twenty-thirty yards beyond that tower."

"You're sure?" When Childress nodded, the motion nearly invisible in the dark, he muttered, "Damn, you've got better eyes than I do."

"You've got a few years on me, sir," Childress said, handing the binoculars back.

Brannigan chuckled softly as he took them. "Santelli was right, you don't beat around the bush, do you?"

"Sorry, sir," Childress whispered back. "I'm trying to work on it. My 'filter,' I mean."

"Never mind, Sam," Brannigan said, bringing the binos back to his eyes. "We ain't in the mil no more, and I wouldn't be 'sir' in the field, anyway." His mind was already on the problem at hand.

He was studying the corner tower, trying to see if there was another static security post there. He couldn't see one, and he'd thought so far that most of the sentry posts had been placed to overlook the city, but he couldn't be sure. "Did you see if there was a sentry on that corner tower?" he asked Childress.

"I didn't see one," Childress replied. "Don't mean there ain't one there."

Brannigan didn't respond, but scanned downward, toward the cliff. It certainly looked sheer; they might have to use the boats. Or, maybe…he squinted. It was too dark to see enough detail, but there might be something like a goat path that they could clamber along. They had ropes and climbing gear; they'd expected to need it to get over the wall. That might just be their way in. Especially if Aziz was still alive, and could get them their diversion at the front gates.

**

The Iranians were being cautious, but they were evidently still relying on the fact that weapons had been illegal on the island for anyone but the Khadarkhi Army for years. The patrol was only made up of four men, armed and loaded out for combat, but with an unarmed populace, they had little to fear, aside from the occasional thrown rock. And from what he had intimated from several of the Al Qaeda fighters' comments, the first few rocks had been answered with ferocious fusillades of rifle fire. No one had dared throw a rock since, except under cover of the daily demonstrations.

Aziz was presently standing in an alley, with Abu Sayf and two younger men, both of whom were also wearing the Wahhabi beard and short pants. Aziz still didn't understand the Wahhabi high-waters. He knew there was some Quranic justification for it, but they just looked ridiculous.

The patrol was moving down the street, just outside the souk, glaring at anyone who came near them. They were about a half mile from the edge of the demonstrations that were choking every avenue of the Old City.

Aziz still only had his Makarov, while the other three were carrying a motley combination of weapons. There was an AMD-65 slung under Abu Sayf's jacket, one of the others was carrying an AKS-74U, and the youngest, whose Wahhabi Beard was a scraggly wisp of hair, had a vz. 23. The message was not lost on him; the jihadis already in place got heavier weapons than he did, until they were sure he was really one of them. That said, they were all watching the patrol, instead of him.

Shit. Fuck! I could pop it off right here and now, except that I don't know if the rest are in position yet. In fact, they probably aren't, because this was just supposed to be recon. Hell, I could be the guy who scragged Abu Sayf. Fuckfuckfuckfuck!

None of the rest had their hands on their weapons; the firearms were backup more than anything else. The real weapon was hidden inside the market stall that the patrol was getting closer to with every step.

Aziz was wracking his brain, trying to think of some way to get himself out of this situation without arousing Abu Sayf's suspicions too much. If the entire city went up in flames that night, it might still be salvageable, but it would be better if it didn't really get down to blood in the streets until the next night, when he could

119

be sure that the other mercenaries were ready to move. And he had to get clear before then, so that he could report in detail and coordinate the final provocation.

While he was thinking, he was, entirely unconsciously, staring at the lead Iranian, a wiry man of average height with a short, trimmed beard. And the Iranian noticed.

The man pointed at the small knot of men standing in the mouth of the alleyway, and shouted. Aziz didn't speak Farsi, but he could interpret the tone well enough, especially considering that his companions were all wearing the Sunni Salafist Starter Pack. The Iranian lifted his rifle fractionally and started to move toward them, his pace increased with a new purpose.

Abu Sayf's eyes had turned to hard flecks of obsidian. Aziz glanced at him, half fearing that the killer might have noticed that he had been the one to attract attention, but the other man hadn't taken his eyes off the patrol. Instead, staring his blazing hate at the Iranians, the terrorist triggered the IED.

The pressure cooker had been concealed underneath the tablecloth covering the lower part of the produce stall. Packed with C4 and nails, it was triggered by a command wire leading to a cell phone stashed in the back of the stall, a cell phone which Abu Sayf had just dialed.

The Iranians disappeared into the ugly black cloud, their bodies pulped and shredded by overpressure and fragmentation as the bone-shaking *wham* smacked the avenue for nearly a hundred yards in both directions. Fragments and shrapnel blasted deep gouges in the opposite buildings, adding to the flying glass from windows shattered by the blast. The shockwave reached the four men in the alleyway, even though they had all ducked back as soon as Abu Sayf had triggered the bomb. Dust and smoke billowed around them chokingly, smelling of explosives, smoke, fire, and other, less-wholesome things.

At first, Aziz nearly despaired. It had gone off too well; the Iranians could not have survived that, and there was no distraction immediately available to give him a chance get clear of Abu Sayf and the others. He was about to reach for his Makarov, to try one last attempt to kill all three and run for it, when he heard shouts from down the alley. And they were in Farsi.

Two more of the Iranians were running toward them, bringing their weapons to their shoulders. Either they were part of a separate patrol that the Al Qaeda jihadists had missed, or they had been a part of the same patrol, who had either gotten separated or were paralleling their comrades. Whatever the case, Aziz thought he'd just found his distraction.

They were still wreathed in smoke and dust, so the Iranians hadn't started shooting yet, somewhat to his surprise. They weren't sure just who the four figures in the haze were, so they were apparently holding their fire. Abu Sayf and his "brothers" had no such compunction.

Abu Sayf turned, and in one motion dropped to a knee and brought his AMD-65 to his shoulder, opening fire in a long, rattling burst. Most of the rounds went high as the recoil drove the muzzle skyward, but the Iranians reacted, ducking and looking for cover in the alleyway, spraying 5.56 rounds down the alleyway, almost blindly. A bullet *snapped* far too close to Aziz' head, and he ducked, pushing past the younger jihadi with the vz. 23 to get out of the line of fire. He briefly considered shooting that one before ducking into the smoke on the main avenue, but then the young man dropped to the street, choking and spitting blood, a crimson hole blasted in his chest, and made it unnecessary.

Ducking around the corner, Aziz ran for his life.

CHAPTER 10

It was getting close to 0400 by the time Brannigan and Childress arrived back at the little gully where they had laid up for the day. Childress exchanged recognition signals with Curtis, who was set up on the lip of the little wadi, his PKP pointed toward the Citadel and the coast road, to their northeast. The bulk of Khadarkh City still glowed to the northwest, but the road was the closer avenue of approach, so that was the direction Curtis was watching. Anyone trying to approach from any other direction had a lot of fairly rough, rocky terrain to cross first.

Brannigan slid into the slot behind Childress, to find Santelli talking to Aziz in a low murmur. Brannigan gave Aziz' shoulder a thump. "Glad to see you're alive, David," he said. "We were getting a little worried."

Aziz looked at him in the dark. "It got a little hairy in there," he admitted. "There are AQ fighters crawling all over the city, and I think most of them have showed up in the last few days, coming in by water like we did. Abu Sayf mentioned Al Jubail like it was a staging area of some sort."

"What's Al Jubail?" Childress asked.

"It's a port on the coast of Saudi Arabia," Brannigan answered. He rubbed his chin. His stubble was getting thicker, and was presently stiff with dust, sweat, and sea salt. "You think the Saudis are sending them?"

"I don't think there's any doubt," Aziz replied. "Which really means that unless the Navy moves in in the next twenty-four hours, we really are the only hope those hostages have. If the Saudi response is AQ fighters, then the hostages are fucked, whoever comes out on top."

"How soon are they going to move?" Brannigan asked.

"They're already moving," Aziz replied. "I damn near got my ass shot off in the process, either by the Iranians or by Abu Sayf when he saw me running away into the smoke." He shook his head. "I could have killed that fucker, you know that? If we'd been one step farther along, I could have been the one to put a bullet in Abu Sayf's fucking head."

"Well, we weren't, and Abu Sayf ain't the mission," Brannigan said. "The hostages are." He thought for a moment, while Aziz sulked. "Do you think you can get back in there to sort of help things along tomorrow night? Or will the risk of compromise be too high?"

Even in the dark, it looked like Aziz wanted to tell him to go fuck himself. But he finally sighed. "I think I can avoid Abu Sayf, and most of the rest of the minions I got introduced to, at least long enough to start some shit and run," he said.

"Wait, you got 'introduced to minions?'" Flanagan hissed out of the shadows. "What, did they give you the full tour? 'Hello, random Arab dude we've never met before, come meet the family!' Really?"

"I might have told them that I was Abdul Rahman al Ramadi," Aziz said.

"Who the hell is that?" Santelli demanded.

"He was an Al Qaeda in Iraq bad boy, about ten years ago," Aziz said. "He was one of the HVIs we were hunting in Diyala. He was actually something of a pro; he usually only hit military targets and actual strategic installations, always pretty clean strikes. I saw his corpse; figured it was a familiar enough sounding name that they might buy that I was a terrorist, and leave it at that. Turns out that while none of them had ever met him, he had more of a rep in the jihadi sewer than I'd thought."

"So, you ID'ed yourself as a Salafist celebrity, and got shown the whole operation?" Brannigan asked. He had to admit, it was hard to believe.

"I don't think I got to see the *whole* operation," Aziz admitted. "And I don't think Abu Sayf entirely believed me, either. But I got to see enough that I got brought along on a bombing."

"So, that's why it took so long to get back here," Hancock observed from the southern edge of the wadi, where he was watching their six.

"Yeah," Aziz said. He sounded thoughtful. "I think I know how to get in and cause some chaos," he said. "Abu Sayf said that the attacks tonight were just the first step. I think they're going to try to turn the next demonstration into a full-blown riot, maybe even try to storm the Citadel. That would be our chance."

Brannigan nodded. "If it works out, I'd agree," he said. He proceeded to describe the breach in the wall. "I'm not sure if we can hit it from the ground, or if we need to use the boats. I'm half inclined to use the boats; if we can somehow secure them to the cliff, it will make for a faster exfil once we've got the hostages."

"Faster?" Santelli asked. "Getting a bunch of shell-shocked hostages to climb down a collapsible caving ladder or a rope into a rubber boat rocking on the breakers at the base of a cliff? I wouldn't expect that to be 'faster.'"

"Faster than trying to overland back to the boats on the south end of the island with a bunch of shell-shocked hostages," Brannigan pointed out.

"I suppose," Santelli conceded. "I can still think of about a dozen ways it can go horribly, horribly wrong."

"So can I," Brannigan admitted, "but unless we want to call it quits and give Tanner his money back, I don't see too many other options."

No one else had a better plan. "Let's get some rest," Brannigan said. "As soon as the sun sets, Aziz will re-insert into the city, and the rest of us will boogey down south to retrieve the boats." He peered at the growing lightness on the eastern horizon, over the water. "It's too late to go get them now."

I just hope the bad guys don't decide to execute any more hostages before tonight.

The crowd was already getting agitated by the time Aziz got anywhere near the Old City.

He was being more careful this time. The first time, he'd been looking to make contact, to get a feel for the atmospherics in the city. He'd gotten that, in spades, and it had soured him on even being seen the second time around. Especially if word of his presence had the potential to get back to Abu Sayf. He didn't want that psycho to come looking for him, not after he'd cut and run in the alley.

The first time, he'd been careful on his initial approach into the outskirts of the city, then had started moving openly, appearing to be a regular pedestrian on the streets. This time, he was trying to stay out of sight, especially since he was considerably bulkier under his man-dress, having pulled it on over his combat vest, and he was trying to conceal his AK-12 under his arm. The dark was helping, but if anyone got close enough to get a good look, he was going to have to kill them or risk exposure.

He had one mission in mind that night. Get to a vantage point where he had a shot both into the crowd, and at the Iranians near the Citadel gate. He would devote one magazine to sowing as much death and chaos as possible, and then he was bugging out, heading for the eastern coast and the rendezvous point.

It occurred to him that if anything went wrong in the Citadel, he was going to be on his own. That was a terrible thought. He thought he could probably find his way back to the rough area of the pickup, but at the same time, would the Russians really honor the agreement they'd made with Brannigan, if it was only him? Or would they just kill him and figure it was better that way?

He stopped in the shadow of a compound wall, leaning against the plastered cinderblock for a moment. The thought was an unnerving one. He hadn't bothered to think about it before. What would happen to him if he was cut off? He started to shake.

Hidden in the darkness, he turned until his back was to the wall, and sank down until he was sitting. The full import of what they were trying to do had just hit him, and he suddenly didn't want to move. Didn't want to go venturing into that powder-keg of a city, where even if the Al Qaeda terrorists didn't find him, there was every possibility that a stray round or an IED could easily finish him off in a split second.

What the fuck am I doing here? Why was I ever so fucking stupid as to say, "Yeah, going into a Middle Eastern country with only eight men—seven if you count the fucking pacifist doctor out— to rescue hostages from a company or more of trained soldiers sounds like loads of fun?"

He wanted to puke. He'd never been so scared in his life. *Fuck these guys. If they've got a death wish, let 'em go storm the fucking castle. I should just hightail it back to the boats and run. I bet I could get back to Sir Bu Nair and find somebody who wouldn't mind taking on another passenger to Abu Dhabi or somewhere.*

He made the decision. The hostages weren't worth his hide. Neither were a bunch of crazy has-beens who wanted to take a last stab at the glory days. They knew what the deal was. For all they would know, he'd gone into the city and gotten killed. It wasn't like he'd be looking them up later. *"Hey, about that mission to Khadarkh! How'd that go?"*

He got to his feet. His knees were still shaking, but, the decision made, he was feeling slightly less sick.

He took two steps back toward the south, toward escape. Then he stopped. His lips compressed into a thin line. *"Fuck!"* he hissed. He turned back toward the Old City and the already growing growl of an angry mob.

***

"Son of a bitch," Brannigan heard Childress whisper. He couldn't say he disagreed with the sentiment.

Our timing really seems to suck, so far. They had, once again, neared the checkpoint at the end of the runway right about at shift-change time. He wondered just what kind of shifts the Iranians were really running; this didn't seem to be at a twelve- or eight-hour mark. *It's probably scheduling by* Insh'allah. Most of the Middle East seemed to operate on two timing schedules: "Later" and "Whenever." Punctuality was not a Middle Eastern virtue. He'd somewhat expected the Iranians to operate differently, but at the same time, he couldn't say that he was surprised to be proven wrong.

127

That didn't make it any less infuriating, though, to be stuck lying flat on their bellies in the rocks and dirt, trying not to even breathe too loudly, while the trucks full of Iranian soldiers pulled up to the checkpoint and began to unload, calling out to each other with loud shouts in Farsi.

He actually had a decent vantage point this time. There were two trucks halted near the checkpoint, both Land Cruiser 79 pickups, each with either a DShK or a W85 heavy machinegun mounted on a pedestal in the bed. A tall man wearing fatigues and a patrol cap had gotten out of the lead truck, and was shouting at the checkpoint guards.

The tall man must have been someone important, an officer or senior NCO. Brannigan suddenly tried to remember if the Iranians really had much of an NCO corps, but couldn't recall if he'd ever heard. It didn't matter, anyway; whoever this guy was, he was giving orders, and the trigger pullers were listening to him.

The guards were rushing out of the guard shack. The one who had been lollygagging by the swing arm was standing rigidly at attention, his rifle held at something close to port arms.

The tall man barked out a rapid speech in Farsi, pointing back toward the lights of Khadarkh City. As if to punctuate his words, a series of *pops,* recognizable even from a distance as small arms fire, could be heard from the same direction. Things were heating up in town.

The man pointed to two of the Iranians, rapped out what sounded like a combination of orders and a warning, and then yelled at the other four, who scrambled to grab their gear and clamber into the backs of the trucks. A moment later, the tall man, yelling a last word to the two forlorn-looking guards staying at the checkpoint, climbed into the cab of the lead truck. The two vehicles turned about and rolled back up the road toward the city and the Citadel.

Childress looked back toward Brannigan, as if to ask a question. Brannigan shook his head fractionally. Killing the checkpoint guards might just alert the enemy to their presence before they were ready. This wasn't a game; as soon as a kill happens on an infiltration, the infiltration has to be considered blown. Their objective was the hostages, so they would have to stay patient and sneaky until they could get to the Citadel itself. That meant leaving these two chumps alone. Just from the body language he could see through the grainy NVGs, they both looked more than a little dejected at being the ones selected to sit on guard, staring at the road, far away from the action.

Childress had started to creep forward again, when one of the Iranians called out to his companion. The other one replied, his answer sounding cautious, but got a dismissive shout in return. A moment later, the Iranian was sauntering up into the rocks, his rifle held sort of ready, apparently determined to patrol their area, and make the most of their misfortune.

From the tone of the back and forth, Brannigan thought he could figure out some of what was being said. The one who was ranging out thought maybe some of the bad guys causing trouble in the city might be trying to sneak in from the south, so he was going to go take a look. The other one was telling him that he was wasting his time.

Unfortunately, he wasn't. Especially since he was walking straight toward Childress. He was going to trip over the lanky point man in the next few seconds.

So much for bypassing the checkpoint.

Brannigan risked looking over his shoulder, trying to spot how far away the trucks were. They were going to run out of time in a moment, and if those trucks were close enough to hear shots, they'd be turning around the instant the mercenaries took the checkpoint guards under fire. Brannigan had no desire to go toe-to-toe with a pair of 12.7mm machineguns on relatively open ground.

The red glow of their taillights could still be seen, but they were a good distance away. And the sporadic firing from the city was getting somewhat more intense. It was possible that they would dismiss any shooting they heard as just more of the same.

Possible. Brannigan didn't like the odds. But they were out of options. He turned toward the man walking toward Childress, and put the red dot of his PKU-2 high on the man's chest.

The guy wasn't looking at the ground; he was scanning the area around them, apparently not imagining that there could be anyone close enough that he hadn't noticed them yet. So he wasn't ready when Childress kicked out and swept his legs out from under him.

He fell to the ground with a squawk and a crash, and Childress was on him in a heartbeat, a knife in his hand. Brannigan saw the point man's arm rise and fall three times, and the Iranian's struggles died away with a faint, strangled gurgle.

The other Iranian called out, a faintly mocking tone in his voice. He probably thought his comrade had tripped and fallen. But when there was no reply, he repeated his query, sounding more worried. Brannigan shifted his sights toward the second man, just in time to see him step out of the guard shack and start walking toward where he had heard the commotion.

Another silhouette was slinking across the ground toward the second man, right on the edge of the road, moving low and fast. The second Iranian stumbled on the rocks in the dark, calling out again, sounding a little scared.

Then Flanagan was on the man, tackling him in a rush. The two figures went down with a muted crash, Flanagan's own knife going into the Iranian's armpit with a fast series of short, vicious stabs. After a moment, the second man's struggles ceased, and Flanagan rose, wiping the blade off on the dead man's fatigues before closing the knife and returning it to his pocket.

Brannigan lifted himself to a knee, looking anxiously back toward the still-receding taillights of the two trucks. They hadn't brightened, and were still dwindling toward the city, so neither the drivers nor the gunners must have noticed anything. He sighed faintly. They'd dodged a bullet, at least for the moment.

He glanced around at his men, mentally nodding to himself. He'd picked the team well. They'd all recognized the imminent disaster and acted quickly, violently, and decisively, without needing any direction from him or Santelli.

It was good to work with professionals.

Villareal moved up to first Flanagan's victim, then Childress'. He checked each man, then returned to his spot in the formation, his face impassive in the brief glimpse Brannigan had gotten.

Brannigan studied the doctor for a moment. His stated confidence aside, Villareal's mental state worried him. He'd been through the anguish of finding those dead kids in Afghanistan; he knew how badly that had torn the man up. Checking the enemy dead like that…he wondered if Doc really was as damaged as some of the others worried that he was. If he really wasn't suited for combat ops anymore.

If he'd freeze up, have an attack of scruples when the real killing got started.

John Brannigan had no problem with conscience. He strove to keep his on the straight and narrow. Scrupulosity, however, worried him. It could make a man hesitate when his moral duty was *not* to hesitate.

He shoved his reservations to the back of his mind. There wasn't time for them, not then. They'd needed a doc, and Villareal had been the best he could think of on short notice. If they made it through this, he'd address the problems later. He got to his feet and moved to Childress.

The point man was standing over the Iranian's corpse, his own knife back in his gear. "You good?" Brannigan whispered.

"I'm fine," Childress replied. "Do we want to try to hide the bodies?"

"No, it'd take too much time," Brannigan answered. "We've got to move fast, now. And if we're still on this rock by morning, we're pretty well screwed, anyway."

Childress just nodded, bringing his rifle back to his front. He'd slung it behind him when he'd jumped the Iranian. He glanced over the formation, then looked at Brannigan.

"Lead on," Brannigan said. Childress nodded again, then turned and headed back south, staying on his feet this time. Unless there were more patrols out on the coast road, they had a pretty straight shot at the boat landing site. And if what they'd just seen was any indication, the Iranians had their hands full in town. They wouldn't have been pulling their security in, otherwise.

Hopefully, Aziz would make sure they were so preoccupied in town that the rest of the op went more smoothly than it had so far.

***

Most of the demonstrations were in the Old City, which presented some difficulties when it came to finding a good vantage point. Aziz was a good shot, but he didn't trust the long-range accuracy of the AK-12 that much, no matter how modernized it was compared to the older AKM or AK-74. Which meant he needed to find a spot within about three hundred yards of his targets, preferably without being noticed. That would be more easily said than done.

One of the high-rise business buildings downtown would have been ideal, especially since downtown lay on the south side of the souk, right up against the Old City. But he was pretty sure that trying to break into one of those places, many of which had private armed security, get to a higher floor, set up, take his shots, and get back out was going to be a losing proposition. And he might have gone against every screaming nerve in his body to get this far, but he wasn't set on suicide.

As he slipped down a narrow, darkened alley, only a few blocks from the yelling, chanting mobs of Al Qays Loyalists and Sunni Salafists, he kept scanning for a good spot. He really should have picked one out on his earlier recon, but getting wrapped up with Abu Sayf had somewhat limited his opportunities for exploration. Abu Sayf hadn't been interested in sniper positions, but in his own attack planning.

And Aziz didn't want to be anywhere near Abu Sayf's operation.

There. Another high-rise was being built, though it was presently little more than a skeleton of concrete pilings and floors. The street was littered with rebar and piles of dirt and sand, scaffolding cutting off the half of the alley that was usually taken up by parked cars.

He jogged toward the construction site, no longer caring that much about his bulk or his AK being spotted. It was dark, and there were probably a lot more armed men in Khadarkh City that night than anyone supposed there should be.

He reached the site without incident. Between the lateness of the hour and the mobs, he had not expected to find a crew still working, but for all his arrogance, Aziz was still enough of a professional not to assume too much when it came to operational details.

He also wouldn't have had any trouble gunning down the construction workers if it had come to that. Brannigan probably wouldn't have liked it, but as far as Aziz was concerned, he was on his own, and what Brannigan didn't know wouldn't kill him.

The site was deserted, as he'd expected. He slipped into the shadows among the square concrete columns in the center of the rising building, looking for stairs. There had to be some; stairs were always one of the first things added to these places. It took him a few minutes, moving from column to column, before he found what he was looking for.

He jogged up to the fifth floor, pausing only just long enough to clear the landings on the second, third, and fourth. There was always the possibility that someone else had had the same bright idea.

The fifth floor provided an excellent vantage point. There were two more floors above him, but he figured that having to fight his way down four floors in extremis was pushing his luck more than enough. He lay down on the dusty floor, set just back from the edge, in the shadow of one of the corner columns, and scanned the souk and the Old City below him.

The Old City was still surrounded by some of the remains of its ancient, tenth-century wall, though it was pierced in multiple places by streets and alleys leading into the tightly-packed hodgepodge of ancient sandstone and new cinderblock buildings. There were three main avenues running through the Old City, all leading to the square just outside the barbican gate of the Citadel.

All three avenues were currently packed with demonstrators, shouting, chanting, and waving Khadarkhi royal flags, along with a few Saudi and even some of the black Al Qaeda flags. He didn't see any of the black and white ISIS flags; that particular franchise's popularity had fallen of late, given the recent setbacks the core group had suffered in Iraq and Syria.

He didn't have a good view of the square, thanks to another taller building that looked like it had been fused together from ancient and modern construction, though he could see the towers flanking the gate. He was pretty sure that there would be armored vehicles in the square, and a quick study through the small pair of binoculars he'd brought showed him that the Iranians had some heavy weapons up in the towers, probably taken from the Khadarkhi Army.

Moving his attention down to the crowds flowing slowly into the Old City, he thought he could pick out a few of the various shooters and provocateurs mixed in with the demonstrators. Abu Sayf and his men had bloodshed on their minds that night, and so long as he didn't get sucked into it, Aziz was just as eager to facilitate all the bloodshed they could stomach.

He wasn't entirely sure of the range to the gate, and momentarily wished that he had paid more attention to learning range estimation. He was pretty sure that the towers were beyond the effective range of his 5.45mm rifle, but then, he rationalized, all he really needed to do was provoke a violent response from the Iranians, and the rest would, more than likely, take care of itself. Abu Sayf and his pack of murderous assholes were certainly eager enough to get the blood flowing in the streets. They wouldn't need much of a nudge.

He settled in behind his rifle, finding that he couldn't lie there comfortably or with much stability without resting the magazine on the concrete. He vaguely remembered that being a bad idea, but then, he thought he'd heard otherwise a few times. He wasn't sure, and frankly didn't care, as long as the Russian gun didn't shit the bed on him. He wasn't much of a gun guy.

Clicking the selector off safe, he put the red dot slightly above the position on top of the southern tower, let out a breath, and squeezed the trigger.

The AK-12 barked twice, the muzzle brake blasting dust and debris off the concrete in front of him, some of it getting into his eyes. He blinked, both against the grit and in some surprise; he'd forgotten that the first position of the AK-12's selector lever was two-shot burst, not single shot. He'd paid enough attention on the dhow to know that the rifle functioned; he hadn't worried too much about the specifics.

Looking down at the selector lever, he couldn't see the gradations, so he shrugged and got back behind the gun. There wasn't time to fiddle with it; he needed to get his licks in and be gone before somebody figured out where he was and decided to light the skeletal hulk of the building up.

There was no sign that the guards on the tower had noticed anything. He was too far away to tell exactly where his rounds had impacted, either. He knew the sight was zeroed for one hundred yards, so he had to assume that they'd hit low, and the impacts had gotten lost in the noise of the mob.

He looked around below him for a moment, hoping that the shots hadn't been heard on the street below. The last thing he needed was someone coming up to investigate. Of course, hopefully, if they did hear him shooting, they would simply dismiss it as another one of their "brothers" shooting at the "apostates."

I've got a little something for you fucks, too. He raised the red dot higher above the tower and squeezed off another two-round burst.

He still had no idea where the rounds went. *Fuck! I need to get closer.* Except that there wasn't a good vantage point that he could see that *was* closer, at least not one that wouldn't take him through a throng of frothing Salafi fanatics along the way. He had no desire to go deeper into that hell. *I've come as deep as I intend to.*

Shit, these fuckers are probably going to touch things off even without me shooting at them. They're certainly eager and pissed off enough, and Abu Sayf would like nothing better than to trigger a massacre in here. He knew he was rationalizing, but he figured that he'd already stuck his neck out far enough, when he'd been well within his rights to cut and run. He'd decided against going back to the boats, and had gone into the city to do the job. He figured he deserved full credit for that.

He still couldn't make out a lot of detail, but there was evidently something happening on the square. He brought his binoculars up, but his line of sight was still blocked.

Shit. He got up and headed up to the roof. He wanted to see.

The roof actually did provide him with a better vantage point of the square. About three quarters of the space around the ancient fountain was taken up by demonstrators, and they were getting rowdy, throwing rocks and other debris at the gates. They

135

weren't shooting, yet, but he knew that Abu Sayf had at least a few shooters and bombers hidden in that crowd. It was only a matter of time.

It took him a second to see what the commotion was about. The gates were slowly swinging inward, even as the Iranians on the wall above fired warning shots into the air. He was surprised. He wouldn't have put it past the IRGC to just open fire on the crowd, mowing down demonstrators with impunity.

The gates swung wider, and the wide, angular prow of an AMX-10P armored personnel carrier pushed out through the gap. The Khadarkhis had gotten a few of the vehicles from the Saudis, as they had been mothballed in the latter's army in favor of the newer American M2 Bradleys. Apparently, the Iranians had commandeered them once they'd murdered the Khadarkhi Army.

The hatches were open, and two of the Iranians were up on the guns, leveling the armored fighting vehicle's 20mm cannon and coaxial 7.62 machinegun at the crowd. The message was clear; the Iranians were done screwing around, and the crowd would disperse or be slaughtered wholesale.

It was a long shot, but Aziz let out a breath and put the red dot above the head of the closest Iranian soldier, his finger tightening on the trigger.

CHAPTER 11

The boats were still sitting where they'd been left, undisturbed. It appeared that, patrols along the coast road notwithstanding, the southern end of the island was deserted.

It was quick work to get them back out into the water. They left one for Aziz; according to the plan, once he had stirred things up, he would exfil out of Khadarkh City, get down to the boat landing site, grab the last boat, and bring it around to join the rest beneath the breach in the Citadel wall, securing the boats for the rest of the team to exfil.

If he didn't make it out, they'd have to adapt and improvise. For the moment, they'd stick with the plan, Villareal climbing into Brannigan's and Childress' dinghy.

Once they were in deep enough water, the coxswains started the motors, the mercenaries holding the boats steady against the swell of the surf climbed aboard, and they were moving, puttering around the east side of the rocky promontory they had used as a landmark and a terrain shield, then heading north, keeping the lights of the airport to their port side.

It was something of a blessing, Brannigan thought, as he kept the boat's bow steady to the northeast, that they had run into trouble at the checkpoint. They no longer had to worry about the guards there hearing the boats and possibly taking them under fire.

They could also stay closer in to shore, reducing the distance they had to cover to get to their insert position.

He was keeping one ear cocked, trying to hear over the slap of the waves, the hiss of water against the rubber gunwales, and the grumble of the engine. If Aziz' diversion took longer to kick off than planned, then they would have to find a spot on the coast to go to ground and wait; he wasn't going to loiter directly under a wall that had Iranian gunmen patrolling it.

Come on, Aziz, give us a good, old fashioned, Middle Eastern street fight.

***

The AK-12 barked, spitting a pair of rounds so close together that they almost made a single sound. His aim was still off. The Iranian standing up in the hatch beside the 20mm didn't go down in a splash of gore. He didn't appear to have been hit at all.

He had noticed, though. Maybe the rounds had hit low, smacking off the armored vehicles' glacis plate. Or maybe they'd gone high, ripping past his head with loud, supersonic *snaps*.

Do 5.45 rounds stay supersonic that far out? Aziz didn't know, and it annoyed him that he'd even mentally asked the question. He started to squeeze the trigger again, even though he had no idea where the rounds were going at that point.

But the Iranian had apparently decided that he was taking small arms fire from the crowd, and began to react accordingly.

He dropped down into the AMX's hull, and no sooner had he disappeared than the 20mm began to depress.

For an instant, seeing only that the cannon's barrel was moving, Aziz was seized with the certainty that they had seen his muzzle flash, and that he was about to die in a hail of 20mm fire. There would barely be enough left of him to bury. He sucked in a breath to curse Brannigan for bringing him along on this suicide mission before he died, only to see the 20mm suddenly gout flame, spitting heavy slugs into the crowd at what amounted to point-blank range.

Wherever those rounds hit, people died. Not in ones or twos, not at that range. The heavy penetrators smashed through stacks of bodies ten or twelve deep, blowing people in half and pulping limbs and organs into fine red sprays.

In a moment, the guards up on the walls were also firing into the crowd. But the crowd didn't disperse in shock, though a lot of the Loyalists were trying to. No, a good chunk of the crowd started shooting back.

An RPG exploded from a nearby rooftop with a puff of smoke and a sluggishly following *bang*. The projectile hit the AMX's flank in almost the same instant; the RPG gunner was that close. An ugly black puff of smoke and debris momentarily eclipsed the armored fighting vehicle, and the 20mm fell silent. A moment later, the AMX was burning fiercely, the crew burning alive inside, presuming that any of them hadn't been instantly killed by the blast and fragmentation of the round as it penetrated the armor.

All hell broke loose in the next few seconds. Someone up on the barbican opened fire with a machinegun, tearing hell out of the rooftop where the RPG had been fired, and everyone else up on the wall with a weapon started shooting. The crowd, what was left of it, was shooting back, flickering muzzle flashes visible even against the growing glare of the burning AFV.

A moment later, the AMX's ammunition started to cook off, at the same time that a volley of four more RPGs slammed into the battlements above the gate.

Aziz decided that that was a good enough diversion. That should keep the Iranians focused on the gate and the Old City. It was time for him to leave, before he attracted any more attention.

He wriggled backward a few feet before heaving himself to his feet and heading for the stairway. He had trotted down two floors when he suddenly froze, listening.

It took a moment before he could filter the sounds through the growing roar of gunfire and explosions half a kilometer away. Someone was coming up the stairs. Several someones.

His heart stopped. His mouth was drier than the Sahara. He was going to die, right there in that shitty, unfinished high-rise, in the middle of some shitty island city that had no right to be its own country in the first place. All because he'd let Brannigan and Santelli talk him into a job that had sounded a bit better than babysitting entitled millennials going to school on their parents' dime, for reasons they couldn't articulate.

He forced his heart to start again, tearing his wide-eyed stare away from the stairway below him, looking for a place to hide, any place. Of course, there were dozens of the thick, square, concrete columns. Cursing himself for a moron, Aziz turned, slipped on the dust and grit on the concrete stairs, almost fell, then got his balance and scrambled out of the stairwell and across twenty feet of bare concrete floor, taking cover behind a column, hoping that there wasn't anyone on the stairs with an angle to see through the presently non-existent walls to shoot him in the back.

The intruders climbed higher, chatting in Arabic in low voices. He recognized one of the voices as the trio got closer. He'd remember that voice until the day he died. *Abu Sayf.*

He was presently crouched with his back pressed against the cement pillar. Taking a deep, shaky breath, he slowly turned, easing one eye around the corner of the pillar.

Abu Sayf and two of his henchmen were climbing the stairs. They weren't moving quickly; there was no urgency there. The sadistic bastard wasn't going to risk his own skin in the hellish firestorm up there in the square. He was looking for a vantage point where he could watch other men fight and die for his bullshit cause.

Aziz almost shrank back behind the pillar to wait until Abu Sayf was gone. He could imagine a platoon of Al Qaeda fighters in the floors below, just waiting to come swarming up and kill him as soon as he made a noise.

But the team could be gone by the time Abu Sayf and his bodyguard left. And if Aziz had seriously contemplated, without scruple, abandoning the rest, the very thought of being abandoned himself almost made him want to vomit.

So, he tucked his AK-12 against his chest and came around the pillar, bringing the weapon to bear as fast as he could, the red dot settling just below Abu Sayf's collarbone.

He hadn't safed the rifle. The two-round burst smashed through the top of Abu Sayf's heart and lungs, and he dropped, spitting flecks of blood. Aziz switched targets faster than he ever had in his life, putting a two-round burst into each of the other two before Abu Sayf had even hit the concrete. It had been an amazing bit of shooting, if anyone else had seen it. To Aziz, though he would never admit it to anyone else, it had felt like frantic spray-and-pray.

He quickly shot each man twice more, just to be sure. Then he was moving, circling around to try to get a shot at anyone else coming up the steps.

Great job, fuckwit. You've now given your position away, and probably trapped yourself on the fourth fucking floor, *with a bunch of rabid Al Qaeda types about to come up and finish your dumb ass off. So much for being the smartest guy on the team.*

But after he had hunkered down behind another pillar, aimed in at the stairwell, determined to sell himself as dearly as possible, he realized that there were no yells of alarm coming up from below, and no one was coming up after him or Abu Sayf.

They're waiting in ambush. They know better than to try to fight up the stairs. That's a nightmare for shit-hot Delta guys, never mind these assholes.

He almost stayed where he was. He was certain that if he started down those stairs, he was going to be shot and killed. And the only other way off was a four-story jump onto a pile of cinderblocks and rebar.

He had no idea how long he stayed there, still aimed in on the stairway, sweating through his fatigues and dishdasha, unwilling to move or even breathe deeply, as the thunder of the fight up the hill intensified. It was probably only five minutes—though it seemed like five years—before he finally forced himself to move. The same horror of being left behind was the only thing that got him moving. Even then, he was sure he was going to die as soon as he descended.

The third floor was empty. So was the second. And the first. There wasn't even a driver in the Kia van parked outside the construction site.

Unable to believe his luck, Aziz plunged into the nearest dark alley and started making his way out of town.

***

The roar of gunfire and the sharp detonations of RPGs were clearly audible, even on the other side of the Citadel and its rocky hill. Brannigan looked right and left, trying to make eye contact with the other coxswains, and then started the boat moving at a faster clip toward the breach. It was time to go.

He just hoped and prayed that the Iranians were being sufficiently challenged at the gate to move all their firepower to the defense. After all, amphibious insertions leading into climbing up cliffs wasn't usually an Al Qaeda technique.

The waves were crashing against the cliffside as they passed under the corner tower, right at the edge of the cliff and the outer curtain wall. Brannigan kept his neck craned to watch that tower, struggling a little to keep the green circle of his NVGs centered on the battlements, looking for any sign of sentries, or simply machinegun barrels poking through the crenellations. If they were spotted, they were dead.

But the tower remained quiet and dark. Maybe the Iranians had never manned it at all, figuring that they didn't really need to worry about the seaward approaches. After all, if they could detect a Navy aircraft, leading to a hostage's death, they must have gotten pretty confident that their only immediate threat came from the Salafists in town.

The seaward wall probably hadn't been really kept up in over five hundred years. For the most part, as far as Brannigan had been able to determine, the Citadel hadn't been a genuine defensive fortification in at least that long. It hadn't even been much of a tourist attraction; the Al Qays kings had used it as a palace and mark of status, little more. So, the breach wasn't all that surprising.

Centuries of waves had slowly eroded parts of the cliffs beneath the Citadel, and at that point, just north of the southernmost tower, part of the cliff had given way, tumbling into the sea. It had undercut the wall enough that a good chunk of the sandstone had gone with it. There was a mound of detritus beneath the breach, now little more than shallows in the ocean, as more years and decades of wave action had washed much of it out into the Gulf.

Brannigan eased his boat a short distance out, trying to get a better angle on the breach itself. In the bow, Childress was behind his AK-12, aiming it up at the gap in the dark expanse of the wall.

142

Movement caught his eye, and he glanced back down, seeing that Hancock was taking his boat in toward the cliffside. The former platoon sergeant was going to take advantage of Brannigan's angle to cover the ascent.

Bringing the boat to a halt, about seventy-five yards out from the cliff, Brannigan hissed at Villareal. "Doc, take the tiller," he said. "Hold us steady."

Villareal nodded and moved to take his place, while Brannigan unslung his own AK and lay down across the boat, setting his back against the starboard gunwale, leveling his rifle at the gap.

He would have preferred to be the first one up the ladder and into the breach. It was the way he'd always approached combat leadership, and he believed, all the way down to his bones, that that was a leader's responsibility; to be the first one into danger, not to ask his men to do anything that he wasn't going to go do first. But at the same time, he was also a believer in small-unit initiative, and he couldn't fault Hancock. He had to roll with the punches and "fill, flow, and go," as the old CQB saying about "initiative-based tactics" had said. There was no other way to work, not with such a small team.

So he gritted his teeth, shoved his pride to the back of his mind, settled in behind his rifle, and covered for Hancock and Flanagan.

***

The caving ladder was little more than a telescoping pole with flip-out rods for rungs and a hook on the top. As Hancock brought the bow of the boat up against the cliff, applying just enough throttle to keep them tight to the rock and keep them from drifting, Flanagan got the ladder out and started extending it.

I hate these things. Flanagan had had to use them on maritime interdiction and a couple of compound raids in Afghanistan. They always felt flimsy, like they would buckle under the weight of a grown man and his kit at any moment. But he knew that there wasn't any better option; Curtis had, of course, suggested ropes and grappling hooks, with "ninja" grappling hook launchers, but the odds of the hooks actually getting a decent purchase on the wreckage of the wall were too long. The ladders would have to do.

Hell, is this thing even going to reach? He peered up the dark, wet rock of the cliff, trying to gauge just how high the breach was. It would really suck if the ladder only extended halfway. Then they were well and truly screwed. They'd have to head back with their tails between their legs, probably give the Tannhauser Petroleum people their money back, just because they'd miscalculated how high the breach in the wall was above the water.

Screw that. He'd never admit it within Curtis' hearing, but Flanagan had brought a collapsible grappling hook along with the decent length of climbing rope in his assault pack. If need be, he'd climb as high as he could on the caving ladder, then throw the hook and rope climb the rest of the way.

Joe Flanagan didn't like to lose.

Carefully, his muscles straining against the poor leverage of the ladder at full length, he started to lift it against the cliff. The aluminum tubing was entirely too flexible at full extension, and bounced with every move. He slowed his movements down; even with the increasingly intense noises of what sounded like one hell of a firefight out in the city, he didn't want the ladder banging against the rocks. Flanagan appreciated stealth; his own silence was often a point of pride. He hadn't had a lot of time to get to know Childress, but there was already something of an unspoken, friendly rivalry developing between them as to just which one could be quieter and sneakier.

He finally got the top of the ladder, waving like a whip antenna, straight overhead. Slowly, trying not to slip on the wet deck of the boat, he eased it against the cliffside. It came to rest with a slight *clink*. Not bad.

He squinted up the cliffside. No, it hadn't made it all the way to the breach, but it looked like it was close enough that he should be able to reach up and pull himself over without needing the rope. He'd still find a way to secure the rope and drop it down the cliff. That would be a better way to ascend than the ladder, with the base set on a boat, that could drift.

Slinging his AK-12 on his back and cinching the sling down as tightly as he could, he drew his Makarov, shaking some of the water off of it and hoping that the Bulgarian pistol would still function despite the dousing it had gotten. He mounted the ladder, making sure his boot was securely on the rung before reaching for the next; the wet aluminum could be slippery. The boat creaked a little under his weight, as all two hundred plus pounds of man, weapon, and equipment was suddenly focused on a point barely two and a half inches across, but Hancock kept it steady.

Neither man had said a word during the entire process. It wasn't a time for talking.

Slowly, keeping his knees as close to the cliff as he could, Flanagan began to ascend the ladder.

Between the unavoidable movement of the boat and the flex of the ladder, it was probably the hairiest climb Flanagan had ever been on. He had to stop several times, clinging close to the ladder, trying to use his weight to press it as close to the rock as he could as the hook scraped against the rocks above him. Twice, he was dead certain that he was about to fall off the side of the cliff. He glanced down, trying to see where he should aim his fall, to give himself a little bit of a chance of surviving the impact with the water and however many rocks were underneath it.

After what felt like an eternity, Flanagan was finally within arm's reach of the breach in the wall. There was actually something of a crack in the cliff where the collapse had occurred, and that, he saw, was the only reason that the ladder *hadn't* slid off to one side and dumped him onto the rocks. The hook was just barely lodged in that crack.

That could have been unpleasant. Flanagan's mental commentary was usually as laconic and dry as his speech.

The sea spray didn't usually reach that high, so the rocks were dry and dusty. That just meant that his own soaked fatigues and gloves were going to be covered in salty mud in short order. Which was also going to present a few problems when it came to climbing the rocks.

Lifting his foot to the next highest rung, Flanagan reached up into the crack, looking for a handhold. His sodden gloves weren't getting much of a purchase; the dust immediately turned to mud and made the rocks slick, and the gloves didn't want to hold. Even when he could get some friction, the gloves squished and stretched, sliding around on his fingers.

Balanced precariously on the top of the ladder, Flanagan pulled his hand down, ripped the glove off with his teeth, and let it fall. He'd probably tear his soaked hands up on the rocks, but at least he'd know that he had a purchase.

After repeating the same procedure with his other hand, he reached up again, wincing slightly as the rocks skinned his wet knuckles. But he found a grip and hauled himself up to where he could let go of the ladder with his other hand and grope for another handhold.

He hooked his fingers on a protruding rock, only to have it shift as soon as he started to put weight on it. After a moment, he figured out that it was a fragment of one of the blocks of sandstone the wall was made of, that had become lodged in the crack during or after the collapse.

Some more exploration got him what felt like a solid handhold, and, digging his fingers in as best he could, he hauled himself up until he could just get his NVGs over the rim of the breach.

He was looking into the lower courtyard. The courtyard was lined with buildings like barracks and possibly an armory bunker on the uphill side. The inside of the outer curtain wall was lined with vehicles and heavy equipment. There was a fair bit of activity, but most of it was at the far end, where figures were scurrying around, heading for the barbican gate carrying weapons and ammunition. Two of the hulking armored vehicles parked just short of the entrance to the barbican, at the north end of the lower courtyard, were rumbling and starting to move.

The southernmost part of the courtyard was empty and dark. The Iranians weren't worried about the seaward wall, apparently.

With a heave, his soggy boots scrabbling against the rock, Flanagan hauled himself over the lip and into the courtyard. He scrambled quickly out of the breach itself, which was, somewhat surprisingly, only about four feet wide at its widest, trying to get into the shadows of the wall as he pulled his AK-12 off his back and scanned for any indication that he'd been spotted.

He crouched there in the dark for a long moment, his rifle in his shoulder, watching and listening. He couldn't hear much over the rattle and thunder of the fight at the gate, but neither did he see much in the way of movement nearby. He didn't think he'd been spotted.

Of course, if one of those AMXs turned a thermal sight in their direction, they were fucked. And there wasn't a damned thing his little 5.45mm peashooter was going to do against one of those behemoths.

He was about to drop his pack and pull the rope out, casting around for a suitable anchor point, when he heard footsteps above him. They were almost drowned out by all the other noise, but something warned him, and he looked up just in time to see a single Iranian soldier run down the wall to the southernmost tower. He had the look of a man who had forgotten something.

There was a flight of stairs leading down from the tower to the courtyard below, flush with the outer wall. Flanagan moved to that corner and buried himself against the stairs, hoping that the shadows would keep him out of sight if the Iranian happened to look down the steps.

After a moment, he started to think that the man was sticking. Which was a problem in and of itself. If he stayed there, it was only a matter of time before he looked down and saw the boats at the base of the cliff. Then the game would be up, and with only one of them through the breach.

Flanagan took a breath. He was about to break out of the shadows and mount the steps, to go up and kill the Iranian in the tower, but descending boots slapping against stone steps stopped him. The man was coming down the stairs.

Leveling his AK at the base of the steps, Flanagan went perfectly still, waiting for the Iranian to turn and see him crouched there. Maybe it would be the faint green glow of the Russian NVGs reflecting off his face that would give him away. Maybe it would simply be the hackles on the back of the man's neck. Flanagan had seen stranger things.

He wished for a suppressor. He really didn't think that, even with the fight going on out by the gate, anyone would be able to mistake an unsuppressed 5.45 shot inside the courtyard for anything else. As soon as he fired, they'd be blown.

Kinda wish I'd learned to throw knives. He knew it was dumb; nobody in their right mind really thought the Hollywood fetish for knife-throwing had anything to do with real combat. But it would be something he could always quietly and smugly rub in Kevin's face, that he'd killed a guy by throwing a knife into his back.

The Iranian came into view, hustling down the stairs, carrying what looked like a MAG-58 and several belts of ammunition. He wasn't moving that quick; Curtis would have been making much better time.

Flanagan's finger was resting on the trigger, the selector lever on semi-auto, the red dot right between the man's shoulder blades. If he turned around…

But the man didn't turn around; he hit the courtyard and kept jogging toward the gate. In another minute, he was a dark blur of movement, a hundred fifty yards away, then he disappeared into the barbican.

There was a faint scrabbling sound behind him, and Flanagan turned, letting out a relieved breath. Hancock was coming up through the breach, dragging himself onto his belly as he got through the gap in the sandstone wall.

Flanagan hustled over and helped the older man the rest of the way up. "Almost had to schwack an Iranian early," he whispered. "I've got a rope in my pack; let's get it secured and send it down."

***

Brannigan was a little annoyed as he clambered up the rope. He was the last man off the boats, and it bugged him. He knew the rest of the men didn't care; he knew he shouldn't care. They were all mercenaries at that point, and equal partners in this crazy job. But it still bugged him.

He clambered up through the breach. The rope was tied off to a stake hammered in the ground; he wasn't sure where it had come from, until he looked up and saw one corner of a nearby camouflage net flapping loose in the faint evening breeze.

Flanagan and Hancock must have cannibalized the stake from there.

The rest of the team was spread out in a line along the wall, hugging the shadows where possible, AK-12s aimed into the courtyard. It looked like the entire stretch was covered. Brannigan was already looking for the sally port that should get them up into the upper courtyard and the keep, preferably without going through the intensifying shitstorm of a gunfight out by the barbican, when Flanagan hissed at him.

"You'd better take a look at this," the lean, black-bearded man said as he detached himself from the shadows along the seaward wall. Even soaked, he didn't seem to make any noise, every footstep a gliding, rolling sort of step that was almost completely silent. He led Brannigan toward where the camouflage net was hanging down.

Lifting the corner of the net, Flanagan stepped aside and held it for Brannigan.

At first, it had looked like there was a row of heavy-equipment haulers or fuel trucks parked along the wall, under the camo netting. But Brannigan quickly realized that those weren't heavy tanker trucks.

They were ballistic missile carriers.

CHAPTER 12

"So," Brannigan murmured, "I think we know what the Iranians are doing here."

"Yeah," Flanagan replied. "This island's well within range of just about every Saudi city on the Gulf coast."

Brannigan took a quick count. There were at least twelve missiles. "This makes things a bit more complicated."

"We don't have time for complicated," Flanagan protested. "It's the missiles or the hostages. We came for the hostages. Frankly, I'm far more concerned with getting them out than I am with the possibility of some Saudi cities getting smoked. Fuck the Saudis, anyway."

But Brannigan was already thinking. While he might generally agree with Flanagan's sentiment—in his experience, the Saudis had taken far more than they'd given, and tended to play the US like a puppet with one hand, while supporting Islamist terrorists with the other—he knew that he'd never be able to live with himself if these missiles flew, hundreds of thousands—if not millions—of people died, and he could have stopped it.

"Back to the wall," he whispered. "We've got to regroup and figure this out."

If they'd still been in the military, the decision would have been entirely on him. Well, not entirely; he would have had to consult higher, possibly as high as the White House, if he'd come into possession of this kind of intel. The ultimate decision would have been made multiple paygrades above his head, he would have passed on the orders, and his men would have executed them. That was it.

This was different, and he knew it, even as the two of them hustled back to the wall next to the breach. "Bring it in!" he hissed, as Flanagan found the darkest spot he could, back in the corner beneath the southernmost tower.

They weren't in the military anymore; they were mercenaries, independent contractors, and he was commander as much by reason of their acceptance as by the fact that he'd effectively hired them for the job. That meant he had to approach this a little differently. He couldn't just order them to risk their lives to save a bunch of faceless Saudi civilians. He had to convince them. And in the middle of the enemy's fortress was hardly the most auspicious place to have that conversation.

"There are at least a dozen ballistic missiles on their carriers here in the courtyard," Brannigan whispered, once the squad was in a tight knot in the shadows, AK-12s pointed outboard and eyes searching for enemies. "Given that they are Iranian, we have to assume that they're aimed at Israel or Saudi Arabia, and they probably have some kind of CBRN warheads." Chemical, Biological, Radiological, Nuclear was every soldiers' nightmare acronym. "I'm not inclined to just leave those in the hands of a bunch of Islamist fanatics. I'm willing to sacrifice some of our Semtex to blow them sky-high."

No one objected. Flanagan had said his piece. "We get to blow something else up?" Curtis asked. "Sounds like a good time to me. Might help cover our exfil, too."

It was a good point, one that Brannigan mentally kicked himself for not thinking of first.

"Somebody has to stay back here and hold the breach, anyway," Hancock said. "They can set the charges, while the rest of us go for the hostages."

"This pig won't be much use inside a damn castle," Curtis pointed out, hefting his PKP slightly. "I'll stay."

"I'll stay with him," Flanagan said, "and set the charges." Brannigan glanced at the quiet man. He suspected that his change of heart had more to do with not leaving Curtis by himself than anything else, missiles or no missiles.

A long, thumping burst of heavy machinegun fire ripped through the night from the direction of the gate, answered by a ragged fusillade of lighter-caliber fire. Tracers were suddenly skipping through the sky overhead, coming from the direction of the Old City. There must have been more Al Qaeda fighters out there than Aziz had thought. They were raising all kinds of hell, trying to get into the Citadel.

Which only made their window of opportunity that much narrower. "All right," he hissed. "Flanagan and Curtis stay here, the rest, with me." He thought he'd seen the route to the sally port; it was going to be a precarious climb, but it beat trying to fight their way into the barbican.

Keeping low, he got up and dashed toward the escarpment, keeping seaward of the old garrison buildings. The rest of the assault team followed him.

**

The sally port had been built into the inner wall as a route for the defenders to slip out and attack an enemy that had taken the inner courtyard. It was not supposed to be conspicuous, and in fact, Brannigan wasn't one hundred percent sure that the spot he'd picked out was the actual sally port. But he thought he saw narrow, zig-zag steps cut into the cliff beneath the inner curtain wall, and if nothing else, they could still use ropes to get over the wall if they had to, provided they could get high enough.

Of course, they'd be exposed, but hopefully, if somebody started shooting from inside the castle, Curtis could quickly tear into them with that PKP.

He hit the side of the long, low garrison building, pointing his AK up at the wall above them, just in case. The rest fanned out around him, Hancock and Santelli covering around the corner, toward the gate, and Childress watching the dark, arched window at the end of the building. Villareal was huffing, but took a knee behind Santelli, hitching his med bag into a slightly more comfortable position.

Brannigan was looking around, frowning behind his NVGs. He'd thought that he'd seen the stairs leading up to the sally port, but now that they were closer, the cliff just looked like a cliff. Had he imagined it? He didn't think so, but then, the castle's builders wouldn't have wanted those steps to be obvious to anyone below them.

Villareal suddenly got up and stepped close, touching his shoulder. The doctor pointed, and then Brannigan saw it. The steps had been cut back into the cliffside, and there was still a gate across their base. He had no idea how old that gate was. Maybe the king had wanted it kept up or restored for some reason.

Brannigan pushed off the wall at his back and moved quickly to the gate, with Childress and Villareal right behind him. Hancock and Santelli followed a few yards behind, always keeping at least one rifle pointed up the length of the outer courtyard.

The gate was shut, but apparently it wasn't locked. Why should it be? The Iranians controlled the outer courtyard. If they even knew about the sally port, they had nothing to fear from it.

The hinges creaked a little as the gate swung open, but the noise was all but inaudible over the crackle of gunfire and the occasional thunder of explosions. The fight in the Old City was waning and waxing, judging by the noise, and it increasingly sounded like the heavier firepower at the Iranians' command had forced it away from the gate. That could be a problem. Brannigan's heart was pounding as he slipped through the gate, aiming his AK-12 up the steps. They had to get inside and get to the hostages while most of the Iranian force still had its hands full.

Unfortunately, he quickly discovered that rushing up the steps was not a good idea. No two steps were the same height, and he nearly tripped and busted his face on the stairs in front of him before falling off onto Childress' head. He just barely caught himself, and realized that he had to slow down and take every step by feel. A muted curse below him told him that Villareal had just learned the same painful lesson.

It could have been by design; asynchronous steps would slow an attacker down, giving the defenders an advantage. But Brannigan had also spent enough time in the Arab world to know that it could just as easily be because whoever had cut the steps simply hadn't cared.

He didn't think about the fact that the Khadarkh Citadel had been a *Persian* fortress. It really didn't matter, and he had other things on his mind.

His legs were burning by the time he reached the sally port. The ancient, iron-bound door was shut fast, and there was no latch on the outside.

He put his shoulder to the gate and shoved, as hard as he could on the narrow landing. The gate didn't budge. It didn't even creak under the pressure, and he felt a boot slip on the dust and grit of the crumbling sandstone steps. Childress had, fortunately, stopped about ten steps below him.

No one had ever accused John Brannigan of indecisiveness. Slinging his rifle, he swung his assault pack off his back and dragged out a block of Semtex and a priming system.

There were no protrusions on the gate that he could try to hang the charge from, and the ancient wood and iron were dusty, too dusty for tape. But the Semtex was sticky stuff, and once Brannigan ripped off the wrapper and jammed the lump of explosives into the corner of the gate and the jamb, it stayed put.

He quickly rigged the priming system, shoved the blasting cap into the slightly deformed wad of plastic explosive, yanked the initiator, and hustled back down the steps as fast as their unevenness and narrowness would allow, praying that the Russian priming system worked the way it was supposed to.

Childress had seen what he had been doing, and hadn't waited around. The younger man was already another ten meters down the stairs, hugging the cliff wall. There wasn't going to be a lot of cover from the blast, and as Brannigan descended, he was counting down in his head. He hit "ten" and flattened himself against the cliffside.

The detonation was a sharp *crack*, and the pressure wave hammered against them as fragments and grit whispered through the air and rained down on the men huddled against the cliff.

Now they really had to move fast. They had just announced their presence inside the Citadel. His legs already starting to ache, Brannigan forced himself back up the steps, forging toward the blasted gate.

The gate was broken and partway open, but even the blast of a block of Semtex hadn't quite managed to completely obliterate it. It had been built solidly, and Semtex, like C4, has a high enough burn rate that it cuts more than it pushes. It had severed whatever latch had been holding the gate open, splintering the thick timbers and pushing the gate almost a foot and a half inward, but that was all.

There wasn't room on the landing for two men to stand, which meant this entry was going to be less than ideal. Well aware that he was about to expose himself, Brannigan pointed his AK at the gap, put his shoulder to the gate, and pushed.

Ancient wood and iron scraped against sand and rock. The gate was mounted flush with the ground, and evidently hadn't been opened in a very long time. The hinges squealed and the grit beneath the edge of the door resisted every inch of movement.

Finally, the gate was open wide enough for a man to get through, even one of Brannigan's considerable size. He pushed through, his rifle in his shoulder, ready to snap it up and engage in a split second, clearing enough room behind him for Childress to follow.

The lanky young man hooked around the partly open gate, to clear Brannigan's six o'clock. Then Villareal, Hancock, and Santelli were coming through. Santelli was puffing a little; he was stouter than the rest, and despite his many miles of weekly running, his shorter legs made it harder for him to keep up with the others.

They were now against the seaward wall of the upper courtyard. The main Citadel loomed immediately to their north, black against the stars. Several smaller buildings had been built against the wall, not unlike the garrison inside the outer courtyard. The arched windows were black and lifeless in the green glow of their NVGs.

A good deal of the courtyard was taken up by the Super Puma helicopter squatting on the helipad. From the markings, dimly visible through the NVGs, it had been the Khadarkhi king's personal helo. It would provide some concealment as they moved toward the Citadel.

As soon as he felt Hancock bump him, signaling that everyone was through and ready to move, Brannigan began to glide along the wall, making for where the Citadel's side entrance was supposed to be. He hoped that it wasn't as hard to spot as the sally port had been.

It was not. Especially once the doors banged open and four Iranians with rifles held at the ready poured out. Someone must have noticed the breaching charge going off.

The mercenaries were in the open, halfway across the helipad. There was no cover, no concealment. So Brannigan did the only thing he could, under the circumstances. Even as their presence registered to the lead Iranian rifleman, Brannigan snapped his AK-12 up and fired.

The two-round burst was a coughing *bark* amidst the thunder of the night, the rifle cycling faster than the recoil could push the muzzle off target. Flame spat from the rifle's muzzle brake, and the Iranian crumpled. Brannigan gave him a second pair, just to be on the safe side, then switched to the next man to the right.

By then, the other three had joined in, cutting the rest of the Iranians down in a rattling storm of rifle fire. Muzzle blasts flickered in the dark of the outer courtyard, and then the four Iranians were down on the ground and the mercenaries were sweeping toward the still-open door.

As they passed, one of the Iranians stirred and groaned. Brannigan looked down to see the man clutching his midsection. His front was dark with blood, appearing black in the greenscale image.

Villareal hesitated, then knelt beside the dying man. Brannigan stopped, even as Hancock and Childress reached the door and set up on it, waiting for the rest before they made entry. He was about to whisper a warning to the doctor when all hell broke loose.

He heard a faint scuffling sound, then Santelli hissed a curse and grabbed Villareal by the med pack and hauled him off the wounded Iranian by main force. That was when Brannigan got a clear enough view of the man to see that he was trying to get a finger into the ring of a grenade. He quickly put his red dot, gleaming a brilliant white in his NVGs, on the man's forehead and blew the top of his head off with another two-round burst. The dead man flopped, the grenade rolling away, the pin thankfully still inserted.

Santelli was pushing the doctor toward the open door, a steady stream of Boston-accented profanity hissing between his teeth. "What the motherfucking fuck were you fucking thinking, doc? You want to get your fucking head blown the fuck off?"

Brannigan ignored the situation for now. When they got in a room and got a breather, he could say something. Right at the moment, they were still exposed. They needed to get through that door, kill anyone on the other side of it, and find a hardpoint for the handful of seconds they could spare to get their bearings.

He got behind Hancock and bumped him with a knee. Hancock took the signal and launched himself in the door.

The double door was wide enough that two men could make entry abreast, without getting tangled up with each other. So Hancock went in first, Childress almost right at his shoulder, with Brannigan and Santelli behind them, their own weapons aimed over the first two men's shoulders.

The entryway was a wide, high-ceilinged anteroom, with tiled columns running along each side. Several expensive couches and chairs lined the walls, a step up from the central floor, and woven wall-hangings, with Arabic inscriptions in gold thread were hanging on the walls themselves. The room was otherwise empty.

They pushed to the far door, Childress turning behind one of the columns to cover back the way they had come. They were in the middle of the enemy's house now, and they had to expect threats from every direction.

Brannigan took a glance out into the hall, flipping his NVGs up as he did so. There were lights on inside, though it seemed as though the Iranians were keeping most of the outer rooms blacked out for the time being.

The hallway appeared to run through the center of the U-shape of the main Citadel building. Like the entryway, the ceiling was high, and there was tile on the floor and in spots on the white and green painted stucco of the walls. There were actual chandeliers hanging from the ceiling, framed by patterned moldings. So far, the hallway was empty, though that couldn't be trusted to last. The Iranians had already sent shooters that they probably couldn't spare to investigate the breach at the sally port; there would be more coming when they didn't report back.

"Doc," Brannigan ground out over his shoulder, without taking his eyes off the hallway in front of him, "I love you like a brother, and I know why you did it. But if you *ever* try to get us killed out of consideration for enemy wounded again, I'll shoot you myself. Understood?"

"Roger that," Villareal said hoarsely from somewhere behind him. From the tone of the man's voice, he had been rattled by the close call. As well he might. He should have known better. "It won't happen again."

I shouldn't have brought him along. As good as he was, I let my respect for his skill keep me from seeing just how deep the damage from Zarghun really went. I should have listened when he told me he couldn't go back.

Of course, it was too late to do anything but roll with the punches. Villareal would rise to the occasion or he wouldn't. They simply had no time for anything else.

The noise of the fighting in the Old City was now muffled by the thick sandstone walls, reaching their ears as only a dull, distant roar. It was deceptively quiet inside the old Citadel that the Al Qays had turned into a palace. That was the only reason that Brannigan could hear the crackle of a radio coming from the other side of the open door, where they'd left the bodies.

A tinny voice asked a question in Farsi. When it went unanswered, the question was repeated, more stridently.

"That's it, we're officially blown," Brannigan muttered. There was no more time. He pushed out into the hall, his AK-12 up and his finger millimeters from the trigger.

"Stairway," Childress called from behind him, where he was facing down the long end of the "U."

"On you," Brannigan replied. He stayed put, blockading the hallway, his rifle covering the corner ahead and the several arched doorways before it. He waited until a fist to the back of his shoulder announced that the last man was out the door and moving toward the stairs.

159

They did not know exactly where the hostages were being kept. The Iranian videos hadn't shown enough detail to pinpoint any particular location inside the palace. Hell, they didn't even have more than the vaguest floor plan for the Citadel. That it rose three stories above ground, with a deep cellar beneath was about the extent of it, though some digging on the Internet had turned up a video recording of a tour from a couple of years before. They thought that the likeliest places would be the grand hall on the second floor, the cellar, or the second grand hall, clear up on the third floor.

There were still innumerable places in that massive edifice where thirty people could be crammed, especially if their captors really didn't care about their welfare. So, the mercenaries were going to have to search as quickly and as systematically as they could.

All of that had been covered in the planning phase. They were now moving according to the plan, as necessarily flexible as that plan had to be.

Few of the doorways lining that ground-floor hallway actually had doors in them, and of those that did, not all of them were closed. That made matters a bit easier; they could quickly check each room and blow past it once reasonably sure that their objective wasn't inside. They swept down the hallway, heading for the stairs, visually clearing each opening as they passed it.

Brannigan was stopping and turning every few steps to check behind him. And it was a good thing, too, because two more Iranians, identifiable by their khaki fatigues and black Type 03 rifles, came jogging around the corner, probably intending to find out why the first group that had gone outside wasn't answering the radio.

The first man saw the group of mercs as soon as he came around the corner. His eyes widened, and he opened his mouth to shout, dragging his Type 03 up from where he'd had the muzzle pointed at the floor.

He was too slow. Brannigan already had his red dot centered high on the man's chest, and stroked the trigger.

His AK-12 rattled and roared in the confined space of the hallway, two-round bursts smashing into the first man just below

160

the collarbone, then the second man in the face as the first one staggered.

The second man dropped like a rock, hitting the floor with a meaty *thud*, his rifle clattering against the stone and hitting his companion in the back of the leg. The first man's knee buckled under the impact, but even with two 5.45mm bullets in him, he still stayed upright, though he triggered a burst into the wall instead of at the mercenaries. Bullets chipped stucco off the wall, and one ricocheted down the hall with a vicious *buzz*, passing close enough that Childress flinched away as it passed him.

Brannigan shot the man four more times, and he finally fell, blood pooling on the tile floor beneath him.

"Come on!" Santelli barked. Brannigan turned to see the rest at the stairway, Hancock covering up the stairs while Santelli and Childress were aimed in down the hallway. Turning, he ran the rest of the way to the stairwell.

"Well, now they definitely know we're here," he said. "We'll have to move quick. Doc, you're with me and Roger; we'll go up. Carlo, take Sam and go down, clear the cellar."

He got terse acknowledgments from all of them. "Let's go," he said. "Hopefully we can get clear before they can recall enough of their shooters from the fight out in the city to give us a problem." He kneed Hancock in the buttock, and the other man immediately started up the steps, Brannigan on his heels.

CHAPTER 13

Ortiz knew they were in trouble as soon as the shooting started out in the city, though he kept his face carefully impassive. Not all of his fellow hostages could face the grim facts of their predicament with as much equanimity as he could, and there was no sense in starting a panic.

In fact, the gunfire and explosions seemed to give some of them renewed hope. They probably thought that it meant there was a rescue mission on the way. They probably had visions of Navy Stealthhawks swooping in, full of Navy SEALs, poised to fast-rope in onto the Citadel and get them out.

Ortiz had lost any such hopes. When there hadn't been an immediate, overwhelming, shock-and-awe op to break them out after Ulrich's execution, he'd known that rescue wasn't coming. They were stuck, just like the hostages in Tehran back in the '80s, waiting until either they were all slaughtered, or some humiliating diplomatic solution was found through negotiation, a resolution that would embarrass the United States and hand the Iranians a moral—and, quite possibly, monetary—victory.

He'd also been paying attention over the last couple of weeks, and knew that the shooting had come on the heels of increasingly restive riots. He'd heard the shouting and chanting down below for days, and had heard it again before the fighting started.

That was no rescue attempt. That was the Sunni demonstrators finally getting violent.

And though he wouldn't give it voice, he also knew that, regardless of whether the noise out in the Old City was an actual rescue attempt or not, it only increased the likelihood that they would all be killed out of hand. Either the Iranians would kill them, to make sure that any rescue attempt, imaginary or not, couldn't get to them, or the Iranians would get overrun by the Sunnis, who probably wouldn't be much better. He didn't figure that anyone in that mob was going to be of a particularly peaceable mindset by the time they reached the top floor of the Citadel.

"Everybody just calm down and shut up!" he barked. "You're giving me a headache."

"But, Captain," Warren Beck remonstrated, "this could be it." Beck was a fat, balding man. Not one of the *Oceana Metropolis'* crew, he had been a tourist come to see the Persian Gulf. He should have stayed in Bahrain.

Ortiz glowered at him. "Yeah, it could be 'it,' all right," he replied. "The question you should be asking yourself is, what is 'it?'" He looked around at the rest, many of whom were still trying to climb up to see out one of the windows. *Screw it, they should know anyway, since none of them has apparently thought that far.* "If nothing else, 'it' could be the guards deciding to come in here and kill us all, just in case."

The room fell silent at his grim pronouncement. A few widening pairs of eyes were turned on him. They evidently hadn't considered that possibility.

When the door scraped open a moment later and Mehregan strode through, in his combat gear and with a rifle in his hands, it suddenly became less of a possibility and more of a reality.

"Against the wall!" the short Iranian said, a fevered look in his eyes. Ortiz recognized the look. The little killer had psyched himself up, and he was out for blood. He waved his rifle muzzle at the crowd of hostages. *"Now!"*

The hostages, however, were standing there, frozen like deer in the headlights, eyes wide and shocked. The combination of Ortiz' warning and Mehregan's sudden appearance had proved to be a bit too much.

"*Do it!*" Ortiz roared. "Do you want him to just gun you down while you stare at him like slack-jawed idiots?"

He wasn't sure why he'd bothered. They were probably all dead, anyway. What did it matter if they bought a handful of seconds before Mehregan gleefully murdered them all?

A quiet, not-quite-so-cynical part of his mind thought ashamedly that he should have done more. Mehregan was alone. If they all rushed him, a few would probably get shot, but they'd get him.

But he couldn't even voice the thought. When he looked into the fanatic's glittering eyes, he saw only death, and could only think of how to buy the next few seconds. The truth of the matter was, he was deeply afraid of Mehregan, after what he'd seen the man do earlier. And he truly didn't want to die, now that his world-weary cynicism was suddenly confronted by the very real imminence of his own brutal murder.

Under Mehregan's basilisk glare, the hostages shuffled meekly to the wall. The Iranian had a look of maniacal, triumphant glee on his face now, as he raised his rifle, and shouted, "*Allahu akhbar! Marg bar Amryka!*"

He was cut off by the bark of a pistol.

The little man staggered, a faintly confused look coming into his dark eyes. He looked down at his side, where a growing red stain was starting to show on his khakis. Then he looked up, toward the door.

Esfandiari stood in the doorway, his Makarov in both hands, pointed at Mehregan.

He advanced into the hall, and the pistol barked twice more. Mehregan staggered as the bullets ripped into his midsection. The rifle fell from suddenly nerveless fingers, hitting the stone floor with a loud clatter. He sank to his knees, his shaking hands clutching the wounds in his belly.

Esfandiari stepped closer and stood over him, staring down at him impassively. Then the Iranian commander put the muzzle of his pistol to Mehregan's forehead and pulled the trigger.

The pistol barked and Mehregan's head snapped backward, a spatter of blood, brains, and bone blasting out of the back of his skull. He fell limply to the floor.

For a long moment, that couldn't actually have been more than a few seconds, the hostages just stared in shock. Ortiz finally forced a tiny bit of spit into his dry mouth, enough to speak.

"Thank you, Commander," he said.

Esfandiari turned pitiless eyes on him, and Ortiz instinctively recoiled. There was no human warmth in that gaze. Esfandiari's eyes were as dead as a shark's. "Do not think that your situation has changed," the Iranian warned. "This Twelver lunatic was simply defying my orders."

Ortiz looked at the floor, rather than meet the Iranian's gaze. His relief at deliverance was waning fast in the face of the fact that their situation was as precarious as it ever had been, especially since Esfandiari now found himself and his men under siege. And there was no reassurance in the man's gaze. While he remained as cool and collected as he had been from the beginning, Esfandiari was still a killer, in the service of a murderous ideology that viewed Ortiz and his companions as little more than barely-human enemies.

For a brief moment, he had the sudden, gut-wrenching impression that Esfandiari was about to make an example of *him*, too, if only to make sure that the rest of the hostages stayed in line while the fighting went on outside. He felt every wasted muscle in his body tense, waiting for the pistol to rise. The faint muzzle flash would be the last thing he ever saw.

But Esfandiari suddenly snapped his head to one side, as if listening. Ortiz had heard more gunshots, but they had been hearing gunfire for some time by then, and he did not have the practiced ear to tell the difference between gunfire *outside* the walls and gunfire *inside*.

Esfandiari abruptly turned on his heel, barking orders in Farsi as he stormed out the door. The guards pulled the doors shut behind him, and he was gone.

Ortiz sank to the floor, shaking.

***

Hancock hit the second floor, going through the door with only the barest pause to make sure Brannigan was right behind him. The two men had both rifles trained down the hallway as they moved to opposite sides of the hall, maximizing their respective fields of fire. Villareal kept close behind Brannigan.

They moved fast, gliding down the hallway as quickly as they could move while still being able to shoot accurately. Their target room was around the corner, at the center of the "U," and speed was their security. They simply didn't have enough guns for any other course of action.

Eyes and rifle muzzles tracked across open doorways as they went past. Strangely, the Citadel, which had been the home of the Al Qays royal family and their retainers, appeared all but deserted. Brannigan could only assume that the Iranians had forced the original occupants out into the city. That had proved to be a bit of a strategic blunder on their part, since doubtless some of those displaced loyalists were presently among the mobs and knots of fighters out raising hell in the Old City. The Iranian soldiers who had replaced them were, presumably, out fighting the Loyalists and Al Qaeda jihadists.

Getting to the corner, Brannigan held just short, until he could see Hancock out of the corner of his eye, rifle aimed at the corner ahead of him. As soon as he knew the other man was in position, he moved, quickly hooking around the corner, his rifle snapping up and ready to engage.

The hallway on the other side of the corner was short, leading to an elaborately decorated, arched double door, flanked by potted palms. Brannigan moved the couple of dozen feet to the door, then paused, his muzzle pointed at the opening, waiting for Doc and Hancock as he listened for any activity on the other side of the doors.

As soon as Hancock was in position on the other side of the double doors, partially squeezed back behind the palm on that side, Brannigan whispered, "Doc, you get the doors. Roger and I will bang and enter."

Villareal nodded, as Brannigan let his rifle hang and dragged a GSZ-T flashbang grenade out of his gear. Hancock held his own muzzle on the door until Brannigan was set, then did the same, dangling the stun grenade by its ring from the pinky of his shooting hand.

Villareal stepped out from behind Brannigan, glanced at both men, then landed a solid kick right at the latch where the two doors met. The doors gave way under his boot and swung inward, and in the same second, both Brannigan and Hancock snatched the pins out of the flashbangs and lobbed them in the widening gap.

The grenades went off with twin thunderclaps and blinding flashes. Brannigan had been a bit leery about using the Russian munitions; while he didn't quite share Flanagan's antipathy for "Communist" arms, he knew that quality control was impossible to account for, especially when it came to black market weapons. It had been entirely possible that they could have thrown two duds in the door, or worse, one of them could have gone off as soon as the pin had been pulled, depriving one or both of them of a few fingers.

Of course, if that had happened, they probably would have been dead in the next five minutes, so the risk was actually more serious than that.

Ears ringing from the blasts, the two men shoved through the double doors, hammering their shoulders into the doors themselves to bash them out of the way, riding the barriers hard against the interior walls as they rushed to clear the corners. Brannigan went left, Hancock went right. Villareal had rolled out of the way as soon as he had kicked the doors in, and was still out in the hall, crouched behind a potted palm until the main room was clear.

Even as he swung through the doorway and cleared his corner, Brannigan's eyes were taking a snapshot of the interior of the room. Two rows of intricately filigreed columns lined the long walls, framing high, arched windows. The floor was tiled in a geometric pattern of black, white, and gold, which was mirrored on the ceiling, between the hanging chandeliers, which were presently dark. The only light in the room came from a couple of flashlights and a pair of battery-powered lanterns sitting on a table.

Four figures were gathered around the long, dark wooden table in the center of the hall. The tabletop was littered with laptops, radios, and what looked like printouts and maps.

In that split-second flash image, he saw that two of the Iranians had apparently looked right at one or another of the flashbangs as they'd gone off; they were blinded, blinking against the tears and the glowing green and purple blotches that were probably obscuring their vision, rocking and swaying with their destroyed equilibrium.

The other two had caught some of the blast, but were still conscious enough to know they were under attack. One was reaching for what had to be a pistol on the table, while the other dove for a Type 03 leaning against a chair.

There were no hostages in the room.

Brannigan halted, pivoted on one foot, and snapped his AK-12 around, his finger tightening on the trigger even before he had it on-line.

The trigger broke just as the red dot settled on the man farthest to the left, the two-round burst putting a pair of bullets within an inch of each other, high in the man's chest. He staggered, but Brannigan was already dragging the muzzle past him, his finger barely letting off on the trigger enough for it to reset before the dot was passing across the second man's torso. Another hammering pair of bullets tore their way through the top of that man's heart and lungs, punching ragged holes just above his sternum.

By the time his muzzle had swung to the third man, that one was already staggering and going down, the pistol falling from fingers that didn't work right anymore, his brain having been transfixed by two of Hancock's shots. Brannigan shot that one again anyway. The fourth man had fallen, and was out of sight.

He tracked his muzzle back across the group. The second man he'd shot had hit the edge of the table and rolled off. He was lying face down on the floor, blood pooling under him. The first one was still moving.

The man was obviously dying, but he wasn't giving up. He was struggling to get the Type 03 up off the floor where he'd dropped it when he'd been shot. Like the one with the pistol, his fingers weren't quite working the way they were supposed to. He was visibly weakening.

Brannigan didn't wait to see what would happen. The man's movement registered in his mind as a threat in the same

169

instant the red dot crossed his crouched shape. The AK-12 roared again, echoes hammering at the ears in the open space of the hall, and the last Iranian crumpled, paired exit wounds, each big enough to fit two fingers in, gaping at the base of his skull.

"Moving," Brannigan called, before he started forward, moving alongside the columns, clearing each bit of dead space as he went. Hancock stayed put, so as to keep both of their fields of fire clear.

There was another door at the far end of the hall, but the room was otherwise empty. Satisfied for a moment, Brannigan stripped the partially empty mag out of the AK-12 and rocked in a fresh one. "Clear."

Hancock and Villareal started moving up to join him. Whatever the Iranians had been doing there, the hostages were either above, or down in the cellar. They had to move.

Villareal paused at the table, looking down at the papers. He frowned. "Hey, John?" he called.

"No time, Doc," Brannigan replied, his rifle already pointed at the door. "We've got to keep moving."

"This is serious, John," Villareal said, still looking down at one of the maps. "I don't think the Iranians brought those missiles here."

Brannigan risked taking his eyes off the door to glance back. "Why not?"

"Because this map has target locations highlighted in Iran."

Brannigan frowned. That didn't sound right. So far, these assholes had acted like stereotypical IRGC fanatics, not MEK or any of the other Iranian splinter groups that hated the Council of Guardians. They sure as hell weren't Green Revolution.

"Grab what you can stuff in a couple of cargo pockets," he said. "We've still got hostages on site, and the clock is ticking."

Villareal started grabbing maps and papers and stuffing them into his pockets. He probably would have taken his med bag off and used that, too, except that it was still packed full of medical supplies.

"Come on, Doc!" Hancock barked, as he reached the door across from Brannigan. The intel that Villareal had found might indeed be important to someone, but right at that moment, intel collection was not their mission.

"I've got all I can get!" Villareal announced, running to get behind Brannigan. "Let's move."

Brannigan started to reach for the doorknob, just before it started to swing open on its own.

He jammed a boot against the door, and there was a surprised yell in Farsi from the other side. With a hard shove, he slammed the door shut again, then jumped back, almost colliding with Villareal, leveling his AK at the door.

Hancock had reacted slightly faster, giving the opening door on his side of the portal a vicious kick before stepping back, flipping the selector to full auto, and ripping half a mag through the wooden door with a rattling roar.

Brannigan followed suit with a burst of his own, before yelling, "Back the way we came! Use the columns! Bounding! Go!"

Hancock and Villareal complied immediately, pivoting and running halfway back down the hall, taking cover behind two of the columns. Splinters blasted from the doors as someone on the far side returned fire, dumping rounds through the increasingly chewed-up wood. The doors were made of solid timber instead of veneer, but they still weren't thick enough to stop bullets.

Hancock might have yelled at him, but the roar of bullets hitting the doors announced that the other man was set as well as any call would have. Brannigan put another four rounds through the door, then spun around and ran, angling back toward the windows to put the columns between him and the line of fire from the doors.

He ran past the point where Hancock was crouched behind a pillar on the opposite side of the room, flame stabbing from his muzzle brake as he hammered away at the doors. So far, they still hadn't opened again, the mercenaries' fire making the doorway a deadly place to stand.

Brannigan hit a column just inside the far end of the hall, rolling around it to point his muzzle back toward the increasingly ventilated doors, just as Hancock's rifle fell silent. Brannigan took up the fire, pouring four- to five-round bursts down the length of the hall, as Hancock started to bound back, stripping out his own magazine and reloading as he ran.

Villareal was suddenly right by Brannigan's side, keeping within the cover of the column. "Hallway's still clear," he yelled in Brannigan's ear. It was still almost impossible to hear him; the acoustics of the hall amplified the gunfire to a hellish, thundering roar.

"Go!" Brannigan yelled, firing another burst at what might have been movement behind the shattered doors.

Hancock was at the portal behind them. "Doc!" he yelled. "On me!"

Villareal clapped Brannigan on the shoulder. "Last man!" he shouted, as he turned and ran for the doors.

"Turn and go!" Hancock was bellowing, opening fire again from the threshold. Brannigan didn't hesitate, but turned and sprinted out the open doors and headed for the corner of the hall, driving forward to make sure no one was coming down the stairs behind them.

He hit the corner and briefly barricaded on it. The hallway was as empty as it had been on their way in. "On me!" he roared hoarsely. His ears were ringing, his sodden fatigues were now also sweat-soaked, his chest was heaving, and his mouth tasted like the desert itself.

As soon as he heard Villareal yell, "With you!" less than a foot from his ear, he was moving down the hall, his rifle trained on the stairway ahead. The gunfire died down behind him as Hancock came around the corner, cutting off the line of fire into the bigger room.

Brannigan moved toward the stairs at a fast glide, the other two mercenaries right on his heels. He was hot, his chest was heaving, and his throat was raw. Adrenaline coursed through his veins, threatening to make his hands and his knees shake.

He hadn't felt so alive in years.

***

Esfandiari guessed that the attackers, whoever they were, had retreated as soon as the stream of bullets chewing up the doors ceased. Abbasi and Ghorbani had reached the same conclusion, and immediately started to push through the doors, intent on pursuit, but a barked order from Esfandiari halted them.

Esfandiari had not been picked to lead this mission solely because of his fanatical devotion to the Islamic Republic. He was also a canny, experienced combat leader, and his mind was racing. "No," he shouted. "Up! They will be trying to get to the hostages! Back to the stairs!"

CHAPTER 14

Santelli's legs were already burning from the climbing they'd done so far that night, and his heart was thudding in his chest. *I really should have kept in better shape.* He was kicking himself for his professions of boredom. The fact that he was in far better shape than most men of his age didn't really count when he was trying to keep up with the long-legged Childress, who was gliding down the stone steps behind his AK at a good clip, keeping his muzzle trained on the next turn. Santelli had to keep stopping to check behind and above them, then hurry to catch up. And, not unlike the steps leading up to the sally port in the inner wall, none of the steps going down into the cellar were quite the same size.

Childress paused at the landing at the bottom of the first flight, leaning slightly to one side to peer around the turn. As Santelli returned from checking their six, he glanced over the younger man's shoulder to see that it looked like the steps took a ninety-degree turn at the landing, following the wall down to the floor of the cellar.

"With you," he whispered. Childress didn't reply, or move his gaze from his sector, but only started to sidestep rapidly down the stairs. Santelli joined him, moving slightly more slowly, trying desperately not to trip on the uneven steps.

As he came out from the shadow of the first flight of stairs, he saw that they were in a vaulted chamber, about fifty feet by fifty feet, cut out of the stone of the Citadel's hill. A single work light, standing on its yellow metal legs next to a chugging generator, was the only source of light in the stone chamber. An arched door at the far end led deeper into the cellars beneath the Citadel.

Santelli suddenly wondered if "cellars" was the wrong word. "Catacombs" seemed to fit better. He shook his head fractionally, annoyed at the distraction.

Carlo Santelli had always been the kind of Marine who had been able to shut out any concern, distraction, or interest that wasn't immediately useful to the mission at hand. Some of his subordinates, doubtless including young Sam Childress, had thought that it had made him the ultimate motard, a wind-up Marine with no life or mind of his own. Everything, even his thoughts, had seemed to be issued by the Marine Corps. If he took the time to think about it, he certainly hadn't done anything to disabuse any of them of the idea. His personal life had always been strictly compartmented to times and places where being a Marine didn't come first.

Those times and places had been extremely rare.

Santelli was not a man lacking in imagination or human feelings. He was a simple man, who gave himself wholeheartedly to his work, because his father had taught him that a man who didn't wasn't worth the title of a man. When his work was soldiering, he gave himself wholeheartedly to it, and let any other elements of life fall by the wayside. It was the way things were, and he didn't bother to worry about might-have-beens, or what he could be missing.

It was probably why things hadn't been working out with Melissa before he'd taken the call from Brannigan. She loved him, but his blunt manner and lack of interest in things that didn't concern him had been hard for her to take.

None of this was actually going through Santelli's head as he and Childress stepped off the stairs and into the vault. The only thinking he was doing was about what could be lying around the corner, and what he had to do next.

The noise of the firefight outside, and even the shooting that Brannigan and Hancock were doing only a couple floors up, was muted in the cellar by the thick stone walls and the very mass of the hill itself. Santelli couldn't hear any of the shooting.

The screaming coming from the other side of the arched door, on the other hand, was all too clear.

The two men angled toward the left-hand wall, keeping close, Santelli turning every few steps to check behind them. It might have looked almost mechanical, but that was simply because maintaining security had become second-nature to the stout old former Marine. He'd hard-wired certain habits into himself to the point that even sitting behind a desk for the last few years of his career—though his time as Brannigan's Sergeant Major had involved a lot more helicopter flights and running around in the bush in combat gear than sitting at a desk in the CP or on ship—hadn't erased them. He would die the Marine he had been since his twenties.

Childress paused just outside the door. Shouts in accented Arabic occasionally overrode the agonized howling. The screams were suddenly muffled, as if the screamer had been gagged or something, though they continued as a nerve-shredding gurgle of pain and terror.

Santelli stepped up beside Childress, fishing one of the GSZ-T flashbangs out of his vest and prepping it. He held it out so that Childress could see it in his peripheral vision, then lobbed it in through the door.

He'd put a bit more *oomph* in the throw than he'd intended. The stun grenade hit the stone threshold with an audible *clank* before bouncing several feet inside, landing somewhere off to the left of the door. A heartbeat later, it detonated.

Childress was through the door while the cloud of smoke from the bang was still boiling up from the floor. Santelli hurried to follow him, his own muzzle held high until the taller man cleared the doorway enough for him to bring it down to cover the room.

The screaming had made him think that the hostages were in that room. But it was too small, and there were only three men inside.

One was stripped naked, hanging by his wrists from a hook in the ceiling. He was covered in blood, and there were burn marks in various places of his anatomy, easily explained by the car battery sitting on the stool nearby.

One of the other men, who was still wincing and blinking from the flashbang, was standing below the hanging man. He was wearing rubber gloves, covered in blood, and had a pair of pliers in his hand. The fresh flow of blood from the prisoner's mouth answered the question of what the pliers were for.

The third man had been lounging next to the far door, his Type 03 leaning against the wall next to him. He had been shielded from most of the flashbang detonation by the bodies of the prisoner and the torturer. He had ducked down, grabbed his rifle, and was turning it to put the stock in his shoulder when Santelli spotted him through the haze left over from the bang's charge.

Santelli had left his rifle on single shot since they'd reached the outer courtyard. *That* might not have been according to most of his old trainers, but just because Carlo Santelli was a simple man and given to certain habits didn't mean he couldn't learn new tricks. He was a sponge when it came to learning more about his profession, and keeping the weapon off safe when in close quarters combat had been a lesson he'd absorbed many years before.

He only had to move the muzzle up an inch before he stroked the trigger three times. The first two rounds hammered into the Iranian's chest, the third one punched through his skull, just below his left eye. Dark fluid splashed against the stone wall behind him, and he pitched forward onto his face.

The man hanging from the ceiling was moaning. He had evidently been worked over thoroughly; there were nasty third-degree burns visible in several places, and he had to have lost a lot of blood. Deep gashes might have been made by the wire whip sitting next to the car battery, and more from the broken glass bottles nearby. The pliers needed no further explanation. Several of his wounds were slowly pumping blood, which was dripping into a wide, sticky pool on the stone floor.

The torturer hadn't moved, even as his vision had cleared enough to see that the two newcomers were holding guns on him.

As Santelli stepped closer, he saw that there was a bloody, broken tooth in jaws of the pliers. That explained the muffled gurgling earlier, just before they'd made entry.

Childress had held his fire, his rifle pointed at the torturer's face. The man was still blinking, tears streaming from his eyes, and looked scared and disoriented.

Now *you're scared. Now that you're not the one with all the power, not the one dishing out all the pain.* Santelli lifted his AK and treated the torturer to the same Mozambique drill he had used to kill the rifleman. Two to the chest, one to the head. The man had already been falling, his heart transfixed by Santelli's second bullet, by the time the third round blasted a half-dollar-sized hole out of the top of his skull. His body hit the bloody floor with a sickening *squelch.*

"He wasn't armed," Childress pointed out, as he moved to the far door. He hadn't said, "Sergeant Major," but the tone of his voice was similar to the one that Santelli had heard him use before, usually when he knew that he was right and a senior officer or NCO was wrong.

But Santelli wasn't having it. He slung his AK and moved to the hanging man, kicking the instruments of torture off the stool so that he could reach high enough to release the victim's bound hands from the hook set in the ceiling. "Yeah, I know," he said, as he lowered the horribly mutilated man to the floor with a grunt. "That wasn't a combat shooting. That was an execution. I've got no sympathy or honor for torturers." He looked down at the corpse. "I find you guilty of torture and crimes against humanity," he told the dead man. "I hereby sentence you to death. Sentence carried out."

He bent over the mangled man. It was hard to tell under all the blood, but he didn't look like one of the hostages. Santelli couldn't think of who else he might be, though. He pulled out his own med kit and started trying to help the man.

"He's dying, SMaj," Childress said. "Doc might be able to help him, but with what we've got, we can't give him more than about five extra minutes."

"Then that's five minutes he wouldn't have had otherwise," Santelli bit out, as he tried to figure out where to start.

The man's chest and back were practically hamburger in places. He didn't have any toenails left, and it looked like that had been the fifth or sixth tooth ripped out of his head.

"We've got another twenty or thirty hostages to worry about," Childress insisted, his eyes still on the doorway, just above his rifle barrel. "We've got to move. What if the guards heard the bang and the shooting? They could be lining up to kill all of the hostages right now."

Santelli's lips tightened as he looked down at the prisoner. "Hang in there, buddy," he said, even though he was pretty sure the man wasn't even aware of him anymore, "We'll go get the rest, then come back for you, all right?" He'd get Doc Villareal to help. Had to put that big-ass med bag to some use. That was why they'd brought the doctor in the first place.

If the wounded man heard him, he gave no sign. Whatever the torturer had done to him, it had gone past the point of interrogation. The man was dying, and as much as he hated it, Santelli could see it. He heaved himself up, blood soaking the knees of his fatigues, and joined Childress at the door.

"What the hell?" Childress asked. "Why would they torture the hostages? What does it get 'em?"

"Probably just for kicks," Santelli growled. "I never yet saw a jihadi who wasn't also a sadistic piece of shit." He bumped Childress. "With you."

They went through the door and found themselves in another vaulted room, not unlike the torture chamber behind them. The far door was shut, and this room was empty, the dust of centuries settled on the floor.

They hurried across the room, Santelli turning halfway to check behind them one more time. As he did so, he saw the alcove with another door in the dimly lit wall to their right.

"Hey, Childress," he hissed, getting a sudden hunch. "Let's go that way."

The layout of the cellar so far did not match the palace above. It seemed to him like a series of chambers, running roughly north to south. If his sense of direction wasn't all screwed up, that door to their right should lead to another chamber beneath the courtyard, between the arms of the U-shaped Citadel.

It was as logical a place as he could think of to store hostages, if you were going to secure them in the cellar.

The door was not large; Childress was going to have to duck to get through it. Santelli figured that was probably intentional.

Since he had spotted it first, he got to it first, stacking up on the door, his muzzle pointed at the edge where the door met the jamb. That was where the handle was; since he couldn't see any hinges, he had to assume that was where the door would open.

Childress slid to the opposite side of the door, pulled out another flashbang, prepped it, and then grasped the door handle.

It didn't budge. Childress pushed harder. Nothing. The handle had no latch. It was barred from the other side.

Well, in Santelli's mind, there were few such problems that Mr. High Explosives could not fix.

Swinging the assault pack off his back, he fished inside and pulled out a block of Semtex, identical to the one Brannigan had used on the sally port gate. His thick fingers moved quickly, mashing the yellow-orange plastic explosive into the joint roughly where he figured the bar should be, then quickly priming it and yanking the initiator. "We might want to get into the next room," he whispered. The overpressure in that confined space was going to be murder.

It was probably going to do a number on the hostages if they were on the other side, too, but if they didn't get in there, the hostages were dead anyway. With the time fuse smoking, the two of them dashed for the torture room, got around the corner, ducked their heads, and opened their mouths to keep the overpressure from rupturing anything.

The *crack* of the charge going off was like the world itself splitting asunder. Even with a wall of stone between them and the explosion, the concussion had nowhere to go but through the passageways of the cellar, and they still got rocked.

It must have really sucked to be on the other side of that door. Santelli found himself hoping one or two of the Iranians had gotten close to investigate Childress' rattling of the door.

They didn't have long to capitalize on the shock of the breaching charge. Santelli led the way out the door, his rifle already up and ready.

As he'd entered the torture room, he'd seen just enough to know that the mutilated man he'd taken down from the ceiling was already dead.

He charged the still-smoking portal. The door had been blasted to fragments and splinters, a smashed collection of shattered timbers still vaguely held together by the iron bars that formed its frame. There was a bite taken out right where the door handle had been. That part of the door was just *gone*.

Santelli's boot thudded into the remains of the door, and he almost put his foot clear through it, drawing back just enough to avoid getting tangled as the remains of wood and twisted iron juddered inward.

His near-entanglement with the door slowed his entry, but as he bulled through the ruins and into the room, it was evident that they still had a few seconds to work with.

As he'd suspected, the room was a long rectangle, that would have almost perfectly fit in the courtyard above. More columns held up the sandstone ceiling, and there were hostages sitting, their hands bound behind their backs, against the columns. Many of those closest to the door had caught fragmentation from the breaching charge, and were bleeding.

One of the guards, a towering, bald-headed Iranian with a thick hedge of black beard, had been standing a bit too close to the door when the breach went off. He was down on the floor, groaning, a chunk of wood embedded in the back of his thigh. Blood was pumping out of the wound, around the jagged obstruction, pulsing in a way that suggested his femoral was cut. He didn't have long for the world.

He must have sensed that, because he rolled over as the two mercenaries came through the door, struggling to bring his rifle up. Childress shot him with a pair of two-round bursts to the chest, the noise of the gunshots reverberating painfully through the room and making the hostages flinch.

The Iranian shuddered under the impacts, but didn't die. Spitting blood, he tried to lift his rifle again, and Childress and

Santelli both shot him in the head, blowing the top of his skull off with a trio of 5.45 rounds.

There wasn't time to dwell on the kill; there was another guard at the far end, who was already behind a column, his Type 03 muzzle sticking out into the room. He triggered a burst at them, more noise hammering back and forth through the room, flame spitting from the barrel and bullets smacking grit and rock fragments off the wall above the door, narrowly missing Santelli's head. He dove for the nearest column, getting behind it as another burst ripped through the air, just inches from his head.

He was sure that the man wasn't really aiming; there was no way he should have missed at that range. Either that, or the Man Upstairs really wanted Mama Santelli's baby boy to stick around a little bit longer.

Childress fired a rattling burst from one of the other columns across the room. The younger man had even less of a shot than Santelli did; he had all of the columns on that side of the room between him and the gunman. But he was providing Santelli with some cover fire, and the shots from the hidden Iranian ceased as the man flinched away from Childress' bullets.

Santelli took a breath, then swung around the back side of the column and dashed down the line, almost tripping over hostages who had shrunk back behind the columns to try to get out of the line of fire. He didn't go the full length of the room; that would have been tempting fate a bit too much. Instead, he recited the old Marine Corps mantra in his head, "I'm up, he sees me, I'm down," and at, "I'm down," he thudded into another column, putting it between him and the guard.

Just in time, too. The Iranian, while having taken cover from Childress' fire, had evidently seen him running, and bullets blasted more fragments off the column even as he took cover behind it. Childress responded with a long burst, emptying the rest of his mag, and in the corresponding lull, Santelli swung around the back of the column behind his AK, looking for his target.

It wasn't an easy shot; the man had huddled back in the shadows behind the column, trying to avoid the roaring, crackling stream of bullets digging pockmarks out of the far wall. All that

Santelli could see was the silhouette of the man's left side, along with about half his head.

It was enough. Santelli was a good shooter; he always had been. He'd considered it vital to being a Marine, and had looked upon other Senior NCOs who no longer bothered with marksmanship as slackers and detriments to the reputation of the Corps.

As Childress ran dry and the Iranian leaned out to open fire again, Santelli squeezed the trigger. It broke as cleanly as he ever expected a Kalashnikov trigger to break, and a single round blasted through the Iranian's left eye, yawed sharply, and blew out the base of his skull. Body and rifle hit the floor with a clatter.

Santelli moved quickly, finishing his run along the long wall, visually clearing the door as he crossed it, and kicked the weapon away from the Iranian's lifeless hands. All that he'd seen in the chamber on the far side had been a sleeping mat, some rations, and a lantern. The room had been otherwise empty, unless there was another man hiding in the shadows. He kept one eye on the door as Childress moved to check on the hostages.

"SMaj?" Childress called out. Santelli was going to have to tell him to cut that out. They were both contractors, mercenaries. He wasn't a Sergeant Major anymore, and Childress wasn't his problem child anymore, either. But it could wait.

"What is it, Sam?" he asked.

"I don't think these are our hostages," Childress said. There was a definite note of uncertainty in his voice.

Without ever taking his eyes entirely off the open door, Santelli moved toward the center of the room where Childress was standing over one of the bound men sitting on the floor, the muzzle of his AK-12 pointed down, away from the hostages, but not too far away. Childress might not have had much of a filter on his mouth, but he was a careful man with his weapons.

The lanky young man was staring down at one of the hostages who was sitting against one of the pillars. Santelli risked looking away from the door he was covering to give the man a once-over.

He stopped, a frown creasing his forehead, and looked again. He scanned the entire group. "Who the hell are you?"

These men were obviously not Americans. They were uniformly Arabs, and they were also in uniform. Or at least the filthy, tattered remains of uniforms. And Santelli thought he recognized those uniforms.

They weren't Khadarkhi Army, either. They were Saudi.

"What the hell is going on here?" Santelli muttered. "Does anyone here speak English?" His Arabic was limited to a handful of phrases that he might be able to remember after a long bit of study and recollection, and they were all in the Iraqi dialect, that was supposed to be damned near gibberish to the rest of the Arab world.

He got nothing but glares.

"You'd think they'd be a bit more grateful that they just got their asses rescued from the torturers," Childress drawled. "Besides, aren't the Saudis supposed to be our friends?"

Santelli shot the younger man a glance. He hadn't known that their backwoods yokel could recognize Saudi uniforms, too. "Saudis ain't friends with anybody," he said. "And I've got a sudden sneaking, nasty suspicion that these guys are a good part of why there's a small army of Al Qaeda fighters out in town right now."

"Well, if these aren't the guys we're looking for, what do we do with 'em?" Childress asked. "Time's a-wasting."

Santelli thought for a moment, then spat out a curse. "We can't just leave 'em here," he said. "I might hate their guts as much as they hate mine, but they're tied up and helpless, and we know for a fact what the Iranians are gonna do to 'em. Get 'em up. We'll take 'em with us." He blew a breath out past his nose. "John and Roger are going to have to find the hostages. They're not down here."

185

CHAPTER 15

Flanagan ducked under the camo netting as Curtis set in in the prone behind his PKP. Presuming the missiles were fueled, he had enough explosives between the two of them to make the whole row go boom, and he was already planning out how to do it. There was no way he was leaving these things in the hands of a bunch of Iranian psychopaths.

It wasn't a strategic decision born of a deep understanding of terrorism and geopolitics, though Flanagan knew quite a bit more about both subjects than his laconic speech usually let on. No, this was a simple recognition that the Iranians, who probably chanted, "Death to America!" on rising every morning, were his country's enemies, and he wasn't going to leave them a weapon when he was already engaged and had an opportunity to take it out of their hands.

It was the right thing to do, so he was going to do it. He certainly didn't have a chain of command worried about political fallout to tell him not to.

As he studied the missile through his NVGs, he started to frown. Something was off. He'd seen plenty of pictures of Iranian missiles, and while he hadn't exactly memorized profiles, these seemed different, somehow. And when he moved down the length of the deadly cylinder, he saw something that convinced him. "Kev!" he hissed. "Come here and look at this!"

"I'm holding security, damn it," Curtis stage-whispered back. "Just describe it to me. I know, too many words make your head hurt, but I've got the machinegun and a line of sight on the gate."

"There's an insignia stenciled on the side of this missile," Flanagan said, ignoring Curtis' jab. "It's a circle, with a palm tree and crossed scimitars inside. Sound familiar?"

"I don't know!" Curtis said. "I'm not an insignia encyclopedia! It may as well say, 'Derka, Derka, Mohammed Jihad' to me."

Flanagan ducked out from under the camo netting and crouched in the darkness beside Curtis. "It's a Saudi military insignia," he said. "Those aren't Iranian missiles."

When Curtis didn't say anything for a moment, Flanagan glanced down at the little man. He knew Curtis well enough to know that the man was more of a thinker than his exuberant party animal persona betrayed. And the fact that he didn't have a flippant comment ready meant that he was rolling the implications around in his head.

"Can you tell what the warheads are?" Curtis asked, his voice serious.

"No, this isn't the movies," Flanagan replied. "There's not going to be a big nuclear trefoil or biohazard symbol painted on the warheads."

"What the hell are Saudi missiles doing here, with Iranians holding the island?" Curtis asked.

"My guess is that the Saudis put them here for a first-strike capability on Iran itself," Flanagan mused. "Which means the Iranians probably came here specifically to capture them."

"You mean the Iranians are the good guys?" Curtis asked incredulously.

Flanagan snorted. "Not hardly. There is such a thing as bad guys and bad guys, you know. If you read more history and fewer comic books you might understand that."

"Then I'd be as boring as you," Curtis replied. "What are we gonna do?"

"Rig the missiles to blow," Flanagan said. "Same as before. Give me your Semtex and cover me."

"Nah, I'll come with you," Curtis said. "You'd just cut off my field of fire." He scrambled to a knee and hefted the PKP. "This is why I have muscles; to run and gun with the machinegun."

"Oh, horseshit," Flanagan retorted. "You didn't know you were going to even touch a machinegun again until a week ago. They're beach muscles, that's it."

"I'll have you know, Joseph," Curtis said, "that I am *always* ready to drop everything at a moment's notice to go on a top-secret commando raid on Val Verde. Don't you doubt me."

"That, or a raid on Macho Grande," Flanagan whispered sarcastically. "Sure." He paused suddenly, throwing up a silencing hand with a sharp, "*Shh!*" before Curtis could retort. "You hear that?"

"Hear what?" Curtis asked. "There's still some shooting going on out in town."

"Yeah, that's what I'm talking about," Flanagan said. "It's dying down."

Curtis cocked his head to listen. "You think our diversion's ending?" he asked.

"Either that, or the Iranians are recalling their forces to come back here and deal with us," Flanagan said ominously. "Whatever it is, we don't have a lot of time. If you're going to be my Semtex mule, then let's go."

"I am nobody's mule!" Curtis hissed. "I am volunteering to help your ungrateful ass out from the goodness of my heart."

Flanagan didn't bother to reply, but got up and headed for the far missile carrier, his rifle at the ready. They hadn't seen any movement in that direction in a few minutes, but that could change at any time.

He could almost hear Curtis fuming behind him at his silence. He allowed himself a quick, tight smile of satisfaction, just for a moment.

There was still quite a bit of gunfire crackling through the night, out by the barbican gate, but at least for the moment, there weren't any Iranian shooters pushing into the outer courtyard. They reached the last missile without being spotted, or even seeing any of the enemy, and Flanagan ducked under the camo netting while Curtis got back down in the dirt with his PKP, aiming it toward the narrow part of the courtyard that led toward the barbican. There were a couple of stairways lining the wall that lead up to the battlements, and he kept glancing up at them, too, but the barbican was the most likely place the bad guys would come from, so that was where he was keeping his weapon pointed.

Flanagan crouched next to the hulking missile carrier, pulling his pack off his back and rummaging around in it for his explosives, fuse, and primers. Flanagan would never style himself an "explosives expert," but the truth was, he knew how to blow some stuff up, using just enough boom to get the desired effect.

Hastily stripping the wrapper off a block of Semtex, he carved it in half with his knife, shoving one half back in the wrapper, then mashing the other against the body of the missile, just above the engines. He hoped that the missiles were fueled, but even if they weren't, blowing a hole in the fuel tanks was going to ground them permanently anyway.

He grabbed his time fuse and hesitated. Set it too long, and somebody could cut it and keep the charges from going off. Set it too short, and they would probably all die before they could get out of the outer courtyard. If the missiles really were fueled, the fireball in that relatively confined space was going to be truly impressive.

And if there were CBRN warheads on the missiles, then blowing them up while the mercenaries and the hostages were still inside the Citadel was probably going to be fatal to all of them, anyway.

He finally figured out what should be a decent balance, cut the fuse based on the test burn he'd done on the dhow, and quickly primed the charge with blasting cap, fuse, and igniter. He thought for a second, then shoved the entire priming system under the missile body. He'd get the rest of the charges set before he pulled the igniter on any of them.

"Joe, you might want to hurry up," Curtis hissed. "I think we've got company coming."

"One's done," Flanagan replied. "Back to the next."

"Did you initiate already?" Curtis sounded like he wasn't sure if he should hope that Flanagan had, or be horrified that he'd pulled already, with the two of them still that close.

"No, not yet," Flanagan answered. "Move!"

Ducking under the camo netting, he dashed back toward the second missile, dragging his pack in one hand instead of trying to sling it over his shoulder again. Time was pressing. He thought he could hear shooting from somewhere up in the Citadel, though it was muffled. Not only were the returning Iranians a problem, but if the rest of the team came tearing back down from the keep with the hostages in tow, they were going to need to get moving with a quickness, and he wanted all of the missiles ready to go by then.

He quickly repeated the process with the second missile, while Curtis dropped to the dirt with a *thud*, training his PKP back toward the barbican. A moment later, Flanagan flinched involuntarily as the night was torn apart by a long, stuttering burst of machinegun fire, flame strobing from the muzzle of the Pecheneg. "We've got company!" Curtis yelled.

Flanagan dropped to the ground, unslinging his AK and scrambling to get it pointed toward the barbican. He couldn't see any targets; whoever had been trying to push into the outer courtyard had been forced back by Curtis' machinegun fire.

It wasn't going to last, though, and he was all too aware of the presence of the hulking APC with its 20mm cannon parked against the wall. Where there was one, there were more, and he suspected that the rest were somewhere out in the Old City, and probably on their way back.

And the RPGs were still stacked back at the breach. If those AFVs came rumbling back through the gate, it was going to be a long, long sprint back to get them. But hauling them along with his pack, ammo, and rifle hadn't seemed like a good idea, if they wanted to stay stealthy.

There was movement in the gap. Muzzle flashes strobed in the darkness, and bullets *snapped* overhead. They didn't seem to be getting very close, though. Flanagan realized that the Iranians were trying not to hit the missiles. *Smart of 'em.*

He fired a burst in reply, his own muzzle blast kicking up dust and grit in front of him. Curtis' machinegun roared again, the blast spattering him with sand. At least one of the dim shapes by the wall crumpled.

Hurry up, guys. We are not going to be able to hold this for long.

***

Stealth was now out. That was why Brannigan came off the stairs and ran down the hall. He wasn't quite sprinting; he didn't want to barrel straight into an Iranian shooter that happened to pop out of a room. But he wasn't being slow and smooth, either. They had to get to that top hall before the Iranians killed all the hostages.

He came around the corner, facing a set of double doors nearly identical to the ones a floor below. If these were of a slightly different shade of green, it hardly mattered. The layout of the portal was the same.

Hancock sprinted up alongside Brannigan, and they hit the doors at the same time. Boots hammered against the central latch, and the doors slammed open with a *bang*.

They were up on their sights as soon as they each got both feet back on the floor, pushing in and spreading out from the doorway. Brannigan shot an Iranian in the side of the head before the man could fire the rifle he had trained on the hostages huddled against the pillars. The man's head snapped to one side and he collapsed, blood pouring from the paired holes in his skull.

Hancock sidestepped out of the doorway and farther from Brannigan's line of fire before taking the longer shot across the length of the room at the guard stationed by the far door. It was a hasty shot, and the two-round burst blew a good-sized chunk of meat out of the Iranian's shoulder. The man slumped back against the wall, dropping his rifle and grabbing his mangled shoulder, and slid to the floor with a scream, leaving a long red smear on the stone and tile behind him. Hancock shot him a second time, unwilling to take the chance that he'd get over his shock and pain long enough to grab for his weapon again. They'd already seen enough evidence that the Iranians were fanatics. The first round shattered the man's forearm before burying itself in the bottom of his lung. The second ripped through his chest, shattering his sternum before yawing to blast out the side of his armpit. He slid the rest of the way to the floor, groaning and dying.

Brannigan hadn't missed a stride as he'd gunned down his target. A quick clear of the corner was enough to assure him that the two Iranians had been the only ones stationed in the room with the hostages, and he moved quickly to the far door, looking for something to use as a barricade. Conveniently enough, there was a crate set against the wall, with a pile of filthy, battered tin plates on it. It looked like it had been used to serve the hostages their meals.

It wasn't much, but it would have to do. Letting his AK dangle on its sling, he put a hand to the crate, set his feet, and shoved. It scraped across the floor slowly; he had no idea what might be in it, but it was heavy enough that it just might do the trick. It took a moment to get it positioned across the double doors.

He got it in place not a moment too soon. The doors banged partway open, hitting the crate after the first few inches, and he heard what sounded like a loud oath in Farsi from the other side. Flipping his selector to full auto, Brannigan brought his AK to his shoulder and hammered a long burst through the doors, bullets chewing holes in the wood, along with any flesh that might be on the other side. There were yells and screams on the other side, and he followed up by dumping the rest of the mag through the doors as he moved out of the line of fire.

Hancock was already at work behind him. "Who's in charge here?" he bellowed. It was a voice that demanded immediate attention and an immediate answer. Roger had been a good Staff NCO, and a good platoon sergeant, and he had the voice to go along with it.

"I guess I am," a stout older man with a mustache replied after a moment's hesitation. "I'm Captain Ortiz, skipper of the *Oceana Metropolis*."

"We're here to get you out, Captain," Hancock said. "Can any of you shoot?"

"Are you Navy SEALs?" a middle-aged woman asked.

Brannigan couldn't help but laugh as he reloaded, taking up a position that offered some cover from one of the columns, where he could still cover the door with his rifle, and keep himself and his gun between the door and the hostages.

"Just answer the damned question!" Hancock barked. "We don't have time. If anyone knows how to run a gun, grab those Type 03s and some spare mags."

"The Iranians killed all of our security contractors," Ortiz said, as he heaved himself to his feet.

"Then you're going to have to fight for yourselves," Hancock said, ripping the Chinese rifle away from the Iranian that Brannigan had killed and shoving it at the ship captain. "There are still too many of them, and not enough of us. Just try not to shoot any of us." He pointed to another man and said, "You! Go grab that other rifle. You ever fired a gun before?"

"Grew up with one," the sailor replied, as he ducked across the room, at least having the good sense to cross the danger area from the doors as fast as he could. He jogged over to the second corpse, where he hesitated for a moment, as if afraid to touch the dead body, then gingerly retrieved the Iranian's rifle. "Never used one of these before, though."

"Figure it out quick," Hancock told him.

Brannigan was frowning as he kept his eyes and his muzzle on the door. The enemy hadn't tried to enter again, and it was making him nervous. "Doc!" he shouted. "You've got thirty seconds to make sure nobody's hurt bad enough that they can't run or climb, then we've got to go."

Villareal hadn't needed the prompting. He had been right behind Brannigan and Hancock as they'd made entry, and had immediately started checking each of the hostages, even before the shooting stopped. "They're malnourished and dehydrated, but none of them appear to be seriously injured," he reported, shortly after Brannigan had finished speaking. "I think we're good to go."

Brannigan nodded without looking back. Villareal might have had some hangups when it came to killing, but he was still no coward. "All right. Captain Ortiz? Come here a second."

The portly merchant skipper stepped closer, and Brannigan spared him a glance. The man's face was drawn and gray, with dark circles under haunted eyes. He'd seen several men he had considered members of his own crew, and at least one fellow hostage, murdered before his eyes. But he was holding it together, and the hands holding the blood-spattered Chinese rifle didn't shake. He'd do, at least for long enough.

"We've got boats at the base of the cliff," Brannigan explained hastily. "I need you and your people to stick close and move fast, and I need you and your crewman to be ready to fight. Can you do that?"

"If it means getting out of here, we can do whatever we need to," Ortiz replied.

"But where are the helicopters?" the middle-aged woman asked. "Aren't the rest of the terrorists dead?"

"Ma'am, we had to come in quietly to do this," Brannigan explained quickly, before Hancock could respond rather more acerbically. "There are only a few of us, and there are a lot more of them." When she opened her mouth to protest in disbelief, he cut her off. "Look, ma'am, it is what it is, all right? We can't change the situation by thinking that it should be different. Just stick close, move fast, and we'll get you out of here alive." *Hopefully*, he didn't add. The continuing quiet from the other side of the door was starting to bother him. He was getting that hackle-raising feeling that the Iranians had decided to change tactics, and were about to spring a nasty surprise on them.

"Ready when you are, Mr..." Ortiz said.

"Brannigan," was the reply. "Roger, lead out!" he called. "Back the way we came!" He was pretty sure that going through the barricaded door was going to lead them into an Iranian ambush.

"Come on, on me!" Hancock barked, turning toward the open door. "You, with the rifle! What's your name?"

"Thomas," was the shaky response. The kid was sandy-haired and beefy, with a corn-fed Midwestern look to him that matched his accent.

"Thomas, stick close to me, and be careful where you point that thing," Hancock said. "If we run into trouble, it's you and me, all right?" The veteran probably wasn't all that comfortable with having such an unknown quantity as backup, but necessity was the mother of sucking it up and making do. "Let's go." With a shuffle of confusion, the hostages started to follow, clumping together behind Hancock and Thomas.

"Stick with me, Captain," Brannigan said. "We'll cover the rear." Keeping his muzzle trained on the blocked door, Brannigan started to side-step after Hancock and the retreating hostages.

**

Esfandiari took a long step back and flattened himself against the wall as the rattling burst of gunfire punched through the doors and ripped into Ghorbani's chest. The man was smashed back into the hall, blood gouting from a dozen wounds as he flopped to the floor, twitching the last few pain-wracked seconds of his life away.

Abbasi started to move forward, but Esfandiari put a hand out to forestall him, just before another burst tore through the wood of the door. To enter that doorway was going to be instant death, and Esfandiari knew it. Especially if the door was barricaded, they'd never manage to force their way through with the four men he had left.

He'd been paying attention to the radio as they had ascended. There were more enemy fighters in the courtyard, near the Saudi Dongfeng 3 ballistic missiles. Losing the missiles was even more of a threat to the operation than the potential loss of the hostages.

Just before Esfandiari had reached the top floor, Farroukhshad had reported that the bulk of the apostate fighters in the Old City had been driven off. Esfandiari had recalled the rest of his forces back to the Citadel immediately. The enemy in their midst was far more of a threat than the poorly-trained apostates outside.

"We must return to the gate and regroup with Farroukhshad," Esfandiari said, coming to a decision. "If we can secure the outer grounds, the infidel commandos and the hostages will have nowhere to go. And we can drive them away from the missiles with the APCs." He turned and started back toward the stairs. "But we must hurry."

CHAPTER 16

"Cover me!" Flanagan snapped. "I'm going to have to do this the hard way."

"What the hell do you think I'm doing?" Curtis replied, between long, hammering bursts of machinegun fire. More Iranian troops were moving around near the barbican, visible as little more than dark shadows occasionally lit by muzzle flashes as they fired at the two mercenaries, though their reticence to shoot too close to the missiles was hampering their efforts. They weren't getting close enough to hit either man. The bullets were either going high, or skipping off the ground off to the right.

Curtis didn't have any such compunctions. Another long burst ripped through the darkness and smashed an Iranian who had stepped out into the courtyard off his feet. The stream of lead, copper, and steel hit right about at knee-level, chopping the man's legs out from under him before slamming into his chest and head as he fell.

Flanagan dug into his pack, pulling all of his demo supplies out and shoving them behind the tire of the nearest missile carrier. He was acutely aware of the nearness of the gigantic bomb over his head; if a stray round were to hit that seven-and-a-half-foot diameter tank of rocket fuel, he was probably going to be instantly vaporized.

Working as fast as he could, getting thumped by the muzzle blast from the PKP, since Curtis had shimmied closer to the missiles as he'd figured out that the Iranians didn't want to shoot too close to them, he started building his charges. If he had to run down the line under fire, slapping charges in place as he went, that was what it would take. But he'd have them prepped first; building each charge as they went didn't seem like a good idea anymore.

He had four more charges ready go when he heard an ominous rattle in the night, and Curtis yelled, "Oh, shit!"

The passage leading to the barbican gate was now filled with a hulking mass of steel and treads, topped by a 20mm cannon. The Iranians had brought at least one of the AMX-10s back inside.

The turret swung, and the cannon belched flame, the thunder of its hammering reports making Curtis' PKP sound like a popgun by comparison. 20mm shells thundered by overhead, the tracers briefly lighting the courtyard with actinic flashes before sailing out through the gap in the wall and over the ocean.

"They still don't want to shoot too close to the missiles!" Flanagan shouted. "We've still got a few minutes!"

"What a time for you to become an optimist!" Curtis all but screamed. "They can still roll up on us and shoot us like fish in a barrel! I can't scratch that fucking thing!"

"Fall back!" Flanagan yelled at him. "I'll place charges as we go! Just stay close to the missile carriers!"

The AMX was advancing, the treads squealing and rattling. The dim forms of more Iranian fighters could be seen jogging behind it. Another raving burst of 20mm fire split the night, but it was still too far off target to be much more than merely terrifying.

Cursing, Curtis scrambled to his feet, hauling the Pecheneg off the ground. He stayed on a knee at first, leveling the machinegun and sending another burst at the oncoming troops behind the APC. Bullets skipped off the vehicle's armored flanks, but did little more than that.

Flanagan was already moving, but he wasn't falling back, not yet. Even as Curtis screamed at him, he dashed forward to the first missile, now only a few dozen meters from the advancing

AMX, reached into the gap, and yanked the igniter. Then he ran back to the next and did the same with that charge before running to the third, slapping a charge on the side of the missile body, and popping smoke.

"You're going to get my ass killed, you crazy fucking cracker!" Curtis yelled between bursts as he fell back alongside Flanagan. "If the fucking *armored vehicle* doesn't get us, then you're going to turn us all into a fucking fireball!"

For once, Flanagan didn't have a comeback, and his silence wasn't calculated to get a rise out of his old friend. He was breathing hard, his AK bouncing against his side, as he ran from missile to missile, pausing only just long enough to pull a charge out of his pack, slap it against the missile, and prime it before running to the next. And that APC was getting closer and closer with each second, advancing faster than he or Curtis could run. As soon as it was close enough, a gunman could conceivably shoot them down from one of the top hatches without risking hitting the missiles in the process.

Movement caught his eye as he ran to the second-to-last missile. Someone was in the breach, and for a second, he thought he was dead. One of the Iranians had somehow managed to get around behind them, and they were cut off.

But then the figure hauled itself the rest of the way up the rope, grabbed the tube of an RPG from the stack they had left next to the wall, and aimed it at the AMX-10. Flanagan had just enough time to throw himself flat before the RPG fired with an earsplitting *bang*.

The projectile bounced off the APC's front glacis plate, hissing into the sky before detonating high above. But it was enough to give the AMX driver pause, and the APC suddenly stopped and reversed, the gunner trying to depress the turret at the same time that the figure with the RPG 27 tossed the spent tube and grabbed for another one.

Flanagan dropped his pack, pulling his AK around to the front and sending half a mag roaring at the turret. The bullets wouldn't do any good against the armor, but he was hoping he might damage the sights or the vision blocks. That was possible, anyway, even if it wasn't probable.

The man with the RPG got the tube back on his shoulder and fired again, before the cannon depressed all the way. The shock of the launch slapped against Flanagan as the projectile roared past him, then it hit the turret ring and detonated.

With a flash and a bone-shaking *wham*, the turret blew off, sending the 20mm tumbling end over end through the air. Flanagan flattened himself against the ground, praying that the cannon wasn't about to land on top of one of the missiles. They probably would not survive the resulting chain reaction.

But the remains of the turret came down on the back deck of the APC with an ear-shattering *clang,* even as the armored fighting vehicle started to burn. The 7.62 ammunition for the coaxial machinegun started to cook off with a loud crackling noise, the bullets hissing through the air when they weren't hitting the inside of the vehicle with muted *pings*.

Flanagan wasn't as worried about the cook-off; contrary to Hollywood, exploding rounds in a fire didn't end up having much velocity. They could still hurt, but it wasn't quite the same thing as being shot. And any that might possibly hit them were getting launched up through the turret ring.

Of course, what goes up must come down, and there was a *lot* of very volatile rocket fuel not very far away. Even so, there simply wasn't time to worry about it.

He got up and continued his dash down the line of missiles, setting charges as he went. The fire coming from the direction of the gate had fallen away to almost nothing, between the shock of the explosion and the simple obstruction of a burning armored vehicle in the middle of the courtyard. Another one could still get by, but none of the Iranians seemed to be in a hurry to get too close to the stricken APC.

Flanagan was grateful that he couldn't hear the screaming that was presumably coming from what was left of the crew.

He got to the last missile, Curtis only a few paces behind him, slapped his last charge in place, and yanked the igniter. He could smell the sweetish smoke of the burning time fuse, and then he ran to join the figure next to the RPGs, who was now on a knee in the shadows, AK-12 up and trained on the far end of the courtyard.

"I was starting to think you weren't going to show up," Flanagan said.

"I almost didn't," Aziz said seriously. "This is still nuts."

"Well, for what it's worth, I'm glad you did," Flanagan said, overcoming his instinctive dislike of the other man enough to say it. "We'd have been toast if you hadn't."

"Does that mean I get a cut of your share?" Aziz asked.

Flanagan looked at him. That hadn't had the tone of a joke, but then, he didn't know Aziz well enough to know if he just had one of those dry senses of humor that made it hard to tell. "Fuck you," he replied.

Aziz just shrugged. "So much for gratitude."

Curtis glanced back at them, first at Aziz, then at Flanagan. He didn't say anything, but his shrug when he looked at Flanagan spoke eloquently enough. *What's this guy's problem?*

Flanagan shrugged back. There would be time enough to confront Aziz about his attitude when they weren't in the middle of a firefight with their backs to a hundred foot drop over the ocean. He got down in the prone and pointed his AK toward the far end, checking his watch.

The rest needed to hurry. Those fuses weren't going to burn forever.

***

Santelli wasn't comfortable with the situation. Childress was on point, with Santelli taking up the rear, and the Saudis between them. He'd distrusted the lot of them enough to have left their hands flex-cuffed behind their backs, but there were still ten of them between him and Childress if things went south, and he didn't trust any of them farther than he could drop-kick them. The kid was way too exposed, but he didn't see any other way to go.

Childress disappeared up the stairs, going around the turn at the landing, and Santelli gave the Saudi ahead of him, who was being slow and mulish, another shove. "Come on, move," he snarled. "Unless you want to stay here and die." The look he got for the shove deepened his suspicion that the Saudis spoke English as well as Arabic, but the skinny man didn't say anything.

He had already picked out a couple of separate groups among the Saudis. There were the tight-lipped, angry-looking ones, mostly with thin beards or mustaches, who gave him and Childress the stink-eye every chance they got. The others were the skinny, scared ones, who deferred to the angry ones. He figured that the angry ones were the officers, or at least whoever was in charge.

The angry ones seemed to be intent on making things as difficult as possible. They'd obviously figured out that their "rescuers" were Americans, and they didn't like it. Which made Santelli that much more suspicious about this whole setup. Between the missiles in the courtyard and the sullen Saudi prisoners in the cellar that seemed to hate their rescuers as much as they hated their captors, he smelled a rat.

"Friendly!" he heard Childress call from up above. He couldn't hear the response, but as he came up around the corner, he saw Brannigan and a portly man, going bald, carrying a rifle, at the rear of a knot of people who were clearly Americans. Hancock was ahead, already stacking on the door to the anteroom that led out toward the helipad.

Childress was moving forward, and Santelli turned his full attention to the Saudis. One of them, a taller man with cadaverous features and burning dark eyes, was watching Childress intently, looking around the hallway as if looking for an opportunity.

"Hey, you!" Santelli yelled at him. When the man turned bitter, contemptuous eyes on him, he moved his AK's muzzle fractionally, just enough to be a threat. "Don't get any funny ideas," he warned.

The Saudi stared at him for a moment. This wasn't the picture of the Saudis that most Americans got. This man was as just as much of a fanatic as the Iranians. But he finally looked away as Santelli stared him down.

Childress moved up and joined Hancock, along with a big, blond, corn-fed kid who was also carrying one of the Iranians' rifles. Together, they flowed into the anteroom, clearing it before bringing the hostages in. Santelli moved up, herding the Saudis against the wall, making sure the American hostages were secured first. He didn't want his charges getting too mixed with the Americans. It might make matters a bit sticky once they got out where bullets were flying again.

Especially if these guys were the hard-core Wahhabis that he suspected some of them were. The Saudis were always treading a fine line between courting the West for influence and supporting the fanatics.

"Carlo?" Brannigan asked, as he paused next to Santelli. "Who the hell are these guys?"

"Saudi prisoners," Santelli explained as they chivvied the Saudis through the door and set up security on the hallway, just in case. "Found 'em down in the cellars. The Iranians were torturing one; he didn't make it. Couldn't just leave 'em there." Although he was already starting to wish that he had.

"Hell," Brannigan muttered. "It's all starting to make sense now."

"What is?"

"Doc found a targeting map upstairs, with targets marked inside Iran," Brannigan explained quickly. "And there are Saudi prisoners here, in uniform. I don't think those missiles out in the courtyard are Iranian, Carlo. I think we stumbled into the middle of a new phase of the Saudi-Iranian proxy war."

"As in, it ain't gonna be quite so 'proxy' anymore?" Santelli asked.

"Looks that way." Brannigan spared a glance over his shoulder. "Captain Ortiz? Can you take up security on this door for a moment?"

The portly man with the rifle complied, asking, "What do I do?"

"Point your rifle down the hall, that way," Brannigan instructed. "If anyone comes down that hall, shoot 'em."

Ortiz nodded. "Easy enough," he said. He stationed himself at the threshold, his rifle pointed back toward the stairs at the end of the hall.

***

Brannigan turned and stared at the group of Saudis, which were now grouped in one corner. He was wet, dirty, his face darkened by smoke, and he towered over all of them, his AK cradled in his big hands, ready to snap into action.

"Who's in charge here?" he demanded. "And don't even try to bullshit me and pretend that none of you speak English. I will kneecap every one of you and leave you here if you try." His voice left no room for interpretation. He was dead serious.

"I am," a cadaverous-looking man with angry black eyes replied, in heavily-accented English.

"Who are you, and what are you doing here?" Brannigan asked. "I'm presuming those are your missiles out in the courtyard, not the Iranians'?"

The man said nothing, his mouth pressed into a thin line. Brannigan brought the muzzle of his rifle up fractionally. "Clock's ticking, friend," he said.

"We have the right to set up defenses on the territory of an ally," the man said tightly.

"Except I don't think those are defenses," Brannigan said. "Let me guess; the warheads are CBRN? Probably chemical. What's the agent? Sarin? VX?"

The man's eyes had flickered slightly. "Sarin, then. No wonder you people didn't want the Navy anywhere near this place. Word might get out that Riyadh's got chemical weapons, and was positioning them for a first strike on Iran."

The sounds of combat from outside were intensifying. Brannigan didn't break his stare, although every eye suddenly jerked toward the door leading outside, as the unmistakable thunder of a 20mm cannon sounded somewhere outside, entirely too close. A moment later, there was a pair of loud thunderclaps that could only be RPG detonations.

"Can we continue this conversation later?" Hancock yelled from the doorway. "It's getting hot out there, and we need to move if we're going to get out at all!"

Brannigan turned a basilisk glare on the lead Saudi. "I'm still half-inclined to leave you here. We came for the Americans, not for you."

"If we leave them here, then the Iranians are going to murder them all as soon as we leave," Villareal protested. "I don't like it either, and it's going to be tight, getting everybody onto the boats, but we can't just leave them to the mullahs' mad dogs." He paused, then added, "Besides, if this situation is as serious as it sounds, they might provide some important intel to somebody back Stateside."

Brannigan didn't say what he thought of that proposition. He'd address it later; Hancock was right. They had to get moving. He jerked a thumb toward the outside. "Get moving. If one of you twitches wrong, I'll blow his head off. I don't trust any of you, understand?"

He *really* didn't like this situation. If the Saudis hadn't been mean-mugging them with every step, he might have been able to simply treat them as nothing other than more hostages than they had planned on. But there was something sinister about the entire setup, and he couldn't help but think that the Saudis would do their damnedest to bury him and his men if they ever found out that they knew about this little operation in would-be mass murder.

He'd deal with that when they weren't about to be overrun by angry Iranians.

Hancock and Childress didn't need any more prompting. As soon as he'd made his decision, they were out the door and moving toward the helipad.

***

Esfandiari was running down the steps toward the barbican as fast as he could when there was a flash and a rumbling *boom* from the outer courtyard. He ducked instinctively, thinking that one of the missiles had been hit and detonated. A sudden chill went through him at the thought; he knew well what was in the warheads, and he had the sudden horrifying thought that they were all dead.

But then he reminded himself that the chemical agent was a binary one, and would not be mixed until the warhead was on its terminal flight path. Damage could still be done, but even if one of the missiles exploded, it would not result in a full release of sarin gas into the fortress.

He looked back toward the courtyard, and saw the sullen glow of flame flickering beneath a growing pall of belching black smoke. The crackle of exploding ammunition soon reached his ears.

The infidels destroyed one of the APCs. He was momentarily incredulous. What had they brought with them, and where had they come from? Any helicopters should have been detected and shot down, riots or no riots.

Straightening, conscious once again of the fact that his men were watching, he composed himself and continued down the steps. Two more of the AMX-10s were rumbling back into the barbican, accompanied by most of Farroukhshad's platoon. He jogged to the nearest APC, which had halted just short of the gate leading to the outer courtyard, the crew doubtless worried about meeting the same fate as the first vehicle.

"Where are Farroukhshad and Jahangir?" he bellowed.

"Here, Commander," the younger man replied. Farroukhshad was little more than a tall, lean silhouette in the darkness, his eyes glinting in the faint light coming from the burning APC.

"Farroukshad, take your platoon and the armored vehicles, and secure the courtyard," Esfandiari ordered. "Jahangir, you and your men are with me; we must secure the Citadel and stop the infidels from escaping with the hostages."

Both men were dedicated officers in the IRGC. They did not ask questions. They simply immediately began to issue their own orders, gathering their respective platoons to follow their commander's instructions. Both platoons were at higher than normal strength; Esfandiari had split the remains of Mehregan's platoon between the two of them.

With forty men behind him, Esfandiari started back up the steps toward the Citadel at a run.

Marg bar Amryka.

CHAPTER 17

Brannigan came out onto the upper courtyard, flipping his NVGs back down over his eyes as he cleared the door. Hancock was already halfway to the sally port, Childress close behind him, but the hostages were lagging and stumbling; it was dark and none of them had night vision.

Hancock looked back and saw that they were outrunning their charges, and quickly took a knee next to the Super Puma, yelling at Childress to get the rest of the hostages and the prisoners around the back side of the helo. If there was going to be opposition, it would be coming from the front of the Citadel.

Santelli, Ortiz, and Brannigan were herding their charges toward the helo as quickly as they could when the first rattling fusillade of rifle fire *banged* into the Super Puma's fuselage.

Hancock shot back, his AK-12 stabbing flame as he fired a long, stuttering burst on full auto in response. Brannigan, still four paces from the helicopter, pivoted and dropped on his belly, his own rifle pointed back toward their attackers. Just in time, too, as another string of 5.56 rounds smacked through the Perspex windshield of the Super Puma, right over his head.

He fired back as soon as he had his AK pointed in at least the general direction of the incoming fire, ripping off another half a magazine at the advancing silhouettes and flickering muzzle flashes. The tactically-minded part of his brain wished that he had a machinegun for suppressive fire, but they had what they had, and they'd have to make do.

He heard a grunt of pain beside him. "You all right, Ortiz?" he yelled, over the ripping roars of gunfire.

"I'm hit." The man's voice, tight with pain, was remarkably calm. The time in captivity must have dulled his sense of shock.

"Doc!" Brannigan roared. "Ortiz needs you!" That was all the attention he could spare; he lined up the running form of another Iranian, and put a two-round burst into the man's center of mass. The charging fighter stumbled, and Brannigan shot him again as soon as the red dot settled. The man pitched forward onto his face. Brannigan switched targets, blasting another four rounds in two trigger pulls at another strobing muzzle blast. Whether the man was hit or not, his rifle fell silent, at least for the moment.

He heard Villareal talking behind him. "You're all right, Captain, I've got you," the doctor was saying. "It's just a scratch, you'll be fine." It was a tribute to Villareal's professionalism and calm under fire that Brannigan couldn't even tell whether he was lying or not.

The wall of the upper courtyard had crumbled in places, and the Iranians were using the rubble for cover as they tried to assault through the gap between the Citadel proper and the inner curtain wall. It was all they really could use, aside from the building itself, since the courtyard was wide open. Of course, that was a problem for the mercenaries and their charges, too. Brannigan was feeling very exposed, lying flat on open ground, vastly outnumbered and taking fire.

They needed to break contact and get through that sally port. They might be vulnerable on the steps going down, but if they stayed put, they would eventually be flanked and annihilated.

He ripped off the rest of the magazine, gripping the forearm of the rifle hard to muscle the barrel down against the muzzle-rise, tracking the long, ravening burst across the gap between Citadel and curtain wall. Then he did a pushup, got his feet under him, and came to a crouch.

Villareal had torn Ortiz' shirt open and slapped a chest seal on the hole in his side. "Get moving, Doc!" Brannigan ordered. "We can't stay here!"

Ortiz, wounded as he was, was still in the fight. He lifted the Type 03 and ripped off a burst, though it was shaky, wild, and probably didn't do much more than make noise and keep some heads down. That was all they needed at that point, though. Brannigan shoved both Villareal and Ortiz toward the other side of the helicopter, then yanked an F1 frag out of his vest.

Please, don't let me frag myself with this Russian monstrosity. He yanked the pin and chucked the grenade as far toward the oncoming Iranians as he could, before ducking around the side of the Super Puma's cockpit.

Even as he did so, he ran smack-dab into one of the Saudi prisoners. He stumbled, almost tripping over the man even as the prisoner rebounded off him and fell. At first, he thought the man had simply panicked under fire, until the prisoner kicked out at his legs, trying to trip him.

The image in his NVGs was blurry, but he made out that it was the cadaverous, angry-looking Saudi, the one who had been in charge. And the man was now actively trying to force him back out into the Iranians' line of fire.

The frag detonated in the next instant, and shrapnel smacked into the side of the Super Puma with a noise like the hammering of the world's hardest rainstorm on a tin roof. More fragments whispered by, inches from Brannigan's back.

The Saudi was still fighting him. Whether he was a Wahhabi fanatic who just wanted to see the infidels dead, or an angry egotist with some twisted desire for revenge after having been threatened and glared down by the big American didn't matter to Brannigan. He dropped a knee in the man's chest, driving the wind out of him with a *whuff* that was barely audible over the thunder of the fight around them.

Taking one hand off his rifle, Brannigan reached down and grabbed the man by the throat. "Either you quit, and live, or I toss your ass out into the open and leave you," he snarled.

The man spat at him and tried to kick him.

Shifting his weight and getting off of him, Brannigan hauled the Saudi physically up off the ground and threw him six feet, out beyond the Super Puma's nose.

More rifle fire roared. Three shots hit the Saudi in the chest and head. He jerked and was still.

Hancock was at the sally port. More machinegun fire was rattling from below. The volume of fire from the Iranians by the Citadel was increasing, bullets hammering at the Super Puma's fuselage relentlessly.

"Go, go, go!" Brannigan yelled. Hancock was on a knee by the sally port, firing back toward the Citadel. Childress was shoving hostages through the gate and down the steps. There was no sign of the corn-fed kid who had picked up one of the enemy rifles; he'd probably expended all of his ammunition and been sent down the steps. Santelli was shooting under the helo. Villareal was half-dragging Ortiz toward the gate.

"Get to the gate and get down!" Brannigan yelled. He was already pulling another F1 out of his gear as he grabbed Santelli by the straps of his vest and shoved him toward the sally port. "Move!"

He didn't know for sure if this would work; even if the Super Puma was fueled, there was no guarantee that an explosion would blow up the fuel tanks. He was hoping it would, though.

More bullets *snapped* overhead and smacked grit off the ground only a few feet to his right. Several of the Iranians had come around the far side of the Citadel, and were trying to flank them. The grenade dangling precariously from its pull-ring, Brannigan snapped his AK-12 to his shoulder and shot back, tearing through another half-mag. He still had seven left, but they were burning through ammo fast.

The Iranians ducked back as his burst ripped through the air at them, but then immediately countered with a ravening storm of fire that shredded the air around him and forced him to hit the ground. He responded with three shorter bursts. One took the lead shooter in the midsection, folding him over his own weapon as he crumpled. The other two only forced the remaining shooters to scramble back, out of the line of fire.

"Come on!" Santelli was roaring. "Last man!"

Brannigan scrambled to his feet, yanked the pin out of the grenade, and lobbed it under the Super Puma before turning and running toward the sally port. Santelli was barricaded on the threshold, firing single shots back toward the Citadel as fast as he could pull the trigger. Brannigan ran through the gate behind him, and almost ran into Villareal and Ortiz, who were shoving the remaining Saudi prisoners ahead of them.

Lifting his muzzle, Brannigan reached back and grabbed Santelli by the vest, pulling him through the gate and into the shelter of the wall, just before the grenade detonated and the Super Puma exploded in a massive fireball. Fragments of fuselage and rotors whickered through the air and chipped out baseball-sized chunks of the wall, which cascaded down on their heads.

***

The crackle of the ammo cooking off in the stricken AMX was dying down, but the volume of fire from beyond it was picking up. Bullets were starting to smack into the seaward wall above their heads, and a few tracers flashed above and sailed out to sea. Flanagan fired a burst down the side of the AMX, blindly, since the fire was whiting out his NVGs.

He and Curtis started up a rhythm as more muzzle flashes flickered at them from the dark beyond the burning armored vehicle. Curtis would fire a long burst, then Flanagan would pick up with a few short ones. Aziz was joining in sporadically, though he was busy prepping the rest of the RPGs and generally keeping his head down.

"Can you hear that?" Curtis yelled after finishing a burst of his own.

Flanagan fired at another muzzle flash before answering, "Hear what?"

"I think there's another APC coming!" Curtis yelled, before tearing the night apart again with another long, stuttering burst. All three men had been nearly deafened by the racket of the fight by then, but if they concentrated between bursts of gunfire, there might have been the all-too-familiar squeal and clank of treads in the background, somewhere beyond the smoke-belching, burning APC squatting in the middle of the courtyard.

"We've only got two RPGs left!" Aziz hollered. "After that, we're fucked!"

"Well, we're fucked now if you don't start using them!" Flanagan snapped back. The dark wedge shape of another AMX-10 was starting to rumble around the side of the burning hulk. "Shoot that son of a bitch!"

Aziz might have cursed. It was impossible to hear over the thunder of automatic gunfire, and the sudden titanic explosion up above, near the Citadel itself. A fireball roiled upward into the sky, and jagged, smoking debris started to rain down on them. Then Aziz fired, the shockwave of the RPG-27 warhead's launch smacking both Flanagan and Curtis with flying grit.

It was hard to see, but the AMX appeared to be trying to maneuver around the burning APC, unable to take a straight-line course through the gap between the wreck and the garrison buildings. The driver seemed to be understandably reticent to drive on the other side, too close to the missile carriers. That same reticence seemed to be affecting the men on foot, as well; Flanagan hadn't seen anyone try to get to any of the missiles, which meant that the fuses were hopefully still burning.

For a moment, the nose of the mobile APC was visible, just past the burning wreckage of the first one, and that was where the RPG warhead hit, almost square against the vehicle's flat sides. Without the angle of the glacis to deflect either the round itself or the plasma jet of its detonation, nearly the full fury of the warhead's shaped charge was spent against the thinner side armor. There was a painful *bang*, a flash, and a shower of sparks.

The explosion must have killed the driver, because the APC, instead of stopping, surged forward and crunched into the garrison building against the cliff below the inner wall and the Citadel itself. A moment later, it started to burn.

The courtyard was now almost completely blocked in that direction by blazing armored vehicles. Infantry could still get through, though, if only through the same buildings.

Even as Flanagan thought it, muzzle flashes sparked from the darkened windows of the buildings, ahead of the burning APCs. More of the Iranians had come through, and were using the buildings as cover. Cover that the three men by the breach in the wall did not have.

Flanagan shifted his fire and ripped off three short bursts at the flashes in the windows, flattening himself as close to the rocky ground as he could get. He didn't dare check his watch, but the fuses were getting low. They had to get out of that fortress soon, or they were all dead, anyway.

Then he saw the figures on the steps, coming down from the sally port. And some of them had guns.

***

The burning helicopter back-lit them as they hurried down the steps, and the fires from the destroyed APCs were lighting up the courtyard, though the growing billows of choking smoke served to cut the illumination, making it hard to see what was going on below. Brannigan and Santelli were close behind Ortiz and Villareal, chivvying the prisoners and the hostages down the uneven steps as fast as they could move. They were exposed as hell, and were going to be as long as they remained on the side of the cliff.

There was more gunfire thundering down in the courtyard, most of it aimed at the small knot of figures huddled near the breach in the wall they'd climbed through. Then a burst of fire smacked chips and grit off the rock above Brannigan's head. Some of the Iranians down below, cut off by the burning vehicles, had figured out that the people descending the steps were not on their side.

He returned fire, though the burst was wild and unaimed, mostly only intended to get their heads down for the few more seconds it would take to get to the bottom.

Then he was rushing downward, hitting the weirdly-spaced steps almost more by instinct than actual agility, plummeting out of the line of fire as fast as he could. He would later consider it a minor miracle that he hadn't fallen off the side of the cliff.

The courtyard was a hellstorm of automatic weapons fire. Hancock and Childress were just inside the gate, firing at the buildings alongside the cliff. The hostages were huddled as close to the cliffside itself as they could get, trying to make themselves as small as possible as bullets crackled past, smacked into stone and earth, and ricocheted with nasty, buzzing whines. There was an increasing volume of fire coming from the buildings, and the three men by the breach were pouring more fire at them in return, until one of them came up to a knee, a tube on his shoulder.

"*Get down!*" Brannigan roared, getting every bit of volume out of his lungs that he could. A moment later, the RPG fired with a *bang*, and the front of the building, not twenty yards ahead of Hancock and Childress, exploded with an earth-shaking *thud*.

A billowing cloud of dust and smoke slammed out from the flash of the detonation, and chunks of stone and brick flew, most of them hammering into the sides of the wrecks of the APCs. Some of it flew at the mercenaries, though, and the shockwave itself was funneled out the open door that Hancock had been firing through, knocking the two men back on their haunches.

For a moment, there almost seemed to be a lull in the fight, though some of it might have simply been the shocked silence of already-brutalized hearing trying to shut down after enduring the shock of an explosion that close. But the brutal blast of that shaped charge would have impacted the fighters inside, as well, and if any of them were still alive, they'd gotten rocked by the explosion, more than the mercenaries outside would have. Those who had been out of range of the shockwave would be blocked by wreckage and debris, at least for a little while.

"Get up!" Brannigan roared, running forward and hauling Hancock to his feet. "Get moving! Get the hostages down to the boats! Childress, go with Hancock! Carlo, you're with me!"

They had a brief breather, but they still had to buy time. The hostages were malnourished, dehydrated, and shell-shocked. It would take a few minutes to get all of them down the rope.

He ran to the corner of the partially-destroyed building. The flames were playing hell with his NVGs; the green view ahead of him was a flickering mess of white flares that rendered almost anything else invisible. He kept them on, though; and just tried to look away from the fires as much as he could.

He stifled a cough. His throat felt like it was on fire from thirst, the smoke was making it difficult to breathe, and now the nearness of the burning vehicles was adding furnace heat to the sweat, salt, and grit that felt like it was abrading away every inch of his skin. He knew that sheer adrenaline was half of what was keeping him on his feet.

The other half was sheer, determined willpower.

He knelt, using the semi-intact corner of the building as a barricade, searching for targets. There might have been movement beyond the flaming hulks of the APCs, but there wasn't a clear target that he could see, and he was getting low on ammo.

Behind him, he felt Santelli take a knee, facing in the open door. The other man's AK-12 rattled off a series of quick shots, but went unanswered. Brannigan stayed facing the way he was, letting Santelli cover his own sector.

Curtis' PKP suddenly roared out a lethal greeting, and Brannigan risked turning his head to look. The little machinegunner was pouring fire down the other side of the destroyed AMX-10s, closer to the missiles. With their approach through and along the buildings relatively cut off, the Iranians were taking the risk of getting closer to the volatile weapons in order to try to keep their hostages, and the infidel mercenaries, from escaping.

But the shooting died back down fairly quickly. Fanatics they might be, but the Iranians had taken a hell of a shellacking already that night, and they must be pulling back to reconsider their attack plan.

Brannigan glanced back again, to see the first of the hostages starting down the rope. They were moving too slowly. He turned his head to look up at the sally port above their heads. There was no movement up there, but he realized that it was only a matter of time. He reached back and grabbed Santelli's shoulder.

"Fall back to the breach," he ordered, "before they come down the same steps we just used and cut us off."

Santelli didn't reply, except to get up, pivot around, and dash as fast as his short legs could take him, back toward the seaward wall. A moment later, Brannigan heard him yell, "Turn and go!"

It was a short dash. He skidded down into the prone next to Flanagan. He and Curtis were covering the courtyard, side by side, while Childress and Hancock got the hostages on the ropes as fast as they could. The hostages were huddled against the wall behind the mercenaries, flat on their bellies while they waited their turn. It was the best they could do with the terrain they had.

"Where's Aziz?" Brannigan asked Flanagan.

"He went down to get the boats ready to move," Flanagan said, before triggering another burst at a flicker of movement near the farthest missile carrier. "Ordinarily I'd think he just wanted to get clear of the shooting sooner, but we really do need to hurry up."

"I know," Brannigan replied, snugging his own AK into his shoulder and sighting in on what might have been another Iranian shape in the shadows beyond the fires. He rapped out a two-round burst, and the shape vanished.

"No, you don't," Flanagan said. "There *might* be five minutes left on that first time fuse."

"Oh, *hell.*"

CHAPTER 18

Esfandiari winced as he got to his feet. The bullet had gone into his side, but he didn't think it had hit anything vital. It only hurt. He could deal with pain, if it meant the infidels were punished.

The searing heat of the burning helicopter scorched his face as he followed Jahangir and one of his remaining squads around the helipad and toward the inner wall. In a moment, they could take the attackers under fire from above, and end this.

With the missiles recaptured, he could still salvage the operation. Riyadh would die, the apostates choking on their own bodily fluids.

***

Brannigan scrambled back to the breach. "Speed it up!" he barked. "We've got to go, *now!* Slide down the rope; I don't care if it burns all the skin off your hands! At least you'll be alive! *Move!*"

Ortiz, wincing visibly with the pain of his wound, immediately started chivvying his people toward the ropes faster. Two more ropes had been staked down and dropped down the cliff face, so they could get more people down more quickly.

One of the Saudis appeared to have taken charge, barking at his fellow prisoners in Arabic. Brannigan wished that Aziz had stayed up top; his language expertise was needed. But the prisoners seemed to become more cooperative after the haranguing, though a few of them still seemed sullen about it. They held out their hands to have their flex cuffs cut, then descended the rope, though more slowly than Brannigan would have liked.

"I can't!" the middle-aged woman wailed. She shrank back from the edge. Two weeks as a hostage of bloodthirsty IRGC thugs hadn't been enough to cure her of fear of heights.

Everybody's got something.

"Hold on to my neck," the big, blond kid said. He'd dropped his rifle, pretty well confirming Brannigan's earlier suspicion that he'd run through all his ammo. "I'll climb down, you can just ride on my back."

Brannigan wondered why the woman's husband wasn't making that offer, then realized that this was probably Trevor Ulrich's widow.

Shaking, the woman wrapped her arms tightly around the young man's neck and squeezed her eyes shut as he grabbed the rope and went over the edge. Her shriek as he fast-roped down to the boats was audible even over ringing ears, roaring fires, and the occasional burst of gunfire that was still cracking through the fortress.

Brannigan returned to Flanagan and Curtis. "Give me the Pecheneg," he said, "along with the rest of your ammo. Joe, give Santelli all but two of your mags. Then get to the ropes and get down."

"Wait a second," Flanagan started, but Brannigan cut him off.

"That wasn't a request, Joe," he said. "Carlo and I will be the last ones down. Move your asses."

The two men were visibly reluctant as they yielded their positions to Brannigan and Santelli and moved to the ropes. Brannigan had handed off his AK-12 and the rest of his mags to Curtis, and got down behind the PKP. A quick check confirmed that he had about half a belt left on the gun, and one more in its ready pouch. It wasn't much, but it was going to have to be enough.

More fire started to *snap* overhead from the far side of the burning vehicles. Brannigan returned it, the PKP rattling and stuttering as flame spat from the muzzle. The barrel was starting to glow a dull, cherry red in the dark. In his NVGs, it glowed a brilliant white.

"Up high!" Santelli warned, turning his AK toward the curtain wall and tearing off a fast series of shots. Brannigan looked, and saw figures against the sky, on the battlements. They'd be sitting ducks down below. He shifted, couldn't get the barrel of the PKP elevated enough from the prone, and scrambled to a kneeling position, burning his hand as he lifted the smoking-hot machinegun, and ripped off the rest of the belt at the top of the wall, dragging the barrel across the battlements, blasting pits in the stone and forcing heads back from the crenellations.

Another roaring burst came from behind them, hammering both men with the muzzle blast, also aimed up at the inner wall. "Last man!" Flanagan roared hoarsely. "*Come on!*"

Brannigan dropped the empty machinegun and turned, running to the ropes. Santelli rapped off three more shots, then followed.

Brannigan went over the edge so fast that he almost missed the rope. He clenched his hands on it at the last moment, feeling the friction sear his grip through his gloves as he clamped down, stopping his fall after nearly three feet. Then, clamping his boots together on the rope beneath him, he loosened his grip just enough to begin to slide down the rope again.

His gloves smoked as he shot downward, almost keeping pace with Santelli, who was cursing loudly as the rope abraded the palms of his gloves away. Flanagan was half a length ahead of Santelli.

Brannigan hit the bow of the left-most boat a moment after the other two go to theirs. The third and fourth boats were already out on the water, lying low with their heavy load of bodies. All four boats were overloaded, almost the point of swamping.

His boot slipped on the wet rubber, and he went over backward, landing on someone who grunted in pain at the impact. But he was aboard, and he yelled at the coxswain, "I'm in! Go!"

"Pull the stake!" Hancock yelled in reply. They'd staked the boats to the cliffside before ascending, to keep them from floating away. Struggling with the weight of his gear, the thrashing bodies under him, and the overloaded rubber gunwale that seemed to want to collapse whenever he needed to push against it, Brannigan managed to sit up, reach forward, and yank on the line holding the boat to the cliff.

It didn't budge. He reached for his knife, praying that it hadn't fallen out and gotten lost. It was still clipped to his belt, gritty and salt-encrusted as it was, and he felt it grate as he opened it. It was still sharp, though, and it took only a couple seconds of sawing to get through the rope. The final strands parted, and they were free. "*Go!*"

Hancock cranked the throttle, and they were pulling back from the cliff and out into the water. They were moving slowly, though. Too slowly. Between the reduced power of the outboard in reverse and the heavy load of the boat, they weren't going to be far enough from the cliff by the time some Iranian poked his head over with a machinegun.

Turning over and trying to get a better position on the gunwale, Brannigan saw that he'd landed on Ortiz, who was already hurting. The man was now crunched down inside the boat. Most of the inside of the hull was a packed, jumbled mass of humanity; the hostages were staying inside instead of riding the gunwales like the mercenaries would have, if only out of habit.

Ortiz managed to get himself partially upright, leaning his head against the bow, and with a wince of pain, wrenched the captured Type 03 out from under him. He shoved it at Brannigan. "Here," he grunted, pain evident in every word, "you probably know how to use this better than I do."

Brannigan accepted the rifle, grateful to have a weapon in his hand. He pulled the magazine, feeling the rounds at the feed lips and weighing it in his hand before driving it back home in the weapon's mag well. About half full, give or take maybe five rounds. "You still have any more mags?" he asked.

"I think I've still got one," Ortiz replied, though it took him a moment to draw it out of a pocket. "Make that two."

Brannigan accepted them gratefully, stuffing them into his vest as he pointed the rifle up at the cliffside. Just in time, too, as a silhouette appeared in the wall breach. Putting what he could see of the sights in the general vicinity, he fired five rapid shots, the brass sailing out over his shoulder to fall into the water.

***

Farroukhshad yelled at his men as the fire from the gap in the wall slackened and died. With the destroyed APCs in the way, that machinegunner had had far too narrow a kill zone, and it had made trying to rush the infidels impossible. The corpses laid out in the dirt were ample testament to that. And he simply did not have enough men to make a human-wave assault practical. Farroukhshad was suitably fanatical; he never would have been appointed as an officer in the Qods Force if he had not demonstrated it sufficiently for the Council of Guardians. Even more so, he never would have been picked for this particular mission if he had not been deemed religiously and politically reliable. But he was also a tactician, much like his commander, and knew that glorious failure was still failure. Even if Allah was ultimately pleased by their dedication, his family would likely suffer at the hands of the Revolutionary Guard and the Baseej. So he held his men back until the fire slackened enough that they could rush through the gap.

The first, the youngest and most viciously enthusiastic of his fighters, were on their feet, variously shouting, "*Allahu Akhbar!*" and, "*Marg bar Amryka!*" They were certain that the attackers were American commandos. Who else could they be?

They were met with no resistance, and Farroukhshad followed, his own rifle in his hands. Some of the other platoon leaders, especially the un-mourned Twelver lunatic Mehregan, preferred to carry pistols in place of rifles, as emblems of their authority, but again, Farroukhshad was a practical soldier.

He saw the first soldier run past the discarded, smoking PKP at the breach, kneel in the rubble, and aim his rifle. Gunfire *cracked* from below, and the man reeled back, blood squirting from his shoulder.

Farroukhshad paused just past the first burning AMX-10. More gunfire was hammering at them from below, bullets filling the gap in the wall with harsh *snaps* and occasionally skipping off the sandstone with showers of grit to ricochet into the courtyard with angry-hornet buzzes. The infidels still had some fight left, even as they fled.

The roar of gunfire, the crackle of the burning vehicles, and the sheer amount of heat and smoke in the courtyard served to mask the faint, sweetish smell of burning time fuse. Neither Farroukhshad nor any of his men noticed the charges plastered against the missile bodies, shadowed by the camouflage netting and the curves of the missile fuel tanks themselves.

When the first missile detonated, hammering Farroukhshad flat on his face in the dirt, it was far too late. He was presumably already dead, crisped by the fireball and his internal organs pulped by the overpressure, by the time the second missile exploded, closely followed by the rest, in a rapid-fire cascade of thundering explosions.

The precursor chemicals for the sarin gas were hardly an afterthought. Any damage they might have done was overshadowed by the sheer, fiery destruction of the exploding rocket fuel.

***

Esfandiari was cursing, calling down every plague Allah could send on the infidels, the apostate Saudis, and even those of his own men who were too quick to hunker down below the battlements when the infidel commando raked them with machinegun fire. It had been a brutal night, so far, and even the hardened killers of the Qods Force were feeling their own resolve being battered by the sheer ferocity of the attackers, and the nearly unthinkable destruction they had already wreaked on the Citadel. It had been hard enough getting past the burning Super Puma, its inferno heat driving them back from the wall twice before they'd managed to mount the battlements. Khadem catching a bullet between the eyes as soon as he'd reached the crenellations had only made matters worse.

The fire from below had ceased, and Esfandiari rose above the battlements and sent a long burst ripping down toward the breach, firing before it even fully registered in his mind that there was no longer anyone there. The commandos had fled down the cliff.

"*After them!*" he screamed, his throat raw from the exertion, the gunfire, and the smoke of the night's fighting. "*Kill them all!*"

Below, he saw Farroukhshad's men already moving forward, rushing the breach in the wall, pursuing the infidels as soldiers of Allah should, without mercy or respite. He ceased his own fire as the men neared the breach; even in his rage, he would not risk accidentally killing his own men. He had lost enough that night already.

He was about to order his men down to join Farroukshad when the missiles began exploding. The shockwave blew him backward off the battlements, even as the fireball that filled the outer courtyard singed his eyebrows and half his beard off. He was smoking as he landed on his back with a brutal impact, staring dazedly at the stars above and wondering what had just happened.

***

Brannigan had just gotten the first burst off when Hancock started turning the boat. They were still close to the cliffs, and there were still rocks close to the surface, but if they were going to get some distance quickly, preferably before the missiles blew up, they needed every bit of power that the little outboard motor could muster. He had to roll onto his side to keep the Type 03's muzzle trained on the breach above, finally setting in lying on his back, facing sternward to shoot over Hancock's head. More rifle fire was coming from the other boats, as the rest joined in, trying to force the Iranians back from the breach by filling it with bullets.

The bow pointed away from the cliff, Hancock rammed the outboard into drive and opened the throttle. The little motor howled, churning the water behind them, but only pushed the boat forward sluggishly, the gunwales too close to the water, the stern nearly sinking under the load of more bodies than the boat had been built for.

Then the night exploded.

The walls shielded them from most of the explosions. Hancock had even angled to the south, getting them out of a direct line through the breach to the missiles. And the inner and outer walls funneled most of the fireball and the shockwave up, toward the sky.

A brilliant, roiling ball of yellow-orange flame boiled up into the sky, propelling a sinister cloud of smoke, dust, and deadly chemicals. There was a chance that there was some sarin in that cloud, but if there was, it was a miniscule amount, as most of the precursors had doubtless been incinerated by the fireball before they could mix. Dust and debris shot out through the breach, pelting the ocean with rocks and bits of metal, narrowly missing the boat. Brannigan heard fragments whicker overhead, far too close for comfort. But the boats stayed afloat, and there were no screams of wounded men struck by shrapnel. There were a few cries of terror from hostages, but they were quickly identified and dismissed.

He realized that that could change, though, as the cloud of debris thrown skyward started its long fall toward the earth. "Get us out from under that crap!" he yelled.

"This is as fast as this sucker's going to go," Hancock bellowed in reply. "Either we make it, or we don't!"

Chunks of wreckage started to rain down out of the sky. In the dark, it was impossible to tell what was what. It didn't matter whether it was a piece of sandstone the size of a fist, or a chunk of rolled steel from a destroyed armored vehicle. At terminal velocity, it could kill a man just as dead. Brannigan hunkered down in the boat with the rest of the hostages, covering his head with his hands, and prayed as debris bounced off the rubber gunwale or hit the ocean with hammering splashes.

Hancock ducked his head but kept his hand on the tiller, the throttle twisted as far as it could go, driving them out of the deadly rain.

***

Esfandiari rolled to his side, narrowly avoiding a chunk of shrapnel that fell smoking to bury itself in the dirt only centimeters from his head. It hadn't been a deliberate movement; he was still too dazed by the shock of the explosions. But another fragment, possibly a stone, struck his calf with bruising force, and he cried out.

The pain shocked him back to consciousness, and with it came a white-hot, burning rage. The hostages had escaped, and the weapons he had been ordered to turn against the apostates had been destroyed before he had been able to force the apostate technicians to re-target their guidance systems.

He was a dead man. He knew it already. Even if he had not been poisoned or otherwise mortally wounded by that explosion, the Council of Guardians would surely order his execution for his failure. He gritted his teeth against the pain as he got his feet under him, debris still raining down out of the night sky. He would *not* simply surrender to failure. He was a servant of Allah, and Allah demanded much of his warriors. At the very least, he would make sure that the infidels and their apostate allies never saw another sunrise.

"*Get up!*" he snarled, hauling Mokhri off the ground. The man was limp, blood flowing from a wound in his head. Too much blood. He was dead.

Esfandiari let the corpse fall in disgust, and began kicking those of his troops who were still moving to their feet. "Get to the gate!" he coughed. His entire body felt like one enormous bruise, his face was smarting from the flash-burns of the explosion, and his throat was raw and on fire. He was probably far more seriously wounded than he knew, but adrenaline and rage were fueling him now. "Get whatever vehicles are left running. We will move to the harbor and take the patrol boats."

"What use are patrol boats, Commander?" one of the soldiers, his face a mask of blood from a scalp wound asked.

Esfandiari almost shot him dead right there. "The infidels are escaping by sea," he snapped. "We will intercept them and kill them all. At least we will have that to offer to Allah when we face the Judgement."

Allah smiled upon those who killed his enemies. That was one thing that he and the apostates could agree on.

Staggering, stumbling, nursing wounds, burns, and a few blast injuries, the surviving Iranians started down toward the barbican gate. The fight was not over yet.

CHAPTER 19

The flames were dying down as the boats lumbered through the Gulf toward the south end of the island. The fires in the outer courtyard were still burning fiercely, and the boiling mushroom cloud was still lit by the sullen red glow from beneath as it climbed into the sky. But the ancient stone fortress supplied little in the way of fuel, and once the remains of the vehicles were burned out, the fires would die.

As they got farther away, Brannigan thought he could see spots where the detonations had breached the outer wall, places where the fires were visible lower than the top of the wall. It had been a hell of a blast. The Old City was probably in even worse repair than it had been from the earlier fighting.

He wondered vaguely how the powers that be were going to handle this. Washington would have to make some kind of statement; they always did, even about things they knew nothing about. Would anyone have figured out that a private rescue mission had been launched? Or would the entire conflagration be put down to the "native" Khadarkhi insurgency, i.e., the Al Qaeda fighters smuggled in by the Saudis?

He suddenly found that he was too tired to care. He would have been struggling to keep his eyes open if he hadn't been riding the bow of a rubber boat, in the Persian Gulf. The weight of the load of passengers kept the bow from bouncing too much; it was more of a wallow. But there was still enough motion from the waves that he was still slammed into the gunwale jarringly every few dozen meters.

"How are we on fuel?" Hancock asked quietly. None of the hostages were talking, or even moving very much, so he didn't have to raise his voice.

Brannigan reached down beneath him to feel the fuel bladder. "Maybe a third," he replied.

"Fuck," was Hancock's response. The word was low and flat, but it carried, and several of the hostages' heads lifted, wondering what was happening.

"Why?" Brannigan asked, wishing that he had some way to have this conversation out of their charges' hearing. The last thing they needed was a bunch of panicky hostages on their hands.

"I still can't see our ride," Hancock replied.

Brannigan looked back out over the Gulf to their south. All that he could see was darkness and the waves. No lights, no faint, dark silhouette of the dhow.

"We're not even past the southern tip of the island yet," he said quietly, looking back at Hancock. The man was sitting up on the gunwale, his hand on the tiller, the Russian NVGs hiding his eyes behind their vaguely insectoid lenses. "They're probably still over the horizon."

"*If* they're waiting," Hancock said. "If you were a mobster, and saw that fireball, would *you* stick around?"

"We'll just have to see," Brannigan replied, hoping that none of their charges suddenly decided that all was lost. "What other choice do we have?"

"On that much fuel, not much," Hancock said. Then he fell silent and drove the boat.

They passed the rocky mount that they had used as a landmark for the initial landing, only about forty-eight hours before. It seemed like a lot longer than that. Then they were on the open water, the island slowly shrinking behind them.

***

It took nearly another hour to get to the rendezvous. The first light of dawn would be starting to spread across the eastern sky in a short while.

And they were alone on the waves. There was no sign of the dhow.

Brannigan didn't cuss, didn't betray any sign that he was in the least bit perturbed, even as his guts twisted inside him. Their options had just become sharply limited. He sat up in the bow, looking over at the other boats, and circled his hand above his head. *Rally up.*

The other three boats motored in, and hands reached out to grab gunwales, lines, and other hands, until they had a little floating pontoon raft of four overloaded rubber boats, not unlike the one they'd formed before casting off that first night, bobbing on the waves.

"All right," Brannigan said, his voice pitched low. There weren't any enemy boats nearby to hear them, but he was going to maintain his field habits until they were out of the field. And being stranded on the water, in his mind, meant they were still in the woods, and caution was called for. "It looks like our friend Dmitri has either written us off or deliberately screwed us. The dhow was supposed to be here until dawn, and there's no sign of it. It's not even on the horizon. So, they've skedaddled, and left us to our own devices.

"We haven't got enough fuel to reach Sir Bu Nair. We might paddle, but that's going to be a *long* haul, and we've got wounded. The other option would be to turn back to Khadarkh, go to ground, and see if we can arrange some other passage off the island. I expect that any of the Iranians who are left are going to be pretty off-balance for a while."

"If we can get to the harbor," Ortiz said weakly, "we might be able to get the *Oceana Metropolis* out of port. Unless they've got it locked down."

"Aziz, did the Iranians appear to have much of a presence outside the Citadel?" Brannigan asked.

There was a pause. "They had some patrols out yesterday afternoon," Aziz finally said, "but who knows, after all that? How many of them can there still be left alive, after the fighting in the Citadel, *and* in the Old City?"

"You might be surprised," Santelli said. He was looking back toward the dark hulk of Khadarkh. "Everybody look off to the east side of the island."

All eyes, even those without NVGs, turned to look. Some of the hostages cried out, and were quickly silenced by their more sensible companions.

They were small and distant, but the two boats shining spotlights on the water and the shoreline could only be patrol boats. And given the situation on Khadarkh, they could only be crewed by Iranians.

It was still possible that the Al Qaeda fighters had commandeered them, but that was no better. Whoever was on those boats, they would not have the best interests of a bunch of American hostages in mind, never mind the mercenaries who had rescued them.

Brannigan's mind was already racing. Their options were sharply limited. Sooner or later, if they weren't found closer in to shore, the gunboats would expand their search out to sea. And the overloaded, wallowing rubber boats would be easy targets out on the water.

He watched the moving lights as the murmurs of fear and despair got louder around him. He ignored the noise. If they were going to stand any chance of survival, he had to plan fast.

"They're searching systematically," he said, his voice low and urgent, "circling the island clockwise. If we move a little farther out to the east, we should be able to get behind them, and move in to shore once they've passed. If we're fast, quiet, and lucky, they might well miss us in the dark entirely." He was all too aware of the nearness of dawn. Once the sun was up, they'd be exposed. And they didn't have much ammo left, either.

But faced with the fact that the only alternative was being hunted down on the open water and slaughtered, it was better than nothing.

The murmurs got louder, especially from the middle-aged woman. None of the hostages wanted to go back to the island they'd just escaped. But Brannigan cut them off. "This ain't a democracy," he said. "If you don't like it, feel free to try to swim to Dubai or Abu Dhabi. You've got a better chance with us, believe me." He looked at his team. "Everybody got the plan?"

There were nods. Aziz didn't respond at first. Only after Brannigan stared at him for several seconds did he finally nod grudgingly. He didn't want to go back to the island any more than the hostages did. And he didn't like the fact that they didn't have any other choice. That much was obvious from his body language.

"Let's go, then," Brannigan said.

The raft broke up, and the coxswains turned their bows back toward the glowing tower of smoke above Khadarkh.

***

Brannigan lay flat against the bow, the Type 03 in his shoulder, watching the distant silhouette of the closest patrol boat, over a nautical mile distant. They were well out of weapons range, but that didn't mean they were out of detection range. So far, there had been no sign that they'd been spotted, but that could change in a heartbeat.

The shore was a dark line ahead, looming higher on the horizon as they approached. And it was starting to get light; the image in his NVGs wasn't quite washed out yet, but it was noticeably brightening. He could even see some of the ocean floor beneath the boat as they got into the shallows.

He took his hand off the rifle's forearm, raised it over his head, looking down at the depth under the keel, then chopped it down sharply. Hancock killed the outboard, then hauled it up before it could plow into the sand and rocks beneath them. Probably pointless; they wouldn't likely use the boats again. But old habits die hard.

In a tight knot, the four boats crossed the surf and beached on a narrow strip of gravel not far from their first landing site. The mercenaries in the bows were out before they were even on the shore, dragging the boats up as far as they could. Which wasn't very far, as heavily laden as they were.

"Everybody off!" Brannigan hissed, echoed by the others on the boats to either side. "Hurry up!"

Ortiz wasn't moving very well, and his face was drawn and pale in the early morning grayness, but he helped chivvy the

231

hostages off. The Saudis were close-mouthed, but generally cooperative, though not one of them lifted a finger to help. Their survival was as touch-and-go as the Americans', and they had to know it. They just wouldn't help if it meant helping the Americans at the same time..

Childress suddenly hissed a warning. Eyes snapped up, to see the nearest patrol boat starting to make a long turn to come around. Either they'd been spotted, or the Iranians had decided they couldn't have gone that far.

"Come on, get off the beach!" Brannigan rasped. "Get up in the rocks and get down!" He didn't know exactly what kind of weapons might be mounted on those boats, but if they were out in the open, the odds were good that they'd be machinegunned to death from well beyond small arms range. *"Move!"*

The sight of that boat turning about was enough of an incentive, even for the Saudi prisoners, to get people moving. In moments, even the wounded were scrambling up the short rock escarpment above the beach, trying to find a hole, a crack, even just a rock to hide behind.

They were still out of range of even a .50 cal by the time they had everyone up off the beach. As before, Brannigan and Santelli had stayed until the last, sometimes physically shoving civilians up over the rocky lip of the high-water line, to where Flanagan, Curtis, Hancock, and Childress were dragging them up, often by main force. There was no time to waste on being gentle.

Finally, the two of them scrambled up and ran for the nearest bit of terrain, a slight, rocky rise with a bit of thorny scrub growing in between the cracks in the stones. Brannigan threw himself down on his belly behind the tiny hillock, even as the gunboat *chugged* into view.

At first, the boat just slowly rumbled past the landing site, as if the crew was only out to take a leisurely trip around the island, and found the four rubber boats pulled up on the narrow beach little more than a curiosity. But then a massive, strobing blast of flame erupted from the M2 .50 caliber machinegun mounted on the bow, and heavy slugs were tearing the air apart overhead, the tracers looking impossibly huge as they floated overhead, the shockwaves of their passage actually physically painful.

They were shooting high, which was a phenomenon that Brannigan had come to expect in the Middle East. He'd never gone toe-to-toe with Iranians before that night, that he knew of, but everyone in the region, be they Arab, Kurd, or Persian, tended to let heavy guns get away from them pretty quickly. Massive, six hundred forty-seven grain projectiles sailed overhead, to impact somewhere off in the desert behind them.

"Hold your fire!" Brannigan hissed. He was sure most of his team would know that, anyway, but everyone was tired, battered, and probably more than a little punchy at that point. Wasting what little ammo they had left by retuning fire well outside of the 5.45mm's range had the potential to be a deadly mistake.

The gunner was joined by a second boat, a few dozen yards behind. More thumping heavy machinegun fire roared overhead, and the mercenaries, the hostages, and the prisoners flattened themselves a little bit closer to the dirt and rocks. Jagged stone dug into chests, hands, and cheeks. Sand filled nostrils already painfully dry from dust and smoke.

"Sooner or later," Brannigan said, just loudly enough that Flanagan could hear him over the thunder of the machinegun fire, "they're going to figure out that they can't finish us off that way, and they'll come ashore after us. When they do, start with grenades. Let 'em get just close enough, and we'll blow 'em to hell. We haven't got much ammo left, so keep the rifles as a last resort."

Flanagan nodded that he understood, and turned his head, without lifting it out of the sand more than a half an inch, to pass the word along to Curtis, who was clutching what had been Brannigan's AK-12. Meanwhile, Brannigan started pulling his remaining F1 frags out of his vest. He had two left. Each of the rest should have three, even four.

They'd come loaded for bear. And it was a good thing, too.

The hammering fire continued for what felt like an eternity. Most of the rounds went harmlessly overhead, but some smacked into the rocks in front of them, the Armor Piercing Incendiary rounds detonating with little flashes and blasts of smoke and grit twice the size of a man's head. Brannigan risked lifting his head just high enough to see over the rise once, but saw no infantry moving onto the beach. For the moment, the enemy seemed content to just sit offshore and blast away at them as the morning light intensified. Most of the mercenaries had already stripped off their NVGs as the dawn reduced the contrast in the image tubes until they were essentially useless.

After a while, the fire started to slacken, then it abruptly died completely. Brannigan risked another look.

One of the patrol boats was moving in toward the shore. It seemed to have circled around the other, and was angling in to come alongside the beach, where they would doubtless unload soldiers to move in on the mercenaries and their charges.

He fought the temptation to open fire. The boat was within effective rifle range now; he could probably hit a few of those figures lining the gunwales, ready to jump overboard and wade ashore. But better to save the ammunition until they were sure.

Let 'em get close enough that you can see the whites of their eyes. He'd never thought, either as an enlisted Marine or as an officer, that he'd ever find himself using that old saw as sound tactical advice. But here he was.

The second boat had had its field of fire cut off by the first. It was a mistake that he hadn't expected the Iranians to make, after the night before, and he momentarily thought that it meant the enemy was Al Qaeda. But the uniform khaki fatigues and the black, Chinese rifles in the hands of the figures dropping into the water confirmed that it was indeed, the Iranians coming after them.

They must have been as tired, shell-shocked, and punchy as he was.

He worked the pin out of a grenade and held it in his hand, clamping the safety lever to the knobbed body with his fingers. He eased one eye back up over the rocky top of the hillock, watching their foes wade ashore and set up on the rocky lip above the beach before starting to clamber over.

Two of the enemy soldiers got down on the rocks and started shooting, spattering the hillock with 5.56 fire. Grit and rock fragments showered down on Brannigan where he lay. They were laying down covering fire for the rest of the attackers to get up onto the flats.

Then, with a ragged chorus of yells in Farsi, alongside the all-too-familiar Arabic cry of, "*Allahu Akhbar!*" the Iranians were charging the hillock, blazing away with their rifles as they ran.

Wait. Don't jump the gun. If you throw too early, they'll land short. Conversely, he knew if he waited too long, the grenades would still go off after the Iranians had run past them.

"*Now!*" he bellowed, lobbing the Russian frag over his head and toward the beach. The safety lever came away with a faint *ping*, almost drowned out by the gunfire and shouting from the Iranians.

The shouts turned to panicked yells, and then were drowned out altogether by the chorus of earth-shaking *thuds* as the grenades detonated, most of them almost right at the charging Qods Force fighters' feet.

Brannigan rolled over, hitching himself just over the top of the hillock, jamming his captured Type 03 into his shoulder, looking for the sights at the same time he tried to see the gunboat through the clouds of dust and black smoke from the exploding grenades. He was looking for the .50 gunner.

There. He imagined that he and the Iranian looked right at each other in that split second before the trigger broke. The Iranian must have been tightening his thumbs on the butterfly trigger of the .50, right before the 5.56mm round zipped just above the machinegun's receiver and blasted a hole between his eyes.

The shoreline suddenly fell silent, except for the pained moans of the wounded and dying Iranians caught in the grenade blasts.

Brannigan lay behind his rifle for a few heartbeats, waiting. The second .50 was still out there, though the boat was presently masked by the rise of the shore to the west. That could change at any moment.

But he also knew that they couldn't stay put. He didn't know how many men the Iranians had left, but it wouldn't take that many to flank them and kill them all. They had to push forward.

He couldn't necessarily have logically explained that right at that moment. He was as gassed as the others. It was just something he knew clear down to his bones, an instinct driven home by decades of training and fighting. When in doubt, attack.

He pulled a second frag out of his vest. He had one left. He pulled the pin, lobbed it at the beach, and hunkered down. The Russian grenades blasted shrapnel farther than a man could reasonably throw them, and fragments whickered overhead as the heavy *thud* shook the ground.

"On me," he rasped, and then he was up and moving.

***

Esfandiari wasn't sure why he was on his back. Or why he was lying on rocks and sand.

A moment later, the memory hazily returned. The memory of the world dissolving in an evil black cloud of smoke, the tiniest fraction of a second before the shockwave of the grenade explosions knocked him flat and rattled his brains for the second time in two hours. And with it came the pain.

He was bleeding; he was sure of that. He realized he couldn't see out of one eye. Everything screamed in agony, a blinding, throbbing, burning pain that told him he'd take more than a few fragments along with the impact of the blast. His bruises and burns from the conflagration in the Citadel were forgotten in the fiery anguish that now wracked his body.

He turned his head and nearly blacked out. He felt around himself and found that he still had his rifle, clenched in his right hand. His left didn't seem to be working quite right.

Then he looked up at the lip and saw the crouched silhouettes of men with rifles. And he knew they couldn't be his.

He couldn't speak. Couldn't form the words, the final battlecry of a warrior of Allah. But he tried, though it came out as a ghastly, gurgling hiss, and his first attempt to lift his rifle resulted in little more than a twitch.

The figures were coming closer, moving slowly and carefully. He didn't know why the machinegunners on the boats hadn't killed them yet. He concentrated on putting every last ounce of strength he had into lifting his rifle. He would die a martyr, die killing the infidels, as was pleasing to Allah…

***

Brannigan, with Curtis beside him, was moving slowly and carefully toward the beach, his rifle in his shoulder and trained on the spot where the second boat should be. He knew he'd gotten

236

lucky, killing that first machinegunner with the first shot. He didn't intend to give the second one the time that the first one had gotten.

The wave of attacking Iranians were down on the sand, a few still moving feebly, groaning as the blood pumped out of them and into the dirt. They had been mangled and pulped by blast and fragments. None of them had long to live. And Brannigan wasn't going to risk any of his men trying to care for them.

The boat came into view. It was a good deal farther away than he'd expected. And its stern was to them, motoring away to the west. The assault broken, the last survivors must have decided that discretion was the better part of valor.

Brannigan's aching eyes narrowed. He hadn't expected that of Qods Force. He'd expected them to die fighting. But he wasn't going to look a gift horse in the mouth, either.

As he neared the beach, he saw a man lying on the sand, apparently knocked off the lip of rock by the grenade blasts. He'd taken a fragment to the head; his face was a mask of blood, and one eye was simply gone, a mass of gore. From the slowly spreading crimson blots on his khakis, he'd taken frag in a few other places, too.

He spat blood, and struggled to bring his rifle up. Brannigan put the red dot on the man's forehead, but hesitated, unwilling to simply shoot a man so badly wounded and obviously helpless.

In that moment, he thought he recognized the face, even through all the blood and gore. The beard, the hawk-like nose, the feverish gleam in the one remaining eye, which was now fixed on him with a burning hatred that would have scorched him to ash if a look was capable of doing so. This was the commander, the Iranian who had ordered the execution of Trevor Ulrich.

Brannigan thought he understood why the last boat had run away.

Suddenly, with a scream, the Iranian wrenched the rifle up off the strand, pointing it with one shaking hand.

And Brannigan shot him through the bridge of the nose from twenty feet away. The Type 03 barked, the Iranian's head snapped back as the 5.56 round blasted a hole through his brain, and his own rifle clattered to the ground.

CHAPTER 20

The first patrol boat was starting to back water, pulling away from the shore, the engine chugging as the water of the Gulf churned around its stern. Brannigan turned from the Iranian commander's corpse, his rifle pointed at the fleeing boat.

The idea came suddenly. "Get to the boats and get 'em in the water!" he snapped.

"We haven't got the fuel to go very far," Hancock said, as he ran past Brannigan to jump into one of the boats. Fortunately, they all appeared to have been sufficiently sheltered from the grenade blasts that they were all still inflated.

"No, we don't," Brannigan answered with a grunt, as he started to push the boat off the beach. "But I bet *that* one does." He pointed at the patrol boat, that was starting to swing around. "And I'd be willing to bet that there are only a couple of 'em still aboard."

It was going to be tight; the patrol boat was almost pointed back north again, and it was starting to pick up speed by the time the mercenaries were all aboard the boats and setting out to try to intercept it. The patrol boat's diesels were considerably more powerful than the outboards, even if they'd had plenty of fuel. If it got any kind of a serious lead on them, they'd never catch it.

239

But the man at the helm was either inexperienced or panicking. Or both. He overcorrected, almost ran the boat aground again, and lost most of his speed trying to turn back and avoid the rocks. In that time, the rubber boats, by then running on fumes, raced to catch up.

Brannigan stayed crouched in the bow, his rifle trained on the retreating patrol craft as best he could, fighting the bouncing of the bow slapping against the waves. So far, no one had tried to get at the M2 on the bow mount, but he wanted to at least get some fire on them as soon as anyone popped out of the cabin.

Then Hancock was pulling them alongside the nearly-stalled patrol boat, using the thrust from the outboard to press the gunwale against the hull. They had scant seconds; the growl of the patrol boat's diesels was growing louder as the helmsman tried to escape.

Brannigan stood up, carefully balancing against the rocking of the boat and the head rush that threatened to make him black out. He hadn't realized just how dehydrated he'd gotten from the night's fighting. He shook it off; he could pass out later.

Slinging the Type 03 on his back, he drew his Makarov, reached up, and grabbed the patrol boat's rail with one hand, hooking his gun hand over with his wrist. The wet metal threatened to slide through his palm as the engines surged, but he clamped down and pulled himself up. His sodden boots slipped and skittered on the hull for a moment, and then he was up, one boot on the gunwale, the other already swinging over the rail and onto the deck.

Childress and Flanagan were boarding on the other side, similarly armed with pistols. They were all nearly out of rifle ammunition, and the Makarovs would be easier to manipulate in the close quarters of the boat, anyway.

Flanagan had beaten Brannigan onto the deck by a split second, and was already moving to the hatch on the starboard side of the pilothouse. Through the portholes, the Iranian helmsman could be clearly seen, trying not to look at the armed men swarming aboard his boat, shoving at throttles already pushed to the stops.

Flanagan wrenched the hatch open, and pointed his Makarov at the Iranian's head. Over the rumble of the engines,

Brannigan could just hear him demand the man put his hands in the air.

Getting no response, Flanagan stepped into the pilothouse and screwed the pistol's muzzle into the Iranian's ear.

The Iranian moved quickly, ducking his head back and slapping at the hand holding the pistol. He'd had some hand-to-hand training, and though it might be a surprise to some, it is actually possible to slap a pistol away from your head before the trigger can be pulled. The pistol went wide, barking out a shot that punched through the Plexiglas porthole just before the Iranian tried to grab it with both hands.

Flanagan moved faster, though. A knee came up and slammed the Iranian against the side of the console, driving the wind out of him. As the man folded, Flanagan aimed an elbow at his head. He ducked under most of the blow, which skipped off the back of his skull. From there, the Iranian lunged at Flanagan, trying to take him down in a tackle. But even as they crashed backward, hitting the edge of the open hatch, Flanagan brought the Makarov crashing down on the base of his opponent's skull.

The Iranian went out like a light, and crumpled to the deck.

All of that had happened in mere seconds. Brannigan, seeing that the pilothouse was under control, turned toward the rear hatch that led down into the hull, where the engine spaces and what meager crew quarters there were on the fifty-foot boat were located.

He yanked the hatch open, even as Childress joined him and Aziz swung over the rail. Pointing his pistol down the short ladderwell, he peered into the relative darkness of the hull, even as he bladed off from the hatchway, staying out of the line of fire.

But no gunfire roared out of the lower spaces, and he saw no movement. If there was anyone down there, they were keeping their heads down. He'd have to go in after them.

Taking a deep breath, he plunged down the steps.

There was a small crew lounge and sleeping area at the base of the steps. As was to be expected from a fifty-foot patrol boat, it was Spartan, at best. It was also empty. There were no signs of any extended crew residence; Brannigan suspected that the boats had been tied up in the harbor for most of the Iranian occupation.

That left the engine spaces, aft. And even as small as that boat was, clearing a holdout down there could be tricky. He hooked around the base of the ladderwell, ducking his head down to avoid peeling the top of his skull off on the overhead, and leveled the Makarov back toward the diesels.

The engine compartment was empty. The diesels were running, but no one was tending them. The helmsman had been the last man on the boat.

It made sense, if he thought about it. The Iranian commander wouldn't have taken the time to round up an actual crew for the patrol boats; he would have piled his own men aboard them, for the sole purpose of hunting down the mercenaries and the hostages. Most of the soldiers had died on the beach.

He started back up the ladder, and had to wait for Childress to get out of the way. Once he was back up on deck, he went to the rail. The rubber boats had fallen back, but were catching up again since Flanagan had throttled back. "Well, we've got a boat," he said to Hancock. "Start bringing the hostages and the prisoners aboard. It'll be cramped, but we can tow the dinghies if we have to."

Hancock gave him a quick thumbs-up, and turned back toward shore.

***

"It's not going to be comfortable," Brannigan told Ortiz, "but it'll get us farther than the rubber boats, since our 'partners' bugged out on us." He rubbed eyes gone gritty and sore. "I don't know if we've got the legs to get all the way to Abu Dhabi, though, not overloaded as we are." The compartment below was jam-packed, and the upper deck was just as covered with bodies. The dead Iranian who had still been lying beneath the .50 in the bow had been heaved overboard, along with the man who had been on the wheel, and Santelli was now manning the heavy gun. Curtis had protested, but Santelli had overruled him.

Flanagan had just smirked, which had sent the shorter man into another tirade.

Brannigan had been glad to hear it. As long as the men, particularly those two, were still bickering, they still had it together enough to survive. And after what they'd already been through, why wouldn't they?

He knew the answer to that question. Even as they continued their verbal sparring, there was a brittleness to the high spirits. The sun was up, it was getting hot, they were almost out of ammo, and they were still in Khadarkhi waters. They were not out of the woods yet.

"This thing doesn't have to get us to Abu Dhabi," Ortiz said, his voice hoarse with pain. "It just has to get us to the harbor."

"I'm not sure that's such a good idea, Captain," Brannigan said.

"My ship should still be docked," Ortiz argued. "And I'm pretty sure they were more interested in us than in the ship. Any authorities are either dead or scattered; the Iranians killed everyone in the Khadarkhi Army when they took over, and the Army *was* the police force. With the Iranians all or mostly dead, we should be able to sail out without anyone even trying to stop us."

Brannigan grimaced. "I'm not entirely sure it's going to be that easy, but you've got a point," he conceded. He looked Ortiz in the eye. "Are you going to be up to it? You've got an extra hole in you."

Ortiz winced. "I don't have to do that much. Most of my crew's still able-bodied enough. That's what a ship's got a crew for, anyway."

Brannigan nodded. "Well, I'll admit I don't have any better ideas at the moment," he admitted. He rapped on the hatch to the wheelhouse. "Head for the harbor."

***

The harbor seemed dead. Gulls circled overhead, but there was no activity on or near any of the ships at anchor or docked to the piers. It was as if the island was in shock after the events of the previous night. The pall of smoke from the destroyed missiles was still hanging over the city and the Citadel, blotting out a good fraction of the sunlight. It was still getting miserably hot despite it.

"How the hell are we going to board?" Curtis asked. "I don't see any ladders on the side of the ship." The *Oceana Metropolis* was looming above their heads, its red and blue hull looking like a steel cliff. An unclimbable steel cliff, without handholds or footholds.

Ortiz pointed. "Simple. We go to the quays where the smaller ships and boats are docked, and get off there, then walk to the gangplank."

"Easy day," Flanagan called from the wheel. "It's only a few hundred yards, so even your short legs shouldn't have a problem, Kev."

"Shut up," Curtis replied.

It didn't take long to get the boat snugged up to a quay and tied up. The long, concrete pier was empty, but Childress, Curtis, and Santelli stayed on security, Santelli keeping the M2 pointed down the length of the pier. Their approach had, apparently, gone unnoticed, but none of them expected that state of affairs to continue indefinitely. Even if the Iranians were beaten or dead, none of them knew just how many Al Qaeda fighters might still be prowling about in the city.

"Flanagan and I will take point," Brannigan said. "Santelli and Childress in the rear. Hostages to the ship-side, Aziz, Villareal, and Curtis on the landward side. Move fast but don't run. Make it look like we belong here, at least from a distance." He looked at Ortiz. "How long are you going to need to get ready to depart?"

"Ideally?" Ortiz replied. "Twenty-four hours. I think I can cut some corners, and get us out of here in six, though."

"*Six hours?*" Curtis exploded. "Do you have any idea what can happen in six hours?'

"After what I've seen in the last couple of days, I've got some idea, yeah," Ortiz replied. "But it's the best we can do. This isn't a car, that you can just turn the key and start. Ship engines are big, complicated, and they have to have time to warm up."

"We should have just taken the patrol boat," Childress muttered. "We're going to get murdered sitting here waiting."

A few of the hostages apparently heard him, because a scared murmur went through the crowd. "We're going to hold security on the gangplank until it's time to get underway,"

Brannigan announced, raising his voice just a little. "We'll protect you. Now, let's go."

With Flanagan by his side, Brannigan started down the pier at a brisk walk, his Type 03 down at his side. He was really wishing that he'd been able to grab some extra magazines from the dead Iranians back on the beach, but time had been pressing. Of course, he hadn't known at the time that they'd have to wait a quarter of a day to get moving, either.

The gangplank wasn't really a plank. It was more of a steep stair, with pipes and hoses for transferring oil on one side, leading up to the gunwale from the pier. Brannigan reached the base of the stair and stationed himself just past it, near a cluster of equipment. "Get aboard," he said over his shoulder. "All of you. Curtis, you and Aziz take charge of the Saudis and make sure they get aboard and stay out of trouble."

He heard some grumbling from both men, but soon there were boots and shoes clattering on the steps behind him, as the hostages, the prisoners, and the two designated guards climbed aboard the ship. Brannigan and the rest of the mercenaries held their positions. They tried to stay casual, keeping the rifles down and somewhat out of sight, though their salt-encrusted, still-soggy battle fatigues and load bearing vests were going to identify them as soldiers quickly enough to anyone who was paying attention.

It was getting hotter by the minute, especially as their clothes and gear dried. Brannigan realized again just how painfully thirsty he was. They weren't going to be able to stay there on the docks, under the sun, for six hours.

After another thirty minutes or so had passed, and the thirst was truly becoming excruciating, Brannigan made a decision. There was still no sign of enemies on the docks; in fact, it seemed as if all of Khadarkh had gone to ground in the aftermath of the explosions in the Citadel. "All right," he croaked. "We're going aboard; we'll hold overwatch on the gangway from the deck. At least we should be able to find some shade and get some water up there, and we'll have better fields of fire."

None of the other three objected. "Joe, Roger, you go first," Brannigan instructed. "Carlo and I will follow once you're set." Extract was always the most dangerous part of a mission, and he was acutely aware of just how far out in the wind they really were. He was determined not to get slack and start taking chances.

Hancock and Flanagan climbed the gangway behind him, their boots clanging heavily on the metal steps. The gulls cried overhead. Sweat trickled down his neck and into his eyes. The smoke stung his nostrils.

"Set!" Hancock called. Brannigan started to turn toward the gangway, pausing to let Santelli go ahead of him. He glanced back as he did so, and stopped. He squinted against the orange-tinted light of the sun.

There was a vehicle sitting at the far end of the pier, near the container yard that sat at the north side of the harbor. He didn't think that it had been there before.

The heat, the discomfort, and his own exhaustion were abruptly forgotten. His gaze sharpened as he watched the HiLux. He was suddenly, uncomfortably aware of just how few rounds remained in the Chinese rifle in his hands.

"Quickly, Carlo," he said, keeping his eyes on the truck. "I think we've got company."

He waited until Santelli was partway up the gangway before turning and following. At first, he tried to maintain eyes on the vehicle, but soon found that, as dehydrated and worn out as he was, he had to concentrate on getting up the steps. His legs were burning and everything ached by the time he reached the deck.

When he looked again, the HiLux was gone.

***

Contrary to the mercenaries' hopes, there was little shade to be found on the tanker's deck. It was a ship designed to carry petroleum, not passengers, and it wasn't set up for sentries to be posted on the gangway, either. Fortunately, there was water aboard, and Villareal set to hauling as much of it as he could up to the men with rifles, helped by a couple of the hostages who weren't needed to get the ship ready to get underway.

The hours ticked by, slowly. After a while, they started to hear machinery noises from belowdecks. They got no updates; the crew were working their tails off to try to get ready on such short notice, and had no time to pass information. The mercenaries just had to sit in the sun, trying not to breathe too deeply of the smoke permeating the air, and watch the Saudis who were also up on the deck, apparently suffering far more than the Americans, who weren't as used to the heat.

There wasn't much talk. Even Flanagan and Curtis had subsided, the combination of the weariness of the night's fighting and the tension of waiting conspiring to dampen anyone's inclination to chat.

***

The engines were turning over, a deep rumble more felt through the deck than heard, when Flanagan called out, "Looks like our friends are back."

Brannigan looked up. Sure enough, the HiLux was back in its position near the containers. It was either the same one as before, or one that looked very much like it; in the Middle East, there were white HiLuxes and then there were white HiLuxes with red decals on the sides. They were a dime a dozen, with little variation.

It did not advance, though. After a few more minutes, the mercenaries simply maintained their vigil, though they watched the pickup more closely than anything else in the port.

***

Brannigan glanced at his watch. They had to be almost ready to go. It was nearly noon.

Motion caught his eye, and he looked up to see the HiLux coming toward them, ahead of three more vehicles, all of them apparently packed with men carrying rifles. Either the locals had scared up a militia in order to try to secure the port now that the Iranians were gone, or the remnants of the Al Qaeda fighters sent from Saudi Arabia had finally rallied. Either way, this could get very bad, very quickly, especially given how little ammunition they had remaining.

"Look alive," he warned. He needn't have; Childress, Hancock, Flanagan, and Santelli were already on the rail, rifles held ready just below the gunwale. Curtis and Aziz were still watching the Saudi prisoners.

The cavalcade of vehicles rolled down the pier toward them, and Brannigan knew they were coming directly to the *Oceana Metropolis*. He pulled the magazine out of the Type 03, checked it for the umpteenth time, then jammed it home again. One thing was for sure; if this came to a fight, it was probably going to be short.

He fought back momentarily against the crushing sense of failure. To have led these men through the hell of the last couple of days, only to die in the last few moments before extract was a bitter pill to swallow.

He refused to swallow it. At worse, they would go down fighting. At best—well, he wasn't convinced that all was lost just yet. The mercenaries still had the high ground, there was only one good approach to their position on the deck, and it was extremely canalized. Furthermore, if the Iranians had been ready to cut and run after the shellacking they'd gotten, he expected the Arabs would be even more flighty. He determined to use that to his advantage.

"Aziz," he called softly. The other merc hesitated, but then came to join him at the gunwale. When he glanced over, Brannigan saw that most of Aziz' mag pouches were still full; he probably had more ammunition than most of the rest of the team combined.

But Brannigan could deal with that later. The vehicles had stopped at the base of the gangway and several of the fighters were getting out.

They were a mixed bag. A few were dressed in man-dresses, one or two were wearing tracksuits, most were in jeans and t-shirts. One was even wearing slacks, an open-collared white shirt, and a dark sports coat, with an AKM in his hands. None of them really screamed "Wahhabi" at first glance, which Brannigan took as a good sign.

The man in the sports coat walked to the gangway and started up. Brannigan looked to Aziz. He yelled down the gangway in Arabic, and the man in the sports coat stopped, then yelled something back.

"He says that they are securing the port," Aziz translated. "He's demanding that we come down and surrender."

"Who the hell is he?" Brannigan asked.

"I don't know," Aziz replied.

"*Ask him,*" Brannigan snarled. Aziz flushed, then complied. The other man barked a long speech in Arabic in reply.

"He says that he is Abdul Abu Bakr al Qays," Aziz reported. "Commander of the Defenders of Islam on Khadarkh."

"Does that mean anything to you?" Brannigan asked.

Aziz shook his head. "No, but I doubt it means that they're going to be especially friendly to a bunch of infidels. I'm a Muslim; I'll be fine. You guys are fucked, though."

"Thank you for the assessment," Brannigan growled. He looked back and studied the Saudis. "Would it change their minds if they knew that we'd rescued a bunch of their brothers from the Iranians?"

Aziz followed his gaze and frowned. "Are you serious?" he asked. "I thought they were detainees. They *were* going to start a war with a preemptive chemical attack on Iran."

"And who do you suggest we hand them over to?" Brannigan asked. "The CIA isn't going to be thrilled about a bunch of private citizens having snuck into a sovereign kingdom and blown up its Citadel. And most of the proof that they were here to gas the Iranian coast went up in a fireball last night." He stopped. Frowned. Then he looked up. "Doc!" he called.

Crouching to stay below the gunwale, Villareal ran to join them. "What is it?" he asked.

"You still got the stuff you grabbed from that table in the Citadel?" Brannigan asked.

"It's a little soggy, but yeah," Villareal replied.

"Keep ahold of it," Brannigan said. A plan was forming in his mind. He turned to Aziz. "Find out which one of the prisoners is in charge, since their old head honcho got smoked."

"That's easy," Aziz said, pointing to a pudgy, balding man at the end of the lineup, sweating more profusely than the rest. "That guy, Abd Al-Aziz Tawfiq."

"Bring him over here."

Aziz just looked at him at first, a puzzle frown on his face. When Brannigan turned his icy glare on the other man, he hurried to comply, moving quickly over to Tawfiq and hauling him to his feet. The Saudi protested, but Aziz snapped, "*Iskut!*" at him, and he shut up.

"Tell him that there's a way that everybody gets out of this alive," Brannigan said quickly. "If he can talk those guys down there into letting us go unmolested, he and his people walk. Otherwise, they all die, and we release the intel that Doc's got."

The balding Saudi studied him as Aziz translated. This guy's eyes had none of the gleam of fanaticism that had characterized his dead boss. "You would do that?" he said, in passable English. "It would destroy the relations between your country and mine."

"I know," Brannigan said. "You people have sworn up one side and down another that you don't have chemical weapons. A lot of politicians would have a lot of egg on their faces if that was publicly shown to be a lie, along with all the other ones the House of Saud has spread around over the years. So, Mr. Tawfiq, that's the deal. Talk these 'Defenders of Islam' down so that we can get underway, and I promise that the intel we've got will be burned. It pisses me off, but if it's the price of getting me and my men out of here alive, I'll pay it."

Tawfiq studied him. "How do I know you will not simply release the information anyway, after you leave?"

"You have my word," Brannigan said. "That's going to have to do. Along with the fact that I'm *not* taking you hostage as safe passage. Take it or leave it."

"What makes you think they will listen to me?" Tawfiq asked.

"Don't insult my intelligence, Mr. Tawfiq," Brannigan gritted. "The Saudis wouldn't have sent nobodies for this mission. You've got rank, and you've got pull. Don't bullshit me."

Tawfiq's manner changed, ever so slightly. He was no longer a nervous scientist. The mask had been pulled away. He glanced down the gangway at the man in the sports coat. Then he sighed.

"You have a deal," he said. He shouted down the gangway, and the man in the sports coat stiffened. The Saudis must have had some direct dealings with the local militias, which stood to reason. They wouldn't have been able to muster the Loyalist and Salafist resistance to the Iranians that they had if they hadn't been going behind the Khadarkhi Army's backs.

"I can buy you an hour," Tawfiq said, after a brief exchange. "But that is all. Then they will come and take the ship by force."

"It'll be enough," Brannigan said. "Get moving."

Tawfiq called out to his subordinates, and in a few minutes, they were getting up and shuffling down the gangplank. There was no great hurry in their movements, but they were getting out of Brannigan's hair, so he didn't worry about it. Their lack of urgency was only buying the Americans more time.

Only once the last of the Saudis was off the gangway did he notice that the skinny man with the protruding Adam's apple, Ortiz' first mate, was crouched near the gunwale, on the other side of Curtis, watching. *Leterrier, that was his name.*

The man hurried over to him. "We'll be ready to cast off in fifteen minutes," he said. "Are we going to be in a firefight before then?"

"I don't think so," Brannigan said. "At least not yet. Though they might change their minds." He glanced at his watch. "Good job; that was quick."

Leterrier shook his head. "We're nowhere near ready for sea, but we can get to Abu Dhabi," he said. "I'll get things moving."

"We'll be here," Brannigan said, "in case our friends down there decide to get frisky."

There was an argument going on down by the vehicles. Brannigan thought he knew what it was about; the militiamen and the Saudis were debating whether or not to just go ahead and break the deal. Tawfiq was doubtless describing their disposition along the gunwale.

He debated sending a warning shot at their feet. That might be enough of an impetus to get them to fall back, at least.

One of the militiamen looked up the gangway, said something strident in Arabic, and started to climb up.

That tore it. Brannigan shouldered the Type 03 and put a bullet into the step right in front of the advancing militiaman. It hit the metal stair with a loud *bang* and ricocheted, buzzing off into the distance toward the city. The militiamen all ducked as it went overhead, and the one on the stairs bounded back quickly.

Good, they were still interested in self-preservation. But they weren't going away, either.

Just another fifteen minutes.

More debate erupted, and more than one rifle was pointed up toward the deck.

"This is gonna get ugly," Hancock said.

Screw it. I've still got my pistol if they try to board. Leaning out over the gangway, Brannigan began putting single shots down on the pier. The militiamen scattered as the first round spat concrete fragments at the feet of a man wearing a dishdasha. The subsequent rounds punched through tires, into hoods, and shattered mirrors.

He wasn't aiming to kill, or even to wound. He was just making them take cover. Buying time.

The mag ran empty and he tossed the Chinese rifle over the side, between the hull and the pier, and drew his Makarov.

Then the crewmen were running past to cast off the forward lines, and the engines were rumbling more deeply, the vibration throbbing through his bones. It was time.

There was a yell from below, answered by a shot from Flanagan. Then the gangway wasn't touching the side of the ship anymore. They were underway.

They stayed where they were, watching as the militiamen milled on the pier, weapons still at the ready, but no fire came their direction, and they didn't need to engage any more. In another twenty minutes, they were past the mouth of the harbor and heading out into the Gulf.

They'd made it.

EPILOGUE

The fire popped loudly as a pitch pocket ignited, throwing sparks into the night.

Brannigan leaned back and puffed at his cigar, before sending a plume of smoke up to join the shower of embers. "Well, now that everybody's here," he said, "I guess you boys want to get paid." He reached into the haversack next to him and pulled out several envelopes. "All cash, as directed," he said, as he handed the envelopes out around the fire. "Don't spend it all in one place."

"So Tannhauser really came through?" Hancock asked. "I'm actually kind of surprised."

"Hector's a good negotiator," Brannigan said. "And he can bring pressure to bear that we could never match. Plus, we got the ship out along with the hostages. That went a long way, believe me."

The mercenaries each took their envelopes, stuffing them in pockets or backpacks. They were gathered at one of Brannigan's favorite campsites, high in the mountains above his cabin. It was as good a place as any to hand out their pay and talk without fear of being overheard.

"So, anybody see any news about it yet?" Hancock asked.

Childress chuckled. "Yeah, I was looking. Supposedly, DEVGRU swooped in from the *Ford* and rescued the hostages just

253

before the Iranians set off a massive bomb to try to take everyone out."

There was a general chuckle at that, one that Aziz didn't join in. No one commented on his silence, either.

"There's another interesting little tidbit," Brannigan added. "Hector told me that they're keeping it quiet, but Prince Bassem bin Bandar has apparently disappeared. Nobody knows where to."

"Who's Prince Bass'em bin Band Aid?" Curtis asked.

"He's one of the Saudi Royals," Brannigan explained. "One known in recent years for his hardline hawkishness towards Iran. Hector thinks that he was probably the one behind the original deployment of the missiles to Khadarkh."

Hancock leaned forward and stirred the fire with a stick. "Did he go rogue, or is he just the scapegoat for an op gone bad?"

"We'll probably never know," Brannigan answered. "I gave Hector the maps and papers that Doc collected, but we'll probably never know what happens with them, either."

"I thought we were going to burn those?" Aziz pointed out.

"That was the deal," Brannigan replied, taking another pull on his cigar. "When old boy tried to rush the gangway anyway, the deal went out the damned window."

"Besides," Flanagan said grimly, "handing it to the government, even if it is through Hector Chavez, just means it'll get swept under the rug, anyway. Nobody in high places wants *that* info getting out."

There was a pause at that, broken only when Curtis blurted, "Damn, Joe, can't you keep your morose cynicism to yourself for once? We had a win! Can't you be happy?"

"'Morose cynicism?'" Flanagan asked, looking up at Curtis, then around at the rest of the group. "Okay, who lent Kev a thesaurus? Because I *know* he doesn't know what those words mean."

"There's one question that we do need to resolve, sooner or later," Brannigan put in before Curtis could get started on his reply. "Hector told me he could keep his ear to the ground for more work for us. You boys did a hell of a job, and there will be a market. The question is, are we in the business, or was this a one-shot job?"

Santelli peered at him from where he sat on a stump, across the fire. He'd already had to move three times, as the smoke seemed to follow him wherever he sat. "Be honest, John," he said. "The real question you're asking is whether or not you're going to have to recruit a new team for the next job." He snorted. "Well, you're not recruiting *my* replacement, I can tell you that."

Brannigan smiled under his handlebar. "I'll admit, as hairy as it was, I kind of liked getting my hand back in," he said. "You've got me there." He looked around at the rest. "Okay, then, who's still in if another job comes along?"

All of the men raised their hands, though both Aziz and Villareal were somewhat slow in doing so. When Childress looked at Aziz in some surprise, the other man shrugged with a fain sneer. "The pay's better than I'd ever make back at the college," he said.

"All right!" Curtis said enthusiastically. "But there's one more thing, something that I brought up before. Now that we're a *real* team, it can't be ignored anymore. The team needs a name!"

Flanagan groaned. Hancock laughed.

"The name's pretty damned self-evident, isn't it?" he said.

There was a pause, all eyes expectantly on him. "Really?" he said, looking around the fire. "Nobody's going to say it? Not one of you dumbasses gets it?" He sighed. "They asked themselves, 'What kind of black-hearted sons of bitches will drop everything to go halfway around the world and do terrible things to bad people, regardless of who they are?' And the next bunch who wants to hire us is going to ask the exact same question. *And* it was one of our old callsigns, too.

"'Brannigan's Blackhearts.'"

Santelli nodded, as if chewing it over. "I like it."

There was a general murmur of agreement. Brannigan's eyes had narrowed. "I don't know," he said slowly.

"Too late, John," Santelli said. "Brannigan's Blackhearts it is."

Brannigan smiled his surrender. "All right, you black-hearted sons of bitches," he said. "I'm gonna turn in. Don't drink all my booze before morning."

READ THE PRELUDE!

THE COLONEL HAS A PLAN

Read it on
americanpraetorians.wordpress.com/free-fiction

Made in the USA
Columbia, SC
24 August 2023